PATRICIA WENTWORTH
THE RED LACQUER CASE

PATRICIA WENTWORTH was born Dora Amy Elles in India in 1877 (not 1878 as has sometimes been stated). She was first educated privately in India, and later at Blackheath School for Girls. Her first husband was George Dillon, with whom she had her only child, a daughter. She also had two stepsons from her first marriage, one of whom died in the Somme during World War I.

Her first novel was published in 1910, but it wasn't until the 1920's that she embarked on her long career as a writer of mysteries. Her most famous creation was Miss Maud Silver, who appeared in 32 novels, though there were a further 33 full-length mysteries not featuring Miss Silver—the entire run of these is now reissued by Dean Street Press.

Patricia Wentworth died in 1961. She is recognized today as one of the pre-eminent exponents of the classic British golden age mystery novel.

By Patricia Wentworth

PATRICIA WENTWORTH

THE RED
LACQUER CASE

With an introduction by
Curtis Evans

DEAN STREET PRESS

Introduction

BRITISH AUTHOR Patricia Wentworth published her first novel, a gripping tale of desperate love during the French Revolution entitled *A Marriage under the Terror*, a little over a century ago, in 1910. The book won first prize in the Melrose Novel Competition and was a popular success in both the United States and the United Kingdom. Over the next five years Wentworth published five additional novels, the majority of them historical fiction, the best-known of which today is *The Devil's Wind* (1912), another sweeping period romance, this one set during the Sepoy Mutiny (1857-58) in India, a region with which the author, as we shall see, had extensive familiarity. Like *A Marriage under the Terror*, *The Devil's Wind* received much praise from reviewers for its sheer storytelling élan. One notice, for example, pronounced the novel "an achievement of some magnitude" on account of "the extraordinary vividness...the reality of the atmosphere...the scenes that shift and move with the swiftness of a moving picture...." (*The Bookman*, August 1912) With her knack for spinning a yarn, it perhaps should come as no surprise that Patricia Wentworth during the early years of the Golden Age of mystery fiction (roughly from 1920 into the 1940s) launched upon her own mystery-writing career, a course charted most successfully for nearly four decades by the prolific author, right up to the year of her death in 1961.

Considering that Patricia Wentworth belongs to the select company of Golden Age mystery writers with books which have remained in print in every decade for nearly a century now (the centenary of Agatha Christie's first mystery, *The Mysterious Affair at Styles*, is in 2020; the centenary of Wentworth's first mystery, *The Astonishing Adventure of Jane Smith*, follows merely three years later, in 2023), relatively little is known about the author herself. It appears, for example, that even the widely given year of Wentworth's birth, 1878, is incorrect. Yet it is sufficiently clear that Wentworth lived a varied and intriguing life that provided her ample inspiration for a writing career devoted to imaginative fiction.

It is usually stated that Patricia Wentworth was born Dora Amy Elles on 10 November 1878 in Mussoorie, India, during the heyday of the British Raj; however, her Indian birth and baptismal record states that she in fact was born on 15 October 1877 and was baptized on 26 November of that same year in Gwalior. Whatever doubts surround her actual birth year, however, unquestionably the future author came from a prominent Anglo-Indian military family. Her father, Edmond Roche Elles, a son of Malcolm Jamieson Elles, a Porto, Portugal wine merchant originally from Ardrossan, Scotland, entered the British Royal Artillery in 1867, a decade before Wentworth's birth, and first saw service in India during the Lushai Expedition of 1871-72. The next year Elles in India wed Clara Gertrude Rothney, daughter of Brigadier-General Octavius Edward Rothney, commander of the Gwalior District, and Maria (Dempster) Rothney, daughter of a surgeon in the Bengal Medical Service. Four children were born of the union of Edmond and Clara Elles, Wentworth being the only daughter.

Before his retirement from the army in 1908, Edmond Elles rose to the rank of lieutenant-general and was awarded the KCB (Knight Commander of the Order of Bath), as was the case with his elder brother, Wentworth's uncle, Lieutenant-General Sir William Kidston Elles, of the Bengal Command. Edmond Elles also served as Military Member to the Council of the Governor-General of India from 1901 to 1905. Two of Wentworth's brothers, Malcolm Rothney Elles and Edmond Claude Elles, served in the Indian Army as well, though both of them died young (Malcolm in 1906 drowned in the Ganges Canal while attempting to rescue his orderly, who had fallen into the water), while her youngest brother, Hugh Jamieson Elles, achieved great distinction in the British Army. During the First World War he catapulted, at the relatively youthful age of 37, to the rank of brigadier-general and the command of the British Tank

Corps, at the Battle of Cambrai personally leading the advance of more than 350 tanks against the German line. Years later Hugh Elles also played a major role in British civil defense during the Second World War. In the event of a German invasion of Great Britain, something which seemed all too possible in 1940, he was tasked with leading the defense of southwestern England. Like Sir Edmond and Sir William, Hugh Elles attained the rank of lieutenant-general and was awarded the KCB.

Although she was born in India, Patricia Wentworth spent much of her childhood in England. In 1881 she with her mother and two younger brothers was at Tunbridge Wells, Kent, on what appears to have been a rather extended visit in her ancestral country; while a decade later the same family group resided at Blackheath, London at Lennox House, domicile of Wentworth's widowed maternal grandmother, Maria Rothney. (Her eldest brother, Malcolm, was in Bristol attending Clifton College.) During her years at Lennox House, Wentworth attended Blackheath High School for Girls, then only recently founded as "one of the first schools in the country to give girls a proper education" (*The London Encyclopaedia*, 3rd ed., p. 74). Lennox House was an ample Victorian villa with a great glassed-in conservatory running all along the back and a substantial garden--most happily, one presumes, for Wentworth, who resided there not only with her grandmother, mother and two brothers, but also five aunts (Maria Rothney's unmarried daughters, aged 26 to 42), one adult first cousin once removed and nine first cousins, adolescents like Wentworth herself, from no less than three different families (one Barrow, three Masons and five Dempsters); their parents, like Wentworth's father, presumably were living many miles away in various far-flung British dominions. Three servants--a cook, parlourmaid and housemaid--were tasked with serving this full score of individuals.

Sometime after graduating from Blackheath High School in the mid-1890s, Wentworth returned to India, where in a local

British newspaper she is said to have published her first fiction. In 1901 the 23-year-old Wentworth married widower George Fredrick Horace Dillon, a 41-year-old lieutenant-colonel in the Indian Army with three sons from his prior marriage. Two years later Wentworth gave birth to her only child, a daughter named Clare Roche Dillon. (In some sources it is erroneously stated that Clare was the offspring of Wentworth's second marriage.) However in 1906, after just five years of marriage, George Dillon died suddenly on a sea voyage, leaving Wentworth with sole responsibility for her three teenaged stepsons and baby daughter. A very short span of years, 1904 to 1907, saw the deaths of Wentworth's husband, mother, grandmother and brothers Malcolm and Edmond, removing much of her support network. In 1908, however, her father, who was now sixty years old, retired from the army and returned to England, settling at Guildford, Surrey with an older unmarried sister named Dora (for whom his daughter presumably had been named). Wentworth joined this household as well, along with her daughter and her youngest stepson. Here in Surrey Wentworth, presumably with the goal of making herself financially independent for the first time in her life (she was now in her early thirties), wrote the novel that changed the course of her life, *A Marriage under the Terror*, for the first time we know of utilizing her famous *nom de plume*.

The burst of creative energy that resulted in Wentworth's publication of six novels in six years suddenly halted after the appearance of *Queen Anne Is Dead* in 1915. It seems not unlikely that the Great War impinged in various ways on her writing. One tragic episode was the death on the western front of one of her stepsons, George Charles Tracey Dillon. Mining in Colorado when war was declared, young Dillon worked his passage from Galveston, Texas to Bristol, England as a shipboard muleteer (mule-tender) and joined the Gloucestershire Regiment. In 1916 he died at the Somme at the age of 29 (about the age of Wentworth's two brothers when they had passed away in India).

A couple of years after the conflict's cessation in 1918, a happy event occurred in Wentworth's life when at Frimley, Surrey she wed George Oliver Turnbull, up to this time a lifelong bachelor who like the author's first husband was a lieutenant-colonel in the Indian Army. Like his bride now forty-two years old, George Turnbull as a younger man had distinguished himself for his athletic prowess, playing forward for eight years for the Scottish rugby team and while a student at the Royal Military Academy winning the medal awarded the best athlete of his term. It seems not unlikely that Turnbull played a role in his wife's turn toward writing mystery fiction, for he is said to have strongly supported Wentworth's career, even assisting her in preparing manuscripts for publication. In 1936 the couple in Camberley, Surrey built Heatherglade House, a large two-story structure on substantial grounds, where they resided until Wentworth's death a quarter of a century later. (George Turnbull survived his wife by nearly a decade, passing away in 1970 at the age of 92.) This highly successful middle-aged companionate marriage contrasts sharply with the more youthful yet rocky union of Agatha and Archie Christie, which was three years away from sundering when Wentworth published *The Astonishing Adventure of Jane Smith* (1923), the first of her sixty-five mystery novels.

Although Patricia Wentworth became best-known for her cozy tales of the criminal investigations of consulting detective Miss Maud Silver, one of the mystery genre's most prominent spinster sleuths, in truth the Miss Silver tales account for just under half of Wentworth's 65 mystery novels. Miss Silver did not make her debut until 1928 and she did not come to predominate in Wentworth's fictional criminous output until the 1940s. Between 1923 and 1945 Wentworth published 33 mystery novels without Miss Silver, a handsome and substantial legacy in and of itself to vintage crime fiction fans. Many of these books are standalone tales of mystery, but nine of them have series characters. Debuting in the novel *Fool Errant* in 1929, a year after Miss Silver first appeared in print, was the enigmatic, nautically-named *eminence grise* Benbow Collingwood Horatio Smith, owner of a most expressively opinionated parrot named Ananias (and quite a colorful character in his own right). Benbow Smith went on to appear in three additional Wentworth mysteries: *Danger Calling* (1931), *Walk with Care* (1933) and *Down Under* (1937). Working in tandem with Smith in the investigation of sinister affairs threatening the security of Great Britain in *Danger Calling* and *Walk with Care* is Frank Garrett, Head of Intelligence for the Foreign Office, who also appears solo in *Dead or Alive* (1936) and *Rolling Stone* (1940) and collaborates with additional series characters, Scotland Yard's Inspector Ernest Lamb and Sergeant Frank Abbott, in *Pursuit of a Parcel* (1942). Inspector Lamb and Sergeant Abbott headlined a further pair of mysteries, *The Blind Side* (1939) and *Who Pays the Piper?* (1940), before they became absorbed, beginning with *Miss Silver Deals with Death* (1943), into the burgeoning Miss Silver canon. Lamb would make his farewell appearance in 1955 in *The Listening Eye*, while Abbott would take his final bow in mystery fiction with Wentworth's last published novel, *The Girl in the Cellar* (1961), which went into print the year of the author's death at the age of 83.

The remaining two dozen Wentworth mysteries, from the fantastical *The Astonishing Adventure of Jane Smith* in 1923 to the intense legal drama *Silence in Court* in 1945, are, like the author's series novels, highly imaginative and entertaining tales of mystery and adventure, told by a writer gifted with a consummate flair for storytelling. As one confirmed Patricia Wentworth mystery fiction addict, American Golden Age mystery writer Todd Downing, admiringly declared in the 1930s, "There's something about Miss Wentworth's yarns that is contagious." This attractive new series of Patricia Wentworth reissues by Dean Street Press provides modern fans of vintage mystery a splendid opportunity to catch the Wentworth fever.

Curtis Evans

Chapter One

THE FRONT DOOR of Sally Meredith's cottage opened straight into the living room. There were a red brick floor, very clean, a much worn Persian rug, and a big open fireplace. Of the two large chairs only one was really comfortable, but M. Frederic Lasalle who occupied it was not really being fair to its well cushioned curves. He sat on the extreme edge, elbow on knee, chin in hand, and looked frowningly into the fire.

Sally thought him altered. His round face was not as rosy as it should have been, but, after all, seven years were seven years, and those between 1914 and 1921 might well count for double.

Sally was sitting on the floor in front of the fire, her lap full of papers which she was sorting. On her right she made a small pile of those she wished to keep. On her left a rubbish heap grew apace.

"It's exactly like dips in a lucky bag," she said. "Cousin Eliza kept everything, and I never know whether I'm going to come across a five-pound note or an invitation to tea in the sixties."

She unfolded a yellow paper as she spoke, and read aloud the endorsement. "'My honoured grandmother's recipe for making black currant jelly. *Very economical.*' I'll keep that."

She laid it down on her right, and Lasalle, leaning forward, picked it up and began to read "Take nine pounds of black currants and nine scant pints of water"—there he stopped, remained looking for a moment at the paper, and then said:

"This old Cousin Eliza, was she good to you? Have you been happy here?"

Sally looked up. Her very candid eyes held a little humour.

"Oh, well," she said, "she simply hated me because I had to do things for her, and she'd always been so frightfully independent. It was very decent of her to leave me everything—"

"Two years you were with her?" said M. Lasalle. Sally nodded.

He rose and walked over to the fire, a little man frowning vigorously. When he had pushed the log with his foot he said:

"And why were you with her at all? Why do I not find you married?"

Sally's colour rose a little.

"Alas, Fritzi, we are both bachelors," she said.

M. Lasalle snorted.

"When last we met," he said, "you were happily and suitably betrothed. To me also it was a happiness. I thought 'Youth is headstrong, but now all will be well.' Always you were a trouble to my mind. Always I felt you a so sacred trust; for, see you, Sally, when your mother was dying she said to me, very soft and earnest, 'Fritzi, we have not been step-brother and sister, you and I, but nearer and dearer than the brothers and sisters of one blood'—and because of that you are to me, in my heart, as if the good God had given me a child, and when you are hurt I am hurt—"

He ran his fingers through his thick grey hair, kicked the log violently, and concluded in a tone of wrath.

"We speak just now of your cousin—I can see she made you no happiness, but I can forgive her before I forgive the other woman who has spoiled your life and broken your betrothal—that Mrs. Stevens-Vine—"

"Vine-Stevens," murmured Sally.

"What does it matter, her name? It is what she has done. To drag a child innocent, unknowing, into an affair of politics—do I say politics—madness rather, and of a publicity, of a scandal—it is this she has done to you, and I forgive her never."

"Just what the magistrate said," said Sally sweetly—"and Bill, and the relations and everyone."

"Speak not to me of her—never. As for your Cousin Eliza—phui—an old maid! Will you be one too?"

Sally regarded him with a dangerous smile.

"Fritzi darling, you are quite out of date. There aren't any old maids now."

"And no suffragettes?"

He hurled the question at her with violence.

"Why, no, since we have the vote."

"The vote!" said Lasalle very angrily. "It makes you happy, that vote? It warms your heart? It is your companion, your support, that vote?"

"Fritzi," said Sally steadily, "you're being a beast."

M. Lasalle ruffled his hair again, with both plump hands this time.

"Yes, yes, my child; but it is because I care. One is not angry like that unless one cares. If I were the step-uncle who does not care, I would shrug my shoulders and say:

"'It is a pity of my niece Sally Meredith. She was betrothed to a fine young man—oh, some years ago now, before the war; and she obstinates herself to be a suffragette, and to break windows with a hammer, and in public places to cry aloud "Votes for Women." Sequel, she is arrested, she is in your Bow Street police court—what will you have? The betrothal is broken—what does it matter to me? It is a pity, that is all.'"

Then, with a complete change of manner:

"Like that I cannot speak, Sally. I have a heart that is torn until I know how it is with you." There was a silence. The ash dropped in the fire. The room was nearly dark. Sally folded her papers, got up, and began to light the lamps. With her back to M. Lasalle, she said:

"Fritzi, it's dear of you to care." Then with a noticeable effort—"It's all such ages ago; need we dig it up?"

"He is alive?"

"Yes, he came through the war all right."

"Do you see him, hear from him?"

"Oh, no."

Sally adjusted the lamp shades and turned, smiling:

"Fritzi, you're an incurable Victorian romantic. Do stop digging, and come and be comfortable."

She altered the angle of the big chair, patted it invitingly, and said,

"Let's talk about you for a change. You know you're ever so much nicer and more interesting than me. What have you been inventing?"

M. Lasalle sat down without speaking. Cousin Eliza's recipe still lay where he had dropped it when he rose so abruptly. He bent now, and picked it up, folding and refolding it in an odd, absent-minded manner.

"Yes," he said after a long pause. "Let us speak about me, but it is not a comfortable thing to speak of, this me."

Sally threw a big cushion on the floor, and sat down on it cross-legged. The little room was full of a warm glow. Yellow shades made the lamplight golden. M. Lasalle sat with the lamp at his elbow, and behind him three little windows showed a strip of sky still warmed by the sunset.

"See then, Sally, if I speak of you, if I tease you, if I am, as you say, 'brute' to you, it is because—"

He broke off sharply, stared at her out of round blue eyes, and then began again.

"There are two of me, Sally. There is the old uncle whom you call Fritzi, kind and peaceable, a good citizen of his Switzerland, a man to be envied, a man, as you say—comfortable. Then there is the other—he who is Lasalle, chemist, inventor, man of science pure and simple. Up to now he, too, has been happy, as one is happy when he does the work which he loves beyond all the world. I say up to now, for now there has come upon this other me, this one who is Lasalle the man of science—"

"Fritzi, what is it?" said Sally.

Her breath came a little faster, her eyes widened. She looked at him with concern and great affection.

"It is—I do not know how to call it—tragedy? Perhaps. A strain beyond what I can bear? Certainly. And this for weeks, Sally, until there is no Fritzi any more, but only this tormented Lasalle. But when I come here and speak of you and think of you—then I am Fritzi again, just for a little. Oh, *mon Dieu*, the relief! And you say, 'Fritzi, let us talk of you and be comfortable.'"

He had taken the same uncomfortable attitude as before—on the edge of the chair, leaning forward, one hand propping his head, the other closing and unclosing on the half sheet of paper which he had picked up.

Sally rose to her knees, and put her hand over his.

"Fritzi, for goodness gracious sake, what is it?"

He pushed her away from him gently.

"I am telling you, but you must stay still. You asked me of my work. Have I invented, have I discovered? And it is as if you struck me upon a wound. And I say, 'Yes, I have worked, I have invented, I have discovered.' And like a fool, I was happy. You are not an inventor, Sally; you do not know how one is plunged in it and lost. One does not think what will I do with this. One thinks only 'This is mine; here no one has passed; I am the first.'"

He gave a sort of groan.

"It was like that with me. It was a gas that I have found, like nothing else, swift, sudden, and deadly beyond what words can describe. Then when the discovery is complete, and I have made my experiments, I think, 'What to do?' I come out of that work dream so absorbing, and I begin to reason, 'My own country, Switzerland, she is neutral for ever. Thank God she needs no poison gases.' After my own country I think of England. With all my heart I love her, and with all my heart I believe that she loves peace. I think to myself, 'England shall have this secret.' And I write to your War Office. All that takes time. We write backwards and forwards, we have conversations. And you will understand I am not yet troubled. Then something happens; there come to me in three separate ways offers from other nations. I say 'No!'

to them. I will not correspond and will not talk. I say they are misinformed. They do not take my answer. First in small ways, and then in big, I am pressed. I cannot describe it; but I begin to feel 'What have I here? What forces are stirring? And can I resist them?'"

His voice sank to a whisper.

Sally stared at him, her face quite pale.

After a moment's pause he spoke again, a sudden energy in his voice.

"After that there began the spying. I cannot tell you. I came to think there were no honest people left. I will tell you of one. He was a refugee from Poland, a youth, violinist by profession, and he came to me with an introduction from one whose name I will not say, because it is a name much honoured. He was sickly and penniless, and for the sake of that honoured name I took him into my house, I got for him engagements and in a week I find him in my laboratory at three in the morning, trying to open, with a false key, my desk. He is impudent beyond words. He says that all these machines of mine inspire his genius, that he has the wish to compose a *Symphonie Chemique*, music futuristic and explosive. I tell him that my machines are to inspire my genius, mine, and not that of chance-come musicians who violate the most sacred laws of hospitality. He departs. But he is only one. I am never safe, I am never free. I say to your War Office that I will come over here, and they must make haste and complete our negotiations. And all the time my trouble becomes greater. I think; I see what it is that I have made, what a fearful thing in wicked hands. And I see how, all the wicked ones of the world, they will never rest until they have it too. I begin to be torn, Sally; I begin to be torn. With all my heart I believe that England guards the peace of the world, and at one moment I think that with this weapon she can guard it safely. Next moment I think of all those others, those who wish for war, driven along terrible paths by what they call ambition. And I think that once this thing is loose in the world they will not rest until they have it too. I shall have set the pattern, and they will work and work until they can follow it. And my dreams—*mon Dieu*, Sally, my dreams!"

He shuddered violently, and was silent.

Sally watched him with a little frown.

"Poor old Fritzi," she said at last. "But if you feel like that, why go on with it? Why not cut the whole thing out, and invent some nice beneficent-uncle sort of thing instead? You know, I don't think poison gas is in your line, I really don't."

M. Lasalle threw out his hands with an impatient gesture.

"You sit there comfortably, and tell me that! To you it is so easy. There is a formula written down, no more than half a sheet of paper, which will burn in five seconds; a match, a flame, a little white ash, and the devils that are plaguing me go back to hell and stay there. To you it seems like that?"

"Well, why not?" said Sally.

She had locked her arms about her knees, and was rocking gently to and fro. Her eyes were sorry for Fritzi who was in trouble; her vivid lips were pressed together in a smile that was just a little scornful.

"Yes, to you it is easy; but for me, I am torn, I walk in a fog and cannot see my way, and in the fog are voices that always say a different thing. When I listen to one, and am at the point when I will destroy everything because of the voice which says 'Destroy!' then comes another voice that says: 'You have gone too far. You are pledged in your honour. To draw back now, it is impossible.' And so it goes by day, by night, and I have no rest. But to you it seems easy—Would you like to make such a decision, Sally? Would you find it easy then, do you think?"

Sally's lips parted on a quickened breath. Colour flickered in her cheeks, and then died again.

"See here," said M. Lasalle.

He undid coat buttons, waistcoat buttons, and appeared to be wrestling with some further complex fastening. In the end, and not without a struggle, he brought into view what appeared to be a cigar case made of red lacquer deeply carved.

"Look, Sally, look well, for in all the world there is not another like it. When I was young I went once to China, and there a very strange thing happened to me, a thing that I tell to no one, ever. I bring away that secret memory and this case, and until now my life has been so easy, so placid—like a Dutch canal. And now, when a thing terrible and tragic comes to me again, I put the secret of it here inside this case which comes with me from China."

He turned, and with a quick movement flung back the falling frill of yellow silk which shaded the lamp, leaving half the little room fully illumined.

"Now see, come close and see, Sally, whilst I show you what no one in all this world knows except myself. Look well, and remember; for, if anything should happen to me, you will have need to remember."

Sally caught the arm of the chair, and pulled herself into a kneeling position. M. Lasalle bent forward, the red lacquer case in his left hand, and over his shoulder the lamplight fell upon it full, and Sally saw the pattern of raised roses and fishes with goggling eyes. Fritzi was speaking in a quick, eager voice.

"Here, in this case, is my secret, my formula; nowhere else, nowhere at all, excepting only in my brain. Now see, Sally, this is the secret of the case. You touch here and here, pressing, and, with the other hand touching this flower on one side and this on the other, you pull. Easy, is it not?"

The case slid into two halves, opening as a card-case opens, but along an irregular line. Metal showed at the edges. From the larger half a piece of paper protruded. M. Lasalle touched it with his forefinger lightly.

"Just a sheet of note paper," he said, "like this one."

Cousin Eliza's recipe still lay folded on the broad arm of the chair, and he touched it with the same finger, the same gesture.

"A sheet of paper and a little ink. They are the same to look at—but one will fill your jam cupboard, and the other will kill you and a million men."

He shut the case. The irregular edges came together with just the faintest click.

Sally looked with all her eyes, but the opening had vanished.

"Clever, is it not? Now, do you remember what I showed you? Take it, and let me see you open it."

Sally took the case, held it as she had seen M. Lasalle hold it, touched what she had seen him touch; and in a moment his strained gaze saw the tiny crack appear, widen—and Sally with a half of the case in either steady hand.

She looked up, smiling in triumph, and saw the sweat stand on his brow.

It seemed a long time before he said rather loudly:

"*Mon Dieu*, what a chance!" Then, as Sally stared—"I only told you half. If you had put just one of your fingers on the wrong place, if you had made any mistake at all, if you had tried to open it by force, there is a spring inside which would release enough acid to destroy that clever paper of mine. The acid is in a glass-lined compartment up here; and I said to myself, 'I will take the chance. If she makes a mistake, and the paper is destroyed, I will take it for an omen.' And you made no mistake."

Sally, kneeling upright before him, had been gazing first at the case and then at his face with its harassed, altered look. But suddenly she looked past him over his shoulder at the three uncurtained windows a bare five feet away. They were black now, for the last of the glow was utterly gone. The unshaded lamplight struck them full.

Sally looked, and caught her breath.

There was a hand pressed against the glass of the left-hand window, a large hand that looked unnaturally white, the blood driven from it by the pressure of a man's weight upon it. The light showed the pale fingers—thick, long fingers—and the still paler palm crossed by a dark, jagged scar.

Just in the instant that Sally caught her breath the hand slipped on the glass. She heard the sharp sound of it on the wet pane, and screamed. Instantly the hand was gone. She heard the gravel grate under a heavy foot, and, as M. Lasalle sprang up with a violent start, she screamed again.

Chapter Two

At eleven o'clock the same evening M. Lasalle was writing a letter. The fire was dying down, but its bed of red-hot ash glowed warmly. The three little windows on the farther side of the room were shut, hasped, and securely curtained. M. Lasalle held his writing pad upon his knee and wrote with a fountain pen. On the small table to his left, full in view, lay the lacquer case, open.

He was alone. Sally had gone to bed. For a while he could hear her moving to and fro, and during that time he wrote at a furious speed, tearing off sheet after sheet and dropping them on the floor to his right. When the sounds ceased he stopped abruptly, his pen poised, his head a little on one side, listening. He remained like this for a long time, his face troubled, his free hand tapping restlessly on the arm of the chair. Once he took up the lacquer case, drew out the folded paper which it contained, and then after a pause during which he unfolded and refolded it several times, he put it back and pushed the case away from him sharply.

When he moved again it was to rise to his feet and gather up all those closely written pages. He crumpled them in one hand, and dropped them on to the red embers where they smouldered for a moment, curling and blackening along their edges before they flared into flame. He watched the thin black ash fly up, starred with sparks. He watched it settle and whiten. Then he turned back to the chair, and wrote again very slowly.

Outside the wind was rising a little. As he paused between the laboured sentences he could hear it, and the sound seemed to add to the trouble in his face. At last he put what he had written into an envelope, addressed it, and, taking from his waistcoat pocket a battered remnant of violet sealing wax, he sealed the flap of the envelope in three places, pressing down the hot wax with an old-fashioned seal which kept odd company with a cheap, modern watch.

There were at least three violet stains upon Sally's lamp shade by the time he had finished, but at last the letter was well and truly sealed. He propped it against the stem of the lamp, and, for the last time, took up the crimson lacquer case.

When ten slow minutes had gone by, he went to the hearth and raked the fire out carefully. Then, seating the outer door ajar, he extinguished the lamp, and stood by it for a moment, waiting until he could see his way. He did not wish to wake Sally by stumbling over a stool or a chair.

As soon as the doorway showed its glimmer, he passed through it, locked the door on the outside, and with a jerk pushed the key under the door.

The moon was shining, and the wind was blowing. All the trees were moving, and their shadows, very black, made restless patterns upon Sally's red brick path and the white dusty road beyond.

M. Lasalle went out of the little wicket gate, and shut it carefully behind him.

He and Sally had walked that afternoon, and he followed the path which they had taken then. After half a mile he left the road for a path that crossed a stretch of moorland. The moon was very bright. It made strange twisted things of what in the daylight had been dead heather and yellowing bracken. The wind blew salt in his face, and the long grating sound of a rough tide that ebbs upon shingle came to his ears. It grew louder. The path rose. There were no trees now, only this empty place under the moon, and the double line where cliff met sea, and sea met sky. A lowering bank of clouds stretched upwards from the horizon and promised storm. No matter, since M. Lasalle had been lighted to his destination.

Twenty yards to the left of the path there was a black hole in the ground. Here, where he was standing now, Sally had stood with him that afternoon.

"They call it Smuggler's Leap," she said.

"Everyone here believes that our great local smuggler, Long Tom Brown, dived into it to escape from the excisemen who were hard after him. Anyhow, he was never seen or heard of again. Nothing that falls into the Smuggler's Leap is ever recovered. Of course they say it's bottomless."

M. Lasalle picked his way across the heather until he stood by the open mouth of the hole. Heather and gorse overhung it. A false step would be so very easy.

He stood looking down into impenetrable blackness.

A person who makes no noise is not necessarily asleep. Sally was not asleep. Instead of getting into bed she put on a warm dressing gown, turned out her lamp, and curled up on the window seat to engage in the time-honoured practice of gazing out into the moonlight.

She could see three elm-bordered fields rising on a gentle slope—background. For middle distance, Mrs. Molton's cottage across the road, with its untidy front garden. She hadn't even cut her lupins down, let alone her hollyhocks. Foreground—Sally's own neat plot with the row of standard roses on either side of the brick path.

Sally began to think about Fritzi. Horrid thing, that hand against the window. She knew just how it had happened. The abominable spying creature wanted to listen, and wanted to see. It was absolutely *brainless* of me to leave those curtains open. If he stood on the path he might see, but he couldn't hear much, even though the middle window was a little open; and, of course, being an expert criminal, he wouldn't be such an idiot as to go and leave footprints on the border which I had just cleared and dug. I only wish he had. But, of course, if you're a mug at that sort of game you die young, or retire to prison. I expect he thought it an awful brain wave to lean across, with one hand on the glass, and his ear up against the open window. I think I convinced Fritzi when I actually showed him how it was done. And poor darling Fritzi holding a guttering candle all over me and my nice raked border, and looking dreadfully solemn and worried! Of course the creature must have heard everything. But, as I told Fritzi, he couldn't *possibly* have seen Fritzi showing me the spring, and me opening it. Thank goodness, Fritzi's nice humpy shoulder spoiled his little game as far as that was concerned. As I said to Fritzi, the only thing he got away with was the quite useful information that, if he did manage to pick Fritzi's pocket—Can you pick a vest, for I'm sure that's where he keeps it?—he couldn't open that wretched case, or even try to, without flooding the whole show with acid—so that's that.

Sally nodded, and went on looking at the moonlight.

Odd for Fritzi to be so disturbed. Why couldn't he make up his mind one way or the other? A creature of quick, passionate impulses and swift decisions, she had never, in all her life, known what it was to hesitate before an emergency. If two ways lay before her, the question of which she should take would settle itself on the instant.

Sally stopped looking into the moonlight, pushed another cushion behind her shoulders, locked her arms about her knees, and stared vaguely into the soft dusk of her room.

Fritzi's talk had brought up the past very vividly. It was years, and years, and years since anyone had spoken to her of her engagement to Bill Armitage. She remembered now how *frightfully* proud she had been of being engaged at seventeen.

It was simply too thrilling to have a diamond ring, and a man at your beck and call. And the rows—the excitement and fascination of them—Bill furious; Sally provoking; and then a delightful scene of reconciliation. Sally frowned and smiled at the recollection. Then Mrs. Vine-Stevens—Sally's mouth twisted a little; the headlong, passionate worship with which she had flung herself at the feet of the famous suffrage leader was just a little bitter to her now. She remembered Bill's "And where do I come in?" Poor old Bill, she wasn't sorry for him then, but now it hurt to remember how he looked when she stamped her foot and flared back at him: "You? Why should you count? You're not in the same street with her. You're not on the same side of the world. Why you can't even begin to understand how I feel about her!"

Yes, it hurt all right. Oh, bother Fritzi for stirring it all up like this.

It was whilst she was bothering Fritzi that M. Lasalle so cautiously shut the front door and pushed the key under the sill. Sally, seven years back in the past, heard nothing. The gate closed noiselessly. Even if she had been listening now, she would not have heard any footfall on a road where the dust lay three inches deep.

Sally went on thinking about Bill Armitage. Presently she dozed, and woke with a start. The wind beat against the window, full of rain. The night was black, and as cold as a seven-year-old love story.

Sally got stiffly to her feet, groped in the darkness, and lit a match.

"Heavens, it's three o'clock!" she said.

She blew out the match and tumbled into bed.

Chapter Three

FOUR AND A HALF hours later Sally became aware of daylight, Mrs. Callender, a rapid flow of conversation, and a bitterly cold draught. She sat up, rubbed her eyes, yawned, and said, "Good morning"—adding hastily, "For goodness' sake, shut something, or I shall freeze, Cally."

"Door or window, Miss?" inquired Mrs. Callender.

"Both," said Sally.

Mrs. Callender fastened the window and banged the door. Everything that could creak and rattle was doing so with great zest. There was a stinging wind and an unbelievably brilliant sun.

Sally detached her mind with a jerk from the prospect, and bent her startled attention upon Mrs. Callender's steady stream of talk.

"What did you say?" she asked sharply.

"At half past seven," said Mrs. Callender without appearing to take a breath, "I knocked at the old gentleman's door like you told me to. And for five blessed minutes if I didn't go on a-knocking and a-standing there like a poor dumb woodpecker which, if you'll remember, Miss Sally, it was only yesterday I told you that there was a tree damaged shameful up at Squire's, and my nephew Bill's eldest son he vows and declares as the 'ole tribe of them did ought to be shot and done away with, only Squire he's fair mushy over birds and animals, and, as my niece Ellen's 'usband 'as often said, if we Christians got the 'arf of it, we'd be well off and no mistake. But I says to him, 'If you'd 'ave known Squire's father, you'd know as you was well off now, for a more ramping, rampageous old devil never cursed a Christian family. No man's job wasn't safe, nor no woman's character, so to speak, not when old Squire was about.' And so I've told my niece Ellen's 'usband many's the time."

Here she drew breath and continued without the slightest change of voice.

"So there's the old gentleman's bed not slept in, and a letter for you a-propped against the lamp downstairs. So I suppose as 'ow he's been called away sudden."

"What?" said Sally with a gasp.

"Just what I've been a-telling of you all along," said Mrs. Callender with an air of virtue. "Sitting late at night means lying late in the morning, and a thing I never did 'old with."

But Sally had leapt from bed and was halfway down the narrow cottage stair.

Fritzi gone! But how? Where? Fritzi whom she had left quite fairly soothed and peaceful. Impossible!

She stood barefoot in her thin nightdress, and tore open the letter which bore her address. The wind whipped in through the open window, but Sally did not feel it. What on earth did it all mean? What on earth was Fritzi up to?

She clutched the letter in one hand, the table with the other, and read:

"Sally, my child, I am going away. This decision, it is too great for me; I cannot make it. I am like a man who is blind; I cannot see which way I should go. But, if I am blind, others have eyes. I think you have the eyes to see and the coinage to choose. Choose, then, and God be with you. For me, I go. Good-bye, little Sally whom I love.

Fritzi.

P.S. The lacquer case, it is behind the second volume of Tillotson's *Sermons* in your Cousin Eliza's bookcase."

Sally found herself breathing very fast. The hand that held the letter was shaking. She was angry, and she was afraid. With a rush of furious resentment she told herself that there was nothing to be afraid of. She turned the letter over; on the back was yet another postscript slanting right down across the page in an almost illegible scrawl:

"It is impossible that I can stay to meet him."

Sally crumpled the letter up, and flung it on the floor. Meet him? Meet whom? Had Fritzi gone mad? Then, in a faint whisper somewhere just beyond her control—had anything dreadful happened? She stamped her foot. Of course it hadn't—of course, *of course* it hadn't. What a perfect fool she was.

Very slowly she went across to the window and shut it. She stood with her hand on the hasp for a moment, looking out. It was the middle window which was open last night, and the man must have stood just there on the edge of the gravel path. A horrid little shiver went all over her. If anything had happened to Fritzi!

With a jerk she drew the curtains, and ran over to the glass-fronted bookshelf which flanked the fireplace. Kneeling on the brick, she flung the doors wide, and dragged both Tillotson's sober volumes from their place on the lowest shelf. There was nothing behind them.

Sally began to feel very cold. She pulled out Jeremy Taylor and Izaak Walton, and there was nothing behind them either. With stiff fingers she added The Reverend Thomas Moggridge's *Remarks on the Uncertainty of Human Existence*, and Bishop Hannington's *Life* to the pile beside her, and gazed in horror at the emptying shelf. Some bound volumes of *Good Words* remained, but there was nothing behind them; and on the next shelf nothing; and on the one above nothing either.

Mrs. Callender opened the door upon a scene of indescribable confusion.

"Enough to make Miss Eliza walk, that it were," as she assured her niece Ellen when she next had tea with her. "Every blessed book on the floor, and Miss Sally, as you may say, 'ardly decent, for her nightdresses is a deal more like what I should think fit and proper for a ballroom, all low in the neck, and short in the sleeve, and no protection at all against those cold bricks, as I said to her at the time. 'Oh, Lor', Miss Sally my dear,' I says. 'What a scramjandrum,' I says. And blest if Miss Sally didn't burst out laughing in my face, and her own as white as a sour curd."

"What's a scramjandrum?" said Sally, scrambling to her feet and sending the books flying.

"I never want to see a worse one," said Mrs. Callender, "not if I was to see a hundred, I don't. Oh, it's all very well to say, 'Go away, Cally,' and you with your bare feet and nothing on."

"Well, put the books back," said Sally shortly.

The gust of laughter which had swept her was gone.

She went over to the crumpled ball, which was Fritzi's letter, and picked it up. The envelope was still on the little table. She took it and turned it over. She had not broken the seals, but had opened it by tearing the top.

She went now to the window, drew back the curtain, and looked long and steadily at Fritzi's three blobs of violet wax. The edges were sharper than they should have been.

Half turning, her eyes went quickly to the little writing table set at an angle between door and window. A small paper knife, dagger-shaped and made of metal, lay on the blotting pad. She picked it up, brought it to the light, and looked closely at it. A little smear of violet wax dimmed the blade. Someone had been here, then, after Fritzi had written his letter and gone away, after she herself had gone to sleep. Someone had been here in this room, and had found the letter and opened it. Quite easy, of course, with a metal paper knife, especially if you heated it.

On the other side of the room Cally was thumping books back into place and grumbling all the time; nice, safe Cally, with her flat back and flatter chest, and the frizzy fringe of a dead Victorian day. She could have kissed her for being so cross, and safe, and respectable.

What a perfectly horrid thing to have happened. The hand, large, pale, and darkly scarred, rose up in Sally's memory. With a rush, the thing that she had been keeping at bay became a clamorous fact, impossible to resist. Fritzi's secret was stolen; the lacquer case was gone!

Chapter Four

MAJOR ARMITAGE walked from the nearest station, Lenton. Chark, of course, hadn't one. A place with a name like that wouldn't have, as Sally had always insisted, much to Miss Eliza Meredith's annoyance.

Bill Armitage was not, however, thinking of either Sally or her cousin Eliza. He had, in fact, not the slightest reason to connect Sally with Chark. He was merely going to meet M. Lasalle who refused point-blank to come to London.

As he walked, he regarded the countryside with a critical eye, and decided that the stretch of moorland on the right would make quite a decent golf course.

"Topping short hole over there, with a plateau green not at all unlike the fourth at Sunningdale," he thought, as he stood for a minute or two where the footpath to the Smuggler's Leap branched off from the road. He walked a few paces up the path to get a better view.

"And that stretch of level ground by the road, with the big gravel pit biting into the far end, would make a good copy of the 'Quarry Out' at North Berwick."

He pursued the path of duty with considerable regret. It ended at a latched gate. He looked over it, and saw very neat standard rose trees, white and red alternately, on either side of a rain-washed brick path. On the left of the front door there was a myrtle, and on the right a fuchsia stiffly trained against the whitewashed cottage wall. The front door was open.

Bill lifted the latch of the gate, walked up the path as far as the doorstep, and there remained rooted to the ground. He could see the recessed hearth. Before it lay a black woolly mat, and in the middle of the black woolly mat a girl was sitting. Her head was turned away, and she appeared to be staring into the fire.

The girl wore a jumper and skirt of grey wool, and her bobbed hair was the exact colour of Sally Meredith's hair, that rather bright chestnut which is not so very common.

He stood looking down at the top of her head and wondering why on earth she did not turn round, since it was quite impossible that she should not have heard his footsteps.

Sally did not turn because she had been trying not to cry, and she did not wish either the postman or someone from the village to see that her eyes were full of tears. She stared hard into the fire and winked vigorously. She also hoped that whoever it was would go away. And then she heard Bill Armitage's voice saying:

"I beg your pardon."

Sally was not conscious of jumping up. But in the same moment that she recognized Bill's voice she found herself on her feet, facing him and feeling exactly as if, somehow or other, she had walked into one of the more improbable kind of dreams.

Major Armitage, for his part, received the shock of his life. The girl's hair was not *like* Sally's; it was Sally's. This was Sally herself, Sally from whom he had parted furiously seven years before. Sally Meredith here, where he was expecting to meet a Swiss inventor!

He exclaimed, "Good Lord!" but Sally said, "How do you do, Bill," exactly as if she had been expecting him. When she had said, "How do you do," she continued, "Won't you come in?" And Bill came in.

Coming in rather intensified his embarrassment. For one thing his head very nearly touched the ceiling and he felt rather as if he had got into a doll's house.

Sally felt immensely pleased with herself, pleased and excited. Not only had she been able to wink away the tears which had been annoying her, but she had achieved a steady voice and a composed manner. This she felt to be highly creditable, and the fact of Major Armitage's confusion ministered still further to her sense of having the situation well in hand.

She advanced a step, and offered Bill three cold fingers.

"We might as well say 'How do you do' properly," she said, "after seven years—it is seven, isn't it?"

"It is," said Bill, and a rush of furious indignation surged up in him.

For six years he had thought quite kindly of Sally, when he had thought of her at all. She was a little devil, of course, but, when all was said and done, he owed her something for having broken off their engagement. And now—the cheek of her, looking at him through her eyelashes and asking in her sweet voice, the one which he very well knew meant mischief:

"It is seven years, isn't it?"

His voice was very stiff as he answered her. And then, quite suddenly, Sally blushed to the roots of her hair, and said, putting out both her hands:

"Oh, Bill, I'm so unhappy. Fritzi's gone."

"Gone!"

Sally nodded.

"Fritzi's gone, and the lacquer case, and the burglar. And I don't know who's got it—the case I mean, not Fritzi. Everything's so mixed."

"It seems to be," said Bill slowly. "I'm sorry, but I really don't understand."

He was on the point of adding, "You always did say I was slow," but checked himself with the feeling of having been on the brink of a precipice. Whatever happened, he must on no account encourage Sally. He knew from experience how very little encouragement she required, and, unfortunately, she was prettier than ever—much prettier.

"If you wouldn't mind explaining," he said.

"I am explaining," said Sally, "but I'd explain much better if you'd sit down. You're such a long way up; it keeps me feeling as if I must shout, and then I lose the thread of what I'm saying."

Bill subsided into the large chair, the only comfortable one.

Sally took the nubbly one, and enquired:

"Where had I got to?"

"I don't really think you had got anywhere. Perhaps you wouldn't mind beginning over again."

"I did begin. I told you Fritzi had gone, and the case; and I don't know who's got it. You see it may be the burglar, the one with the horrid white hand, or one of the spies; or Fritzi may have taken it himself after all; and it's simply too harassing not to know which, because, of course, I'm responsible now—you do see that, don't you?" Sally looked earnestly at him out of her dark grey eyes. Her cheeks were very pink.

Bill forgot about not encouraging her.

"My dear child, I haven't the foggiest idea what you're talking about," he said.

Sally was liking him a little bit better every moment. She had liked him when he turned brick-red and hadn't a word to say, and she liked him still better for forgetting all about the seven years which were gone. ("And thank goodness they are gone, and no one can ever make one live them over again," murmured Sally parenthetically.) Bill had always called her "my dear child" when he wanted to be impressive and superior, and it used to annoy her a good deal when she was seventeen; but somehow now, after the war and Cousin Eliza, it was not unpleasant.

The pink in her cheeks burned a little deeper. The feeling of being in a dream persisted.

"Look here," said Bill, "begin at the beginning, really at the beginning. Start by telling me who Fritzi is, and where he has gone to."

"I don't know—I only wish I did."

"Do you mean you don't know who he is, or you don't know where he's gone?"

"I don't know where he's gone. Of course I know who he is. Don't be so stupid, Bill."

"Well, suppose you tell me who he is. I came here to meet M. Lasalle, and you tell me Fritzi is gone—is Fritzi M. Lasalle?"

"Of course."

"He's been here?"

"Yes, yes, of course, I told you so. He was here last night in that very chair."

A dreadful idea flashed into Bill's mind.

"You're not—he isn't—I mean you're not married to him, are you?"

Sally's eyes opened until they were perfectly round.

"My dear Bill! What on earth are you talking about? Fritzi?"

Bill began to experience acute exasperation. Sally had developed a dimple and a giggle, and he was not sure which annoyed him more.

"Look here, be rational," he said. "I don't see anything to laugh at. If you're not married to him, you're not."

"Poor Fritzi," said Sally, drying her eyes. "I can't think why you don't know all about him; but I suppose we were always too busy quarrelling. Anyhow, I'm never very good at explaining Fritzi; I'm always game to try though. If you don't understand, it'll be your fault. I warn you it's complicated."

She let her voice drop to a sort of singsong, and recited with great rapidity, "My grandmother was left a widow with a little girl of six; and she married Fritzi's father, who was a widower, when Fritzi was eight; and the little girl was my mother—I don't mean when she was six but later; and she and Fritzi were step-brother and sister, and frightfully fond of each other, but no relation; and I've always called him Uncle. That is to say," said Sally, slackening speed, "I *call* him Fritzi, but I always talk of him to people as my uncle. It sounds more respectable, especially when he comes to stay with me alone. I say 'My uncle, M. Lasalle,' and then everyone's quite happy."

Bill received this flood of intelligence without any alteration in the rather blank expression with which he had been contemplating Sally. His rugged features did not, in fact, lend themselves to much play of expression, and the effort to repress a just annoyance was having its usual stiffening effect.

"Now, to begin at the beginning," he said. "He was here last night?"

"I keep telling you so," said Sally, aggrieved. "And then the hand came on the window, just as he was showing me how to open the case. And of course, that upset him a lot; and goodness knows, he was quite enough upset before. But I did think I'd got him soothed down before I went to bed. And then, when I came down this morning, there was his letter propped up against the lamp, and he was gone."

Instantly Bill clutched at the letter, emerging like a point of solid rock from a whirlpool.

"A letter? What was in it?" he said sharply.

Sally jumped up, ran to the writing table, rattled open a drawer, and came back with Fritzi's letter in one hand and the envelope in the other. She thrust the letter at Bill, and stood watching him as he read it, her colour flickering and her breathing quickened. Bill read slowly, turned the page, and at last—it seemed to Sally at last—looked up.

"He was bothered about this?"

Sally nodded.

"Horribly," she said with something that was just not quite a sob.

"Then why did he go on with it?"

"Of course I asked him that. And he said he couldn't see straight. He's most frightfully conscientious, and sometimes he thought it was his duty to go on, and sometimes he didn't, and he couldn't sleep."

Sally's gaze was rather piteous now. It searched Bill's face, seeking for reassurance.

Bill realized this quite suddenly, and found himself saying: "He's all right, you know, he's bound to be all right. There's nothing to worry about."

"You're sure?" The words were just breathed.

This was a Sally he did not know, a little soft thing who wanted comforting, not the Sally who provoked and resisted.

"Yes, of course," said Bill, rather loud.

Sally pushed the envelope into his hand.

"You see it's been opened," she said. "Here, under the seals with a hot blade. Whoever did it used my paper knife; the wax has marked it."

Bill whistled.

"Yes, it's been opened," he said. "Who did that?"

"It might have been Fritzi," said Sally, "but I don't think so. I expect it was the person with the hand."

"What hand?"

"The hand. The hand on the window. I go on telling you about it."

"Well, it hasn't got there yet," said Bill.

"It was just after Fritzi had been telling me how absolutely distracted he was, and all about the horrible thing he had invented. He pulled the red lacquer case out of where he'd got it all mixed up with his vest, and told me the formula was inside; and then he showed me how to open it. No, sit back a little more. Now you're Fritzi. Put your elbow on the arm of the chair just here—no, your shoulder's too high, flat it down a little. And I'm kneeling like this with the case in my hand. Now can you screw your head round without changing any of the rest of you, right round until you can see the window? That's it. Right in the middle of the left-hand window, quite suddenly, there was a hand, a perfectly horrible hand with a scar. I mean I saw it suddenly. Someone must have been leaning across to look in, and to hear what we were saying. Well, he must have heard every word, but he couldn't possibly have seen anything, that's what I want you to get quite clear. He heard Fritzi tell me that the formula was in the case, but he couldn't see Fritzi open it to show me how. And he heard Fritzi tell me, if anyone meddled with the case or tried to force it, or even made a mistake over opening it, that a spring would let out enough acid to destroy the formula."

"Well, you saw the hand. And then what happened?"

"Oh, I screamed," said Sally, "like a railway whistle, the very loudest sort. And we heard someone running away. And then I screamed again. And by the time Fritzi and I got into the garden there was no one there."

Bill took up M. Lasalle's letter and read it again. "He wrote this afterwards?"

"Yes."

"And the case—the red lacquer case?"

"Gone," said Sally—"I told you that the very first thing."

Bill got up and went to the bookcase.

"Oh, I've had all the books out," said Sally, sitting back on her heels to watch him.

It was, of course, exactly like Bill to take them out again. He shook each one carefully, and, unlike Sally, when he had finished he put them all back.

He turned to find Sally on her feet, frowning, but he brushed past her and went to the window.

Sally considered that he filled the room up dreadfully, and that he was even more obstinate than he used to be.

"I told you it was gone," she said, but Bill was not listening.

"This window has been opened from the outside," he remarked. "Those catches wouldn't bother a child. Someone has slipped a thin knife in here and pushed the catch back; you can see where the paint is scratched. The question is, when did M. Lasalle go out?"

"I was sitting at my window till three, but I think I did go to sleep—I'm not sure. Anyhow, he had locked the door and slipped the key under the sill; and Mrs. Callender found it there, but she can't remember anything about the windows, for I asked her. I suppose,"—very sweetly—"that you would like to ask her all over again?"

Bill shook his head.

"No, I'm going back to the station," he said. "The first thing to do is to find Lasalle. If he went by train, they'll know where he went to. You see, it's just on the cards that he changed his mind and came back for the case himself."

"Then he wouldn't have left the letter," said Sally.

Chapter Five

THE FEMININE OCCUPATION of waiting at home whilst the man goes out and does things, was one which had never commended itself to Sally Meredith. As Bill had, however, refused point-blank her offer to walk with him to the station, pointing out with unanswerable truth that he could walk three times as fast without her, Sally had been forced to accept the situation. She reflected that men were the most uncomfortable creatures in the world. Take Bill, for instance. When he was here he filled up the room and ignored you and rode roughshod over what you wanted to do. And when he was gone, and anyone would think you'd be thankful to have a breathing space, you felt limp, and lonely, and left behind. That was a man all over; horribly in the way when you'd got him, and horribly out of it when you hadn't. Oh, bother men; and bother, bother Bill! The time went very slowly.

Mrs. Callender came in and asked: "What about lunch, if you please, Miss Sally?" and Sally bit her head off, and then, conscience-smitten, penetrated into the kitchen to apologize.

Cally was soothed, and lunch spoiled, by the time that Bill returned. And, even as Sally ran to the gate and lifted the latch with shaky fingers, she knew that he had no good news for her.

The fact that he quoted the horrible old chestnut about no news being good news frightened Sally more than anything. If Bill produced reassurances, it must be because he thought that there was need for reassurance.

"Well, he hasn't gone by train," he said. "They've telephoned all the stations which he could possibly have reached, and they're all quite sure that no one in the least like him had boarded any train from eleven last night onwards."

"But I didn't give you a description."

"You didn't need to, I've been twice to Switzerland to see him. Didn't he tell you?"

Sally shook her head. How extraordinarily deceitful of Fritzi! So this was why he had started digging things up last night.

"No, he didn't say a word." This with sudden energy, and then in tones as nearly ice as possible, "Why should he?"

Bill, it is to be feared, was not attending. He ate a hasty lunch, and Sally, a very perfunctory one. Sally's efforts at conversation fell into bogs of silence and drowned there. They ate overdone beef and a burnt milk pudding, and were glad when lunch was over.

As soon as they were alone, Bill recovered his powers of speech.

"Look here, I've been figuring it out," he said, "but I didn't want to talk about it till you'd had something to eat. Women always think they can go on without anything to eat when things are happening, and that's just the exact time you want about double." He frowned gloomily at her, and added: "You don't eat enough to keep a guinea pig going."

"Guinea pigs overeat," said Sally. "What does it matter anyhow? If you were going to say something, for goodness' sake say it."

"Well, I was thinking," said Bill, "if he didn't go by train, he may be somewhere in the neighbourhood still. He didn't hire a car or a trap, that I can find out, either. I've been keeping the telephone pretty busy, and he's a noticeable sort of person— foreign accent, and so on—"

He broke off and seemed a little uncertain how to proceed. Finally he said:

"Did he know the neighbourhood at all? Ever been here before?"

"No," said Sally.

"Any friends within reach?"

Sally looked at Bill, and looked away. She shook her head.

"No," she said in a low voice, "he didn't know anyone. He only arrived at lunch time yesterday, and in the afternoon I took him for a walk, and in the evening everything began to happen."

"Where did you take him?" said Bill Armitage.

"Oh, just along the road, and over the moor to the Smuggler's Leap," said Sally, and on the last word her voice wavered suddenly, and she caught at Bill's arm and shook it.

"No, no, no!" she cried passionately.

"No, no, of course not."

It was plain enough that the thought so vehemently repelled by Sally was one which weighed on him.

"Oh, I *hate* you!" she cried, and swung round to hide eyes in which anger was suddenly drowned. The certainty that Bill was being sorry for her slid forlornly into her consciousness. How dared he be sorry when there was nothing the matter? How dared he speak in that kind, hesitating way?

"I didn't mean that—no, Sally, do listen to me. I'm really only trying to help you—but he might have gone out for a walk to clear his thoughts; and if he didn't know the neighbourhood he would most likely have taken the one path he did know and might have lost his way, or fallen down somewhere—something like that—I don't mean anything serious. I thought perhaps I'd go and have a look at the place—just stroll up there, you know."

"Not alone?" There was a faint relenting in her voice.

Bill continued to hesitate.

"Well—I rather thought—it's quicker, you know."

"I'm coming with you," said Sally. "I simply won't stay here by myself, not if you talk for ever. You don't know what it's like—just waiting."

As she spoke she had the door open, and after calling down the passage, "Cally, we're going out," she ran upstairs, and was back in an astonishingly short time with a grey woolly coat, a little grey felt hat crammed down on her head, and a bright violet scarf.

"I'm ready," she announced rather breathlessly, and they went out together.

As they emerged into the road and turned to the right, two women were coming slowly up from the opposite direction. They looked with eager interest at Miss Sally and the gentleman from London.

"Look at 'er violet scarf," said the younger of the two who was Mrs. Callender's unmarried niece, Gladys.

The stout, elderly woman, a second cousin once remov-ed, nodded.

"Ellen told me as she'd got one, but it's the first I've seen of it," she said gloomily.

"Of course it suits her," said Gladys.

"Suiting ain't everything," returned the cousin. She watched Bill and Sally out of sight and then lifted the latch and turned in for a word with Ellen Callender.

The village, though fond of Sally, considered that she should still be wearing black for Cousin Eliza. In Chark when you bought mourning you wore it out, and with care it could be made to last two years for best; hence the violet scarf weighed heavily upon the communal conscience.

Bill and Sally turned up onto the moor. The sky rose above it, very blue, very full of light, absolutely cloudless. On either side of the path, the scorched heather faded from amethyst to brown, and the hollow places of the moor where the bracken grew thickest looked as if they were full of a pale fairy gold. The keen air, the sun, the clear light that bathed everything made their cheering way into Sally's mind and drove the shadows out of it. Bill might be kind to her now if he liked; she would not mind; she might even be kind to him.

They had walked in silence until they left the road, but with the sudden change in Sally's mood the silence broke and Bill was asking her:

"How long have you been here? All through the war?"

"Oh, no!" Her eyes were wide with dismay. Two years in Chark were bad enough, but seven—

"What did you do?"

Sally put up a bare right hand, and ticked off the fingers one by one. "Working parties—you know the sort of thing—nightshirts made from the Prince Consort's pattern, and woolly socks with all the feet different. Two"—down came the second finger—"washing dishes and scrubbing floors. Three, V.A.D., and I quarrelled with the matron. After that I learnt to drive an ambulance, and they wouldn't have me over here because I was too young; so I went and drove for the French Red Cross who didn't mind whether you were nine or ninety so long as you could drive. That's four, and five was Cousin Eliza after the armistice."

"And your suffrage friends?"

Sally's chin lifted.

"All doing ditto."

"Yes, I know. I didn't mean that—what I meant was—"

"Well, what did you mean?"

"Oh, hang it all, Sally, I only meant—"

"Yes?"

"Well," said Bill in what Sally called his nice voice, "I thought it sounded rather strenuous and lonely, and I was wondering whether you'd been able to keep up with your friends, or whether you'd made new ones, or what."

Sally looked at him through her eyelashes. He was really taking an interest, she decided, really being nice and friendly. An impulse moved her to frankness.

"When you say old friends, what exactly do you mean, Bill?" she asked quite simply.

"Well, I suppose I meant Mrs. Vine-Stevens," said Bill Armitage.

Sally gave a little slow nod.

"I thought you did. I never see her now—" a pause—"I haven't seen her or heard from her for years. As for the others, I haven't much in common with them. The only one I ever see is Etta Shaw. Do you remember her? She used to be rather pretty. I do see *her* sometimes, but it isn't exactly a feast of reason and a flow of soul. She's gone crazy about a new society she's taken up with. They call themselves 'The New Party of Peace,' and she bombards me with tracts about it. I went to one of their meetings, and I thought some of them looked a pretty shady lot. But all Etta's geese are swans. She's that sort, you know; like I used to be, only with Etta it's chronic."

"And you've got over it?"

"Yes," said Sally, "I've lost all the fresh enthusiasms of youth."

She looked soulfully at Bill as she made this statement, but there was a dimple at the corner of her mouth. Bill remembered Sally's dimple of old. It usually meant deviltry, but he was amazingly glad to see it again.

"I am old and disillusioned, and very, very good now," said Sally. "I belong to a Village Institute, and go to Mothers' Meetings. I used to read Tillotson's *Sermons* aloud to Cousin Eliza in the evenings. I know quite a lot of theology."

Her limpid gaze continued to rest upon Bill, and the dimple flickered in and out.

"It's been very, very dull," she said, "and that's why I'm talking to you like this. You've no idea how nice it is to talk to someone who knows the very worst about one. You couldn't possibly think worse of me than you do, so there are no appearances to keep up. It's awfully *restful*," concluded Sally.

"Do I think badly of you?" said Bill rather seriously.

"Well, you said so—seven years ago."

"Isn't there a statute of limitations?"

"Not for that sort of thing, and not with you. You're the world-without-end kind. If you make up your mind about a thing, it stays made up, whereas, mine—" Sally smiled her sudden, brilliant smile.

"What about yours?"

"Mine isn't so monotonous," said Sally. "It's fresh and various and—and open-minded. I should simply hate to have a mind like a War Office sealed pattern. If I hate a person one minute, it's quite on the cards that I may be loving him like anything in a little while." And then and there Sally stopped short and blushed scarlet.

"You said you hated *me*", said Bill.

"That," said Sally, recovering herself, "was a figure of speech."

They had come up over the top of the rise, and for a moment they stood looking out to the edge of the cliff and the dazzling line of sea beyond.

"Is this the place?"

Bill's voice had not changed, but the atmosphere had. In spite of the flooding sunshine, coldness and shadow seemed to sweep between them.

"Is this the place?" he repeated.

Sally pointed. All her flow of words dried up.

"Over there," she said, and led the way across the heather.

They came to the black hole in the hill. It had been black at midnight. It was black in the daylight. Furze overhung it on crooked, twisted stems, and the heather huddled about its rim.

Sally stood quite still, looking down. The silence held her, and, as she stared down into the darkness, the colour slowly drained away from her face. She was afraid—oh, she was very much afraid of this place, but it had nothing to do with Fritzi, it could not possibly have anything to do with Fritzi.

As she stood there she was vaguely aware of Bill moving to and fro, now stooping down, now rising and walking on a pace or two; but the impression made by these movements of his remained, as it were, upon the surface of her mind. Within were fear, and the shadow, and her desperate struggle against them. It shook her, but she resisted. She was still resisting when an exclamation from Bill startled the surface of her mind into attention. She looked at him, and saw him rise from his knees with something in his hand.

It was a fountain pen; Bill had it in his hand. There was distress on his face. He came towards her quickly.

"It's a Swiss make. Did he drop it yesterday afternoon?"

"No," said Sally, "I saw it afterwards. He was writing with it. Yes, it's his."

The short sentences came stiffly from her lips. The struggle within had grown sharper. She wanted to stop struggling, but she mustn't.

"I'm afraid—" said Bill in a low, unhappy voice.

Quite suddenly the struggle was over.

"It isn't true, and I'll never believe it!" she cried.

She caught at Bill with both hands, and burst into tears.

Chapter Six

DURING THE WEEK that followed, those who knew of M. Lasalle's disappearance became tolerably well convinced that it was a final disappearance, and that whether it had been effected by his own determination or by some outside agency, the chances were that he and his secret lay somewhere in the depths of the Smuggler's Leap.

Sally continued to say that it was not true, and that she did not believe it. She said it to Bill Armitage, and she said it to Detective-Inspector Williams who came down in plain clothes from New Scotland Yard. Bill said nothing at all. And the inspector said, "Yes, Yes," in a perfunctory sort of way, and went on asking her questions, more questions than she could have imagined that anyone could possibly think of.

With singular unanimity the press ignored M. Lasalle and his disappearance, but in Chark interest ran high, and tongues ranged unchecked.

To Hannah Preston, the cousin who had disapproved of Sally's violet scarf, Mrs. Callender, of course under seal of secrecy, had confided her own version of M. Lasalle's farewell letter to his niece. The sister-in-law to whom Mrs. Preston subsequently imparted it—"between you and me and no one else"—asserted to her next confidante "that the 'ole thing fair made her creep."

To her niece, Gladys, Mrs. Callender merely described the hand on the window which she had not seen, and Sally's scream which she had not heard.

Her married niece, Ellen—niece and goddaughter—was privileged with the sight of an old snapshot of Bill and Sally, abstracted, or let us say borrowed, from Sally's photograph album.

Chark, it will be seen, had plenty to talk about. It watched Sally with intense interest, and wondered when she would go into mourning, and whether she would wear out the black which she had bought for Miss Eliza which must still be quite good, or wastefully purchase something new.

On the Saturday of that rather long week Major Armitage walked into the cottage, and sat down with rather a purposeful air. He did shake hands with Sally, but it was a very incidental hand shake.

"No, there's no news," he said, "but I want to talk to you. Is the door shut? And is that Callender woman really out of the way? I expect I should kill her if I saw her very often, so it's just as well I don't. I suppose you know that she tells her relations in the village everything that has and that hasn't happened, and, as the entire population appears to be related to her in one way or another, we are rather, as you might say, living in the open."

"I suppose it's that dried-up inspector who's been setting you against her?" said Sally hotly. "I hated him the minute I saw him. I simply couldn't do without Cally, and it isn't her fault she's got a lot of relations. I am sure they're not things anyone would choose to have a lot of if they could possibly help it. I think Cally must be an angel not to quarrel with them. I know I always quarrel with mine."

"But then you're rather good at quarrelling, aren't you?" said Bill. He said it with just a trace of a smile, but his eyes dwelt rather sternly on Sally, or she thought so. Her colour rose brightly.

"Am I?" she said. "Well—I suppose you ought to know whether I did it well or not. Did I? I like doing things well, if I do them at all."

"I haven't time for old quarrels," said Bill shortly.

He was sorry for Sally and he wanted to help her, but if she imagined that he was going to dangle about and be flirted with, she would find herself mistaken.

"I've come down on business, serious business; and I want to get on with it."

Sally folded her hands.

"Well, but I've been waiting for you to begin," she said.

Major Armitage pulled a copy of *The Times* out of his pocket.

"This is the first thing," he said. "Do you know anything about it?"

He held the folded paper out. She leaned forward and read in the Agony Column, just above his large, blunt thumb, "From Sally to F. L.: Please, please write. Dreadfully unhappy and anxious."

"Oh," said Sally.

The sparkle of anger was gone from her eyes; they looked in frank bewilderment from the paper to Bill, and back to the paper again.

"Who put it in?" she asked sharply.

"We don't know, if you don't."

"I? Certainly not. But it's quite a good idea; I wish I had thought of it."

Bill took the paper from her.

"The notice was sent to the office with one of your cards enclosed."

He produced a card and held it out.

"Is that one of your usual cards?"

Sally nodded, frowning.

"Yes, it is—but how on earth, and why?"

"Well," said Bill, "someone hopes to get information of M. Lasalle's whereabouts through you. That's tolerably certain, I think. You didn't advertise, so they've done it for you. They hope he'll write to you. And, with your Mrs. Callender in the house, the rest is easy."

"She's perfectly loyal."

"She talks. My dear girl, her motives may be excellent, but her tongue is a yard and a half too long. Don't get angry, or at any rate not for a minute. There's something else I want to talk about."

"Business first, and pleasure afterwards in fact," said Sally. Then she laughed and leaned back in her chair. "All right, go on," she said.

"Well," said Bill. Then he stopped, got up, and went and stood in front of the fire. "It's this way. My connection with this affair is—well, in fact, it's over. You know the conclusion that Williams came to. He's a very able fellow, and, and—well, that was the conclusion he came to. I know you don't share it. And, of course, I don't want for a moment to urge on you any point of view that would—that would, in fact, distress you. But I think it's only fair to say that my own personal view coincides with his, and that the War Office accepts it. In fact, we don't think there's anything more to be done. The attempt to drag the water at the bottom of the Smuggler's Leap failed, as you know. But there it is. As far as M. Lasalle personally is concerned, we don't think there's anything more to be done."

"Yes," said Sally in a very little voice.

Her hands were holding each other tightly.

"As regards his invention, we incline to think that he took the secret with him. We have had a man over at Berne, and he reports that before leaving home M. Lasalle burned a good many papers and destroyed all the materials with which he had been experimenting."

"That would be because of the spies," said Sally with decision.

"It—it rather points to premeditation."

"It points to spies," said Sally.

His half-unwilling admiration for the pluck with which she defied probabilities rose a point or two as he watched her steady eyes and little, shaking hands. After all, there was something about Sally, even in her most exasperating moods. It was something that made it rather hard to keep one's head, and be calm and judicial. With one side of him Bill desired very much to be cool and detached in fact, to stick to the point. Another side of him yearned to comfort Sally, envisaged ways of comforting her, and was, in fact, in some danger of forgetting how fortunate a thing it was that he and Sally had escaped marrying each other.

He went on speaking.

"It's possible, of course, that the case has been stolen; the bogus advertisement points to something of the sort; but, of course, that's not really in my line at all. That's a job for Scotland Yard, and we've asked them to keep a sharp lookout. So you see my business here is over"—he waited a moment and then added, "my official business."

A dreadful wave of forlornness flowed in upon Sally. Bill was the sort of person who made you feel as if he would always be there, angry and disapproving perhaps, but so blessedly safe.

Her eyes widened suddenly like those of a startled child, and the forlornness showed in them as she said with a little gasp:

"You're going away—and not coming back?"

"Do you want me to come back, Sally?" said Bill, watching her.

Sally was silent. Pride and independence urged her to intimate to Bill that his coming and his going were matters of perfect indifference to her. On the other hand, something did so ache at her heart, and that something made her want to put out both hands to him and say, "Oh, Bill, be friends again and stay."

So Sally was silent and after a moment, Bill went on.

"What's the good of beating about the bush?" he said. "If we had met for the first time a week ago, it would all be different; but, as it is, I want to know where we are. I seem to have a knack of annoying you—we never have been able to steer clear of quarrelling—and so—" Bill stuck.

After a long pause, during which Sally sat with her chin in her hands and her eyes fixed on the black woolly mat in front of the fire, he made another effort.

"You see it's this way. Up to now I have had an official connection with your affairs—that is, as far as M. Lasalle's disappearance was concerned. Now that's over. If I go on coming down here, it would be on my own—as a friend; and I don't know whether you want me or not. Once," said Bill rather gruffly, "you told me not to butt in on your affairs—that you liked managing them yourself, in your own way—and—well, it's not the sort of thing one wants to hear a second time."

"Did I say that?" said Sally's smallest voice. "*How rude!* Why did I say it? Were you trying to manage me?"

"I expect so. And we weren't bothering about being polite to each other just then."

"No?" said Sally. Her eyelashes just flickered up and down again. "No—I remember you called me a vixen, and a hoyden, and a little fury. Our manners are *much* nicer now," she concluded with an air of virtue.

Bill found himself watching to see if the dimple would appear. With an effort he looked out of the window. If he went on looking at Sally, goodness knew what might happen. It was much safer to look away and go on talking.

"What's the good of raking things up?" he said impatiently. "It's now, not seven years ago, that concerns us. Am I to leave you to manage for yourself, or do you want my help? That's what it comes to. It's up to you."

Sally stole a glance at his profile; "nubbly but nice," she reflected. Then she contemplated the mat again, and maintained a maddening silence. Bill turned at last with a jerk.

"My dear girl, I wish you'd say something."

And at that Sally looked up.

"What do you want me to say?" she said.

"What you really think," said Bill.

"Shall I? Really tell the truth?"

"Please, Sally."

"One hardly ever does—not really. But I will if you like. After all, as I said the other day, you can't think much worse of me than you do, so what does it matter? What I feel at present is that everything is slipping—like being in the middle of a landslide, with a perfectly horrible nobody- knows-what's-going-to-happen-next sort of feeling about it. And—and you *are* something solid to take hold of—"

Bill put out his hand. It met Sally's, and found it very cold and small.

"All right, I'm here. Hold on, my dear," he said.

Sally blinked rapidly three times, and jumped up. "I'm an idiot," she said, stamping her foot and pulling her hand out of Bill's—just in time, for, even as she did it, Mrs. Callender came in with the tea.

Chapter Seven

AFTER A SUNDAY of the most blameless description Sally felt at peace with the world and in an angelic state of conscience rather unusual for her. Bill and she had parted friends, "for about the first time ever" as Sally put it; she had sat through a very dull sermon without going to sleep; and on Sunday afternoon had spent an hour and a half reading aloud to Mrs. Preston's bedridden mother. What she had not bargained for was finding the cottage filled with a nice selection of Cally's relations. Hannah Preston was, of course, to be expected—and endured. She was a person of many mournful disapprovals which clung like a mist and always made Sally feel limp. One went braced to meet her, and gave her credit for being a devoted daughter; but Cally's married niece, Ellen, and her unmarried niece, Gladys, were, she felt, superfluous. The cottage was not really big enough for them all. In fact Sally had for a moment hesitated upon the doorstep when she heard their voices, and was only kept upon the path of virtue by the conviction that if they had not seen her come up to the door, they would certainly see her go away from it.

As she hesitated for that moment, and just before she raised her hand to the knocker, she heard Mrs. Preston say in her deep, carrying voice:

"No, not to say foreign, she wasn't, Gladys, and wonderful interested."

"Lor'!" said Gladys, and, as Sally knocked, there was a loud "Ssh" from Ellen.

Mrs. Preston's mother was so glad to see her that Sally did not regret having clung to the path of duty. She considered that she had earned the comfortable feeling with which she encountered Monday morning.

She came downstairs; had breakfast; waited for the post; read a dull letter from Cousin Eliza's solicitor; picked up *The Times*, and there was the bombshell staring her in the face from the Agony Column. Sally stared back, and felt her heart pound against her side.

Friday's advertisement, the sham advertisement, had elicited a prompt reply. There was no mistaking it.

"F.L. to Sally: Don't worry. Messenger will meet you Chark-Strudwick road eleven-thirty today. Absolute discretion."

Sally jumped up and looked at the clock. It was nearly half past ten. Her eyes went back to the paper. Everything seemed to be shaking a little, but she steadied herself, and read the message again. It was from Fritzi. That meant Fritzi was alive. She had always said that he was alive. Bill didn't believe it. Now he would have to believe it. Would he?

Just the faintest little shiver of doubt came into Sally's excited mind like a little draught penetrating into an overheated room. If Bill were here what would he say? He might say— Sally frowned, but her mind was clearing—he might say, if one advertisement was bogus, why not the other? He might say that.

Sally crumpled up the paper, and let it fall onto the floor.

If Bill were here, he would probably say any number of stuffy, prudent things; but he wasn't here, and she was certainly going to walk along the Strudwick road, and meet the messenger who might have news of Fritzi.

She ran upstairs for her hat and the violet scarf, and hurried out. As she unlatched the gate she heard a man's voice answering Mrs. Callender, and wondered vaguely why Cally was in the garden gossiping. She went on down the road.

The person with whom Mrs. Callender was conversing was Mr. James Preston, who combined the duties of village postman with those of obedient husband to Mrs. Callender's cousin, Hannah. Having left the letters half an hour before, he had returned at the moment when Sally was coming downstairs, thus missing her.

Whilst she was considering who on earth was talking to Cally, he was explaining at great length and with much detail, how it had come about that, having a telegram as well as a letter to deliver to Miss Sally, he had entirely forgotten all about the telegram until well upon his homeward way. He was a little, rosy man, and it amused him very much to think that he had remembered the letter and forgotten the telegram. He and Mrs. Callender laughed together for some time before she thought of going to see where Sally was. To do her justice, however, it must be stated that she already knew the contents of the telegram, having elicited from Mr. Preston that it did not contain bad news. "Something about an appointment," he explained, "nothing to signify, so to speak. But perhaps you'd better just give it to 'er, Ellen, and—yes, if you are making a cup of tea, I don't say as I shouldn't be glad of one."

But Sally was well away down the road, and Bill Armitage's telegram, "On no account keep appointment," failed of its purpose.

Sally walked along the road. A slight feeling of exhilaration, a sense of escape, quickened her steps. There was no one to interfere, no one to stop her, but she hurried as though someone might try.

At the four-crossway near the Prestons' cottage she turned at right angles and took the road that ran inland towards Strudwick. It was a long, straight road, all on the flat, with a bank upon either side, and on the top of each bank a hawthorn hedge. Nothing duller could possibly be imagined. The grass was brown, and the road dusty.

Sally walked on, and by the time she had gone half a mile she began to wonder how far she would have to go, and to wish that Fritzi's messenger had thought of any road but this one. Of course it was a good place for a meeting, with those high banks on either side and not even a farm within sight for a couple of miles at least.

At eleven-thirty Sally was nearly two miles from Chark and beginning to be bored. The sort of things that Bill would be likely to say began to come into her mind. Half a dozen drops of rain fell, and there was a pebble in her shoe. She sat down upon a tree stump, took off her shoe and shook it out, and was just making up her mind to sit and wait instead of walking any farther, when a distant humming sound made her look round, and far down the long, white road a car came into sight. It was travelling fast, and as it drew near she saw that it was a two-seater Standard driven by a woman.

It slowed down, stopped, and the driver leaned over the side, asking, "Can you tell me, am I far from Chark?"

Sally got up and came forward. Her boredom was gone. She looked hard at the woman, and saw very little—a black felt hat crammed low over the eyes, a nondescript tweed coat whose collar hid the chin, and fold upon fold of navy blue motor veil, hands in leather gauntlets.

As she came up to the car the woman spoke again. "Is it Miss Meredith?" And, as Sally nodded, "I am glad you have come; it was short notice, but I wanted you, and no one else."

"Well, I'm here," said Sally. "May I ask whom I am speaking to?"

"A friend," said the woman.

"Of my uncle's?"

"Certainly, and of yours."

The voice puzzled Sally. It was low, rather muffled, perhaps by the veil, and singularly lacking in vibration. She received the impression that it was being used a good deal below its natural pitch. She began to feel at once excited and irritated. The child in her—and there was a great deal of the child in Sally—thrilled to the secrecy, the lonely meeting; but something else, just as much a part of her, something that stood for intelligence and experience, was repelled and very much on the alert.

With her hands behind her, leaning on her stout ash stick, she stood about a yard from the car, and asked:

"Have you a message for me?"

"But certainly," said the woman. She had no foreign accent, but each time that she spoke, her "r" was not quite the slovenly English "r." Her words were pronounced, they did not just slide one into the other.

"Will you give me the message?" said Sally, "I mustn't stop."

"It is a message from your uncle. No, I have not seen him; it would not be safe. Above all things it is necessary that we should not be connected, but he has sent me a message. Even that was a risk, but he could not bear to think that you were grieving, and besides there was the case."

"What case?" Sally's tone was cool and detached, but the hands that rested on the crook of the walking stick pressed it hard.

"The red lacquer case," said the woman. "You know; he told you; he showed you how to open it, and in his letter—"

"Yes, in his letter?"

"He said he was leaving it in the bookshelf, but after all—"

"Yes?" For the life of her Sally could not keep the word steady.

"Oh, he took it with him; you must have guessed that," said the woman coolly, "didn't you?"

"Perhaps. What about it?" said Sally.

The woman looked back along the empty stretch of road before she answered. Then she leaned a little farther over the side of the car.

"He took it, but of course he couldn't keep it; it wasn't safe. He passed it to me," and now she spoke low and rapidly. "Now he wishes that the case should be opened, and the paper sent through the post—that is the safest of all—to an address which he has given me."

Sally remained silent for some moments, her eyes fixed on the blue motor veil. Behind it there were eyes that would not show themselves, lips which she could see moving, but whose expression was withheld from her. She spoke at last in simple, puzzled tones.

"Well, if he wants it opened, he can open it."

The clumsy, grey tweed coat did not quite conceal a very slight shrug of the shoulders.

"He has not got the case. How can he open it? He has passed it to me, and his message is this: 'Tell Sally she is to open the case and give you the paper. Then I am safe.'"

As it were through opposite doors, there came into Sally's mind two apparently unconnected sentences. One: "Her tongue's about a yard and a half too long." That was what Bill had said about Cally. And the other: "Not to say foreign she wasn't, and wonderful interested." That was Hannah Preston—about—?

With the sound of those careful "r's" still in her ears, Sally wondered whether Hannah had heard them too. She remembered Ellen had said, "Ssh."

Then she spoke. Her voice sounded a little strange to herself, a little higher and louder than it needed to be.

"You have a written message from my uncle?"

A leather-gauntleted hand tapped impatiently.

"I tell you, even a message by word of mouth, it is a risk—and you say: 'Has he written?'"

"Why should there be any risk?" said Sally.

The hand tapped again.

"Do you doubt that I come from him? Is it that?"

Sally smiled. She was pleased to find that she could smile.

"Oh, no," she said.

Bill would have thought her tone too sweet. He had reason to beware of Sally when she spoke sweetly and raised limpid eyes. The woman looked behind her again.

"We must not waste time," she said. "If you will open the case, I will take you now to where it is. Believe me, if you wish to help your uncle there is need for hurry."

Sally stopped leaning on her stick, and stood up straight.

"If there is anything that my uncle wishes me to do, I will do it—when I have his written authorisation. And now I must be getting home." There was a little electric pause before the woman said: "Can you not understand? I tell you there is danger, I tell you there is need for haste; and you talk to me of a written authorisation."

"I'm sorry," said Sally, "but I can't do anything without it."

She smiled again, adjusted her scarf, threw a good-bye over her shoulder, and began to walk briskly in the direction of Chark. Her heart was beating a good deal faster than usual, but her uncertainty had vanished. Like a little white-hot flame there burned in her the conviction that the woman was lying, that she did not come from Fritzi at all; so she stuck her chin in the air and walked away, and with a soft purring noise the car came after her and drew alongside.

"You do not care," said the woman, "how much you injure him, your uncle? You will not move a finger to help when he asks for help? I am to go back and say 'Sally washes her hands of you, she will not help.' I am to say that?"

Sally turned her face towards the car for a moment. Her brows were arched over scornful eyes. Her colour was high.

"You can go back and say, 'Sally isn't a fool,'" she said, and with a little nod she turned, scrambled up the bank on her right, squeezed through a gap in the hawthorn hedge that topped it, and, with a parting wave of the hand, struck out across the fields for home.

Chapter Eight

AT HOME she found Bill's telegram. "On no account keep appointment." To persons of Sally's turn of mind it is very pleasing to find that you have done a thing which some-body forbids.

She sat down and wrote Major Armitage a faithful account of the forbidden interview, and she did not tell him that his telegram had arrived a day after the fair. If Bill supposed that just because they were friends again he could start ordering her about, he would have to be shown the error of his ways. Sally smiled and sparkled as she wrote.

When the letter was ready she asked Mrs. Callender to take it to the post, and, as it chanced, Mrs. Callender met Mr. Preston and gave him the letter instead of going on to the pillar box with it herself.

"Just drop it in as you go along, James, and I'll step in and see Hannah," she said. And Mr. Preston, acquiescing cheerfully, put the letter in his pocket and forgot all about it until next day, when he found it with a guilty start, and posted it twenty-four hours late.

He thought it best not to mention the matter, either to Hannah, his wife, or to her cousin, Ellen Callender, "least said, soonest mended, and I 'ates unpleasantness," being his ingenuous thought.

He was on his way up to the cottage with another telegram.

"Ellen, she do talk," he continued to himself. "She makes a good cup of tea, but she do talk, and between her and Hannah I shouldn't hear the last of it this side of Easter."

He came round to the back door with a cheery "Mornin', Ellen," and produced the orange envelope.

"A wonderful lot of telegrams your Miss Sally keep a-having," he remarked as he handed it over to Mrs. Callender.

"And a turn they always give me, whether or no." Mrs. Callender took the telegram gingerly as she spoke.

"And what is it this time?" she said. "Waste of money is what I call it, and all in the pockets of them in the Government as keep a-lumping on of the taxes. What do they do with it all? That's what I want to know, with stamps enough to ruin you, and linen pillowcases double what they was before the war, to saying nothing of pins and cotton. A scandal is what I call it, and time it was seen into. And what did you say it was this time, James?"

Mr. Preston's slightly bewildered eyes, which had been roving as if in search of something, here came to rest upon the familiar orange envelope.

"Meaning in the telegram, Ellen?" he inquired. "Oh, it's only to say as e's coming down this evening, arriving six-thirty at Lenton, and wants 'er to meet him." Mr. Preston stopped and chuckled. "It'll be a match, I suppose," he said complacently. "Hannah, she says no; says he gave her the chuck once, and once off is never come on again. But I says a match it'll be, for it isn't in reason to suppose as 'e'd be so free with his train fares and his telegrams if 'e wasn't meaning business."

"Ah," said Mrs. Callender enigmatically, "them as lives longest'll see most."

Sally walked to Lenton to meet the six-thirty. It was very dark as she stepped into the lane, and she stood for a moment looking about her and watching until she could distinguish the sky-line above the trees. Her torch was in her pocket, but she did not wish to use it. Presently the trees and hedges stood out like ink blotches on a dense, even dusk, and Sally stepped out, with the wind blowing in her face, soft with a hint of rain to come. She loved walking in the dark; everything so large, and quiet, and vague, and the wind moving on enormous gentle wings. It gave her what she called a world-without-end feeling. She felt as though she would never quarrel with anyone again, not even with Bill. "We ought always to go to church in empty fields at midnight," she reflected.

Presently she permitted herself to think about Bill. Nice to be going to meet him. Nice to feel there was a person like Bill somewhere about, ready to weigh in with appropriate telegrams, and to catch a dull local train after office hours if you wanted him. It was even nicer to think of the tons of good advice he could place at your disposal. She would try and remember all Bill's niceness so as not to quarrel with him tonight. But, on the other hand, supposing he was too nice, supposing—Sally wrinkled her brow in the dark and then laughed. "He very nearly forgot and kissed me last time he went away!" She laughed again. "Are you going to pretend that you would mind if he did? You needn't be a hypocrite as well as a flirt." Then, with a sudden change of mood, "Sally, you're an idiot. You had your chance, and you threw it away, and you needn't think you're going to have fool's luck and another chance, for that sort of thing simply doesn't happen. Bill will marry a nice fat girl who takes sevens in shoes and never powders her nose. She'll adore him out of pale blue eyes, and he'll get wind in the head, and finish up by being eighteen stone, and he'll always remember what a lucky escape he had from you."

It was at this moment that Sally saw the beam of light. It sprang out of the dark—dazzling, brilliant—shifted, and fell in a long ray across the lane, making footmarks in the dust look like craters, and pebbles like boulders, each with its hard inky shadow.

Sally stood still and stared. The beam came from the headlight of a motor bicycle. She could just discern the vague outline dote in under the hedge. The ray of light seemed to bar her way, and as she hesitated a man stepped through the lighted patch and came towards her.

"Miss Meredith?" he said.

His voice was strange to Sally, and the light had showed her no more than a pair of legs in drab overalls. Except for the fact that he seemed to have large feet, she might, as she put it to herself, just as well have seen him in the dark. She slid her right hand into her pocket, and rested it on the electric torch. She meant to see something more than boots and legs before this interview was over, if luck would serve her.

"Miss Meredith?" said the man, and she noted the trilled "r" again.

"I am Miss Meredith, but I am afraid I have an appointment."

"With Major Armitage—exactly. I will not keep you long."

"What do you want?" said Sally, a little sharply.

"My dear Miss Meredith, do you really need to ask me that?"

"It would save time if you would come to the point."

"Oh, I'm not pressed for time—not in the least. It is you who are in a hurry. For myself, I find it a charming night for a talk."

"Let me pass," said Sally, and found herself caught by the left wrist.

"Your pardon—not yet," said the man. "But I will come, as you say, to the point. You sent on Monday a message. It was to say that you were not a fool—a very interesting message, and in response to it I am here to deal with a young lady who is not a fool, but of sufficient intelligence to see when good terms are offered her."

"Let go my wrist," said Sally, in perfectly colourless tones. A white fury was upon her, which completely purged her of fear. She felt as deadly as an electric wire. The man released her, but stood his ground.

"Good terms," he repeated.

"Yes?"

"For yourself, and for M. Lasalle."

"Yes?"

"Shall I state them?"

"If you like."

"For M. Lasalle—safety and release, and for you also safety and—" He leaned forward and mentioned a sum of money that fairly took Sally's breath away. She started involuntarily, and the man continued to speak in a low, rapid fashion that was more un-English than his accent.

"For this you will do one thing, one simple thing. You will open the red lacquer case. M. Lasalle he has consented, he takes what has happened as an omen. To him it is Fate that has intervened, and he accepts what Fate has done. Only—you know him, he has a scruple of con-science—he will not himself open the case. He washes his hands of the whole thing. He has a new idea—something beneficent that shall make his name known. The inventor's fever is upon him again, and for the formula in the lacquer case he no longer cares. He says 'Go to Sally, she will open it for you. Leave me in peace.'"

"Is that all?" said Sally, quietly.

"Is it not enough?"

"Oh dear, no."

"What more then?"

"The simplest thing in the world. A written authorisation from M. Lasalle."

The man swore under his breath. "You cannot have it."

"Then—" Sally made a slight gesture. The man's hand touched her shoulder, and lifted again.

"Miss Meredith, I do not think you understand. That formula we most solemnly intend to have. You say you are not a fool. Then reflect. Those who can offer such a sum as I have offered you, is it that they will accept the present situation? I will be frank with you, as one person of intelligence with another. We have the case, and in the case we have the formula; but we cannot open the case without risking the destruction of what we seek. Our experts have examined the case, and they announce that they cannot recommend an attempt at forcing it."

"No," said Sally. "That's just what M. Lasalle told me. I expect you heard him. By the way, was it you at the window?"

The man threw out an impatient hand.

"That report of the experts decides the matter. The lacquer case must be opened. You alone know how to open it. Therefore it must be opened by you. If you open it, you are rich and safe, and if not—you are—"

"Yes?"

"I do not threaten—I beg you to understand that I do not threaten—I deal only with facts. It is a fact that if you open the case you will be rich and safe; and it is a fact that if you refuse to open it there is no safety for you anywhere. It is a fact that if you do not open it, it is better for you that you were never born. In the end you will open it—that goes without saying—but first you will wish, as I have said, that you were never born. Does a person of intelligence hesitate between such facts as these?"

"I'm not hesitating," said Sally calmly. "*Nothing* would induce me to open the case without M. Lasalle's authority. Is that quite clear? I don't mind repeating it if it's not, and I don't mind in the least how often I say it."

"I suppose," said the man, "that you now expect me to admire your spirit. You think, perhaps, that I am impressed. Believe me when I say that so unintelligent a position merely arouses in me contempt; and if I have any other feeling it is, perhaps, a little, yes, just a little pity, because, after all, you are young and charming; and to waste youth and charm is always a pity, is it not?"

"I really don't know," said Sally. "If you've said all you want to say, do you mind letting me pass? I want to get to the station."

"To meet Major Armitage? Yes, you may pass now. Was it not Shakespeare who said that journeys end in lovers' meetings? Pleasant, but not always true. *Au revoir*, Miss Meredith."

Sally stepped back a pace, and threw up her right hand with the electric torch in it. Her finger pressed the switch, and the sharp little beam flashed out upon the man whom she had up till now seen only as a dark blur. The light showed her a figure of medium height, a leather jacket, and a head most effectually disguised by a leather cap and motor goggles; the chin was sunk in a dark muffler. So far as recognition was concerned she had gained nothing, and, as the light fell upon him, the man gripped her wrist and turned it back upon herself.

The sudden dazzle and glare made her call out. The man's touch seemed to be forcing fear upon her, a fear which up till now she had not felt.

He stood looking at her with the light on her face. Then he said gravely:

"I shall be quite sure to know you again, but I do not think that you will know me. Think a little of what I have said. Think intelligently. Good-bye, Miss Sally."

He dropped her wrist, turned his back, and walked over to the motor bicycle under the hedge.

Sally stood where she was, and heard him start the engine. She did not move when the noisy, thudding thing came by within a yard of her but as soon as it was past she flashed her torch upon the number plate, and stamped her foot with sudden fury. These people took no chances. A fold of newspaper covered the plate, adjusted, no doubt, just before he met her, and removable as soon as he was out of sight.

Sally could have cried with pure rage as she put her useless torch back in her pocket and set out for the station; but behind the rage there was fear, and presently her anger died down and the fear rose about her like a cold mist. When the lights of the station came into view it was all she could do to keep to her steady walking pace. She wanted to run, and she knew that, if she began to run, panic would take hold of her.

She came up to the station just as the London train came in. Only three passengers alighted at Lenton. One was an old woman, another a girl in her teens, and the third a young man with a carpetbag. There was no Bill. Sally stood on the platform and stared at the train. Bill had not come.

She sat down on a hard, wet station seat. She sat down because quite suddenly she did not feel as if she could stand any longer. She wondered when it had rained. The seat was quite wet. It hadn't rained at Chark. There must have been a shower here just now. Why hadn't Bill come? What on earth had happened?

Sally shut her eyes. The feeling which she had described to Bill as "everything sliding" came upon her with renewed force; and there was no Bill to take hold of. No Bill here, and nearly three miles of dark lane between her and home. She got up, and walked through the little anteroom with its smell of fish and its bright, hard light and out through the open door beyond. She stood there and looked at the dark.

When she had stood there for five minutes and had called herself every sort of a name that she could think of, she went back into the station and telephoned to the White Hart for a cab.

Chapter Nine

BILL ARMITAGE got Sally's delayed letter on his arrival at the War Office next morning. It was the third or fourth letter in a fairly big pile, and when he had read it he pushed the others on one side and rang up Scotland Yard. After a little delay he got Inspector Williams on the line, and to him imparted the details of the interview on the Chark-Strudwick road as set down by Sally.

Inspector Williams said, "Yes," at intervals. Sometimes he said, "Yes, Yes," and at the end he said, "Quite so." An efficient person, but not conversational.

"I shall go down this morning. There's an eleven-thirty. What about you? Inquiries at Strudwick about the car? All right. You'll take your own line then? I must get back to town tonight, but I don't think Miss Meredith ought to be alone in that cottage. What about her coming to London? Better not? Well, perhaps you're right. But someone ought to keep his eye on her. You'll take that on? Good. I may understand, then, that from now on it won't be possible for these people to get her by herself. All right then."

Bill hung up the recover and reached for Bradshaw.

Sally, meanwhile, was getting into the London train at Lenton. She had passed the sort of night during which one does not seem to sleep at all, and yet manages to experience a succession of vivid and rather terrifying dreams. First, she and Bill were eloping on a motor bicycle. Bill wore a blue motor veil and enormous leather gauntlets. The motor bicycle bumped very much, and between the bumps Bill kept explaining to her that he was passionately in love with a fat girl whose feet were larger than his own. In the middle of the explanation he kissed her. Sally woke up. Then she and Fritzi were running, hand in hand, down a very dark lane. They were trying to catch Mr. Preston who hovered in the air just overhead and pelted them with telegrams, and Fritzi kept saying, "You'll be an old maid, Sally; I fear it with all my heart." Sally woke up. Then she was standing in the dock at Bow Street, and the magistrate had three little rows of tight grey curls like Cally's. He put on a black cap over the curls, and sentenced her to death because she wouldn't save Fritzi's life by opening the lacquer case. Sally woke up. This sort of thing went on all night.

In her last dream she heard Bill calling her name in a tone that changed from appeal to violent anger. So vivid was the impression that she woke to find herself halfway to the door, with the tears running down her face. After that she washed in cold water, and dressed herself.

By the time she was dressed she had firmly decided that she would go up to town for the day and see Bill. She considered her decision very fortunate when a telegram interrupted her breakfast. It ran, "Unavoidably detained in town. Anxious to see you. Can you come up today? Will meet ten-thirty from Lenton. Bill."

The telegram took a weight off her mind. Bill was all right then. He wanted to see her; she wanted to go up; and the day, instead of presenting itself as full of veiled anxieties, suddenly cleared up and disclosed a very pleasant prospect.

Sally put on the hat she liked best, and told Mrs. Callender that she was going to shop and might be back late.

Mrs. Callender told Mr. Preston, who told his wife, who told her cousins, Ellen and Gladys, that Miss Sally was off to town to meet her young man, to which Gladys replied, with a haughty toss of the head, that she didn't hold with running after the men, and hadn't never found she needed to neither. They spent a very pleasant half hour disapproving of Sally.

At Lenton, Sally, after passing two rather crowded compartments, ensconced herself in a third-class carriage, the only other occupant of which was a schoolboy of twelve or thereabouts. She had settled herself comfortably in a corner seat, and was looking idly out of the window when she saw, advancing along the platform and scanning every compartment by turn, a person upon whom her gaze rested, at first with bewilderment, and then with something like horror.

The person was a woman, a quite ordinary-looking woman, but she wore a shapeless grey tweed overcoat and a dark blue motor veil over a black felt hat, and she looked into every carriage.

Afterward Sally might accuse herself of being jumpy and imagining things. At the time she jumped up without hesitation, opened the carriage door, whisked out, and plunged into the most crowded of the compartments which she had previously rejected. There were women in it with market baskets, there were children eating bull's eyes, and a workman smoking shag. Sally took her seat thankfully in the crowd, and was impervious to the fact that her advent aroused no enthusiasm.

When they all had to change she again chose a full carriage. She caught another glimpse of the woman in the blue veil, and after she had got into the train she edged her way to the window, and stood there looking out. The woman was walking up the platform. There was a man with her, a man in a Burberry, a leather cap and motor goggles. Sally took her seat hurriedly. She did not, therefore, see that only the man got into the train. The woman went down the steps, crossed to number one platform, entered the telegraph office, and despatched a telegram addressed to Miss Etta Shaw at a club in London. It ran: "Coming up by ten-thirty as arranged. Please meet." It was unsigned.

Sally sat in the train and struggled against a feeling that the day had clouded over. Bill would meet her, and she would tell him all about everything, and then they would have lunch, and after lunch perhaps they would do a show together. It was simply ages since she had seen a play. Instead of being depressed and feeling flat, she ought to be simply full of pleasant anticipation. She told herself firmly that she was full of pleasant anticipation, and then sat back and hoped that no one would notice that her eyes were full of tears.

"Oh, Sally, you *are* an idiot!" she said to herself. "You really are!"

The journey seemed to take a long time. When the train slid into the terminus, Sally felt as if she had been sitting in it for hours and that she hated trains and never wanted to see one again. She got out of her carriage, and looked up and down the platform for Bill. There was a crowd of hurrying people all completely and utterly strange to her. She began to walk towards the barrier; Bill of course would be waiting there. And then something made her look round, and there, a few yards behind her, was the man in the motor goggles. He was coming up on her right-hand side. Now he was abreast of her. He turned his head, and, for a sickening moment, Sally thought he was going to speak. Instead, he pushed against her ever so slightly and then passed on. Sally followed, gave up her ticket, and passed the barrier.

The man had disappeared. She looked around for Bill, and there was no Bill. A horrid blankness came upon her. Only last week she had run upstairs in the dark. When she came to the top she had thought there was still another step and there wasn't; her foot came down hard with a jerk. That same blankness was upon her then. To expect something very confidently and to find that it isn't there, that was the feeling in both cases. It gave one a jolt and then that blankness. After last night, too.

Sally gave herself a little shake, and, still looking about her, began to cross the station. She was looking for a man, and so did not recognize Etta Shaw until she fairly bumped into her.

"Why, Sally," said Miss Shaw, "what a surprise!"

And Sally found herself taken warmly by the arm, and was conscious that she was much more sincerely pleased than usual to see this old and rather outgrown friend. Ten years ago Etta Shaw had been a very pretty girl. Curiously enough, it was just that epithet that was always applied to her. People said at once, "Etta Shaw, oh, a very pretty girl." Now she was one of those people who had ceased to be a girl without becoming a woman. The slimness of ten years ago had degenerated into thinness and a poke. The bright colour was just as brilliant, but there was a hard edge to it. The blue eyes were even bluer than they had been, but one looked in vain for any hint of a nature enriched by experience. There was no grey in her hair, but it had a dry and faded look under a noticeable blue hat.

She pressed Sally's arm, and reiterated her pleasure at this unexpected meeting.

"I have come up for the day," said Sally.

"So I see, my dear. Shopping?"

"Well," said Sally doubtfully, "I suppose I shall shop."

"Or are you meeting anyone?" said Miss Shaw brightly. "Am I in the way?"

If Bill were to turn up, Etta Shaw would most certainly be very much in the way. The thought flitted through Sally's mind and was immediately followed by another. If Bill didn't turn up? She routed this thought, but it left behind it the faint impulse to detain Etta.

"I must telephone," she said abruptly. "Are you in a hurry? I don't really know what I'm doing till I've telephoned. If you could wait a moment it would be rather nice; I really haven't seen you for an age."

Miss Shaw was most amiable about waiting. It appeared that she also felt it to be an age since she had seen Sally and had a good talk.

"Life's so interesting just now, don't you think so?" she said. "So full of movement and development; such wonderful new ideas abroad! Don't you think so, Sally darling?"

Etta's enthusiasms were apt to leave Sally cold. They not uncommonly centred upon oddish young men, rather weirdly dressed and without visible family connections.

Sally disengaged herself, therefore, without replying, entered a telephone box, and having shut the door, rang up the War Office, gave the number of Bill's extension, and received a rather serious shock.

Miss Shaw, waiting outside heard her say, "What?" in tones of sharp incredulity, and then "Called out of town suddenly? What? You don't know where he's gone? Are you sure he's out of town? Quite sure? Do you know at all when he'll be back? Not today? You're certain of that? Oh—no, there's no message, no, thank you very much, except perhaps you might say that Miss Meredith rang up."

Sally came out of the box looking pale and bewildered.

"Plans any clearer, dear?" asked Miss Shaw. Sally turned to her with relief. It was something not to be alone in this crowd which might at any moment give up the man with whom she had spoken in a dark lane.

"Well," she said, frowning a little, "I'm afraid my plans have all gone to bits. I came up to see someone on business, and they've gone out of town for the day; so really and truly, I suppose, I'd better just get something to eat at the station and go home again."

"Oh, but how *dull!*" said Etta Shaw. Her voice was pitched rather high. It produced an effect of bright monotony which the stress she laid upon many of her words hardly served to break.

"Yes, it is rather," said Sally, "but I don't really want to shop, and I expect I'd better be getting home."

"Oh, but you *can't,* not when you're actually here. Come and lunch with me at my club. Whatever happens, you *must* have lunch."

"But you?" said Sally.

"I was going there, anyhow. I've got a really *delightful* plan, in my head, only I won't tell you about it until we get to the club. I think we'll take a taxi. I've got the car up in town, but it's having something done to it and won't be ready till half-past four—tiresome, but, of course, I don't really want it today."

Etta continued to talk as she and Sally crossed the station and got into a taxi.

Sally was still rather bewildered. She followed Etta, partly because of that vague inclination to stay with someone that she knew, and partly because she was hungry and the idea of having lunch was a pleasing one.

As they drove away and Etta went on talking, Sally began to experience feelings of extreme resentment against Bill. To fail her twice was really too much. If he imagined for one moment that he could just send her telegrams whenever he felt inclined, and make appointments only to break them—well, Sally thought she could trust herself to put Major Armitage firmly in his proper place. "If anyone is going to do anything of that sort, it'll be me, not him," she thought vigorously, if ungrammatically. She gave a little determined nod of the head, and, for the first time since leaving the station, became aware of her surroundings.

The taxi, wedged in a block, was moving slowly forward at the rate of about two miles an hour. Sally looked across to her left and exclaimed.

Miss Shaw stopped with some offence in the middle of an enthusiastic description of the prodigies performed on the violin by a new Polish genius with a name like three sneezes in rapid succession. She was not, of course, aware that Sally had not heard a single word of it.

"What is it, Sally? How jumpy you are!"

"I'm not. It's Eleanor Farquhar, there on the island. Oh, I *should* like to see Eleanor again. I thought she was in India. Etta, I'm going to get out."

The colour rushed into Miss Shaw's face. Her arm went firmly round Sally's waist.

"You can't, Sally; how mad. Besides I thought you'd quarrelled with Mrs. Farquhar. She's Major Armitage's cousin, isn't she?"

"Yes, yes, she is. I did, but it doesn't matter in the least; I *love* Eleanor."

Sally got the taxi door an inch or two open, and just then the car in front of them shot ahead. Etta Shaw, leaning forward, pulled her back, and the island fell away behind them.

Mrs. Farquhar on the curb, waiting to cross, watched the taxi out of sight. "That was Sally Meredith," she thought. "I wonder if Bill ever sees her. I ought to know the other woman's face, too—a hideous hat, anyhow." She plunged into the traffic, and Sally faded from her mind.

Chapter Ten

IT WAS AFTER lunch that Etta Shaw propounded her plan.

"You know, Sally," she said, "you really *are* my oldest friend, and I never seem to see you at all."

"Cousin Eliza," murmured Sally. She was looking round the room, thinking what very odd people belonged to Etta's club. There was a woman just opposite to them who wore what looked like a white Viyella nightgown and a hat covered with purple ostrich feathers.

"Yes, I *know*. *I'm* tied like that, too, with Aunt Emma. Not that she's really *ill*, you know, but she doesn't get out of bed. She just lies there, and has her cats and her birds; and sometimes she knows me, and sometimes she doesn't. Of course it's a *tie*."

Sally removed her fascinated gaze from the nightgown, looked at Etta with real sympathy, and said:

"Yes, it must be."

"I can't get away for more than one night, but I can do that; and I was thinking if you *could* have me—" She paused, and went on with heightened colour and just a shade of something odd in her voice, "We're *such old* friends, I know I need not stand on ceremony—what do you think of my plan? I could drive you back in the car, stay the night, and then wander home across country? It would be rather fun finding the way."

Sally did some rapid thinking. She didn't want Etta, that was the first thought. On the other hand, nothing would annoy Bill more than to arrive and find Miss Shaw at the cottage. Perhaps he was there now, waiting to see her. It would be extremely pleasing to arrive with Etta. Behind these thoughts there were others like faint shadows. "I hate trains. I don't want to travel alone. I hate the Lenton road. It will be pitch dark."

Thought is a very rapid process. There was no perceptible pause before Sally said aloud:

"Oh, Etta, could you really?" and was immediately assured that Etta not only could, but would.

It was while they were having coffee that Miss Shaw suddenly put her cup down and remembered that she had promised to telephone to a friend.

"About our meeting next week, dear," she explained, "our *big* meeting—you know, I sent you the papers about it." At this point she lapsed obviously into quotation: "The opportunity for the great heart of the country to become vocal, and to demand not the *shadow*, but the *reality* of peace."

At the door she nodded brightly and made her way to a telephone box.

Having got the number she asked for, she burst out volubly, "It's all right, she'll come. I've invited myself to stay the night at the cottage, and offered to drive her down. Yes, quite pleased. I told her the car was being mended and wouldn't be ready till half-past four or so. If we don't start till five, it will be too dark for her to see which way we go. You're sure she won't recognise *you*?" She listened eagerly for a moment, and with a parting "Then you'll bring the car round at five?" hung up the receiver.

Sally, left alone, had decided that she felt exactly like a cat on a strange roof. She didn't think that she liked the roof very much, but she found the other cats distinctly intriguing. Really Etta's faculty for drifting into odd environments was amazing. The woman in the nightgown and feathers had just been joined by a fat pillow of an old lady whose cropped white hair and horn-rimmed spectacles looked much too modern when taken in conjunction with a black cashmere dress and a crossover shawl of yellowish woollen crochet. A cigarette was the last discordant touch.

Etta came back rather breathless.

"And now we're going to have a *treat*," she announced. "This isn't like a *formal* club, you know. We all know each other, and have the same aims and interests, the same *soul sense*, in fact; and some of our more gifted members are going to *give out* to us this afternoon."

"Give out?" repeated Sally, endeavouring to control a suddenly obstreperous dimple.

"Yes," said Etta earnestly with the gesture of one who hands food to the starving. "Don't you think genius is like that? It must give out, impart, in fact, *radiate*."

"I see," said Sally. "Yes, radiate makes it quite clear. Who's going to do it?

"Well, Sascha's going to play for us—"

"Sascha?"

Etta repeated the name that sounded like three sneezes. "I call him Sascha," she added, "it's easier, and we are *very* intimate."

"It's certainly easier," said Sally.

She settled herself down to enjoy her afternoon, and to watch the people who now began to fill the room. Etta seemed to know them all, and, according to her whispered comments, practically every one of them was either the greatest thinker since Schopenhauer, or a really divine musician, or almost *too* brilliant an intellect. Rivals to Shakespeare and Shelley jostled sculptors whose work would simply eclipse Rodin. In fact, Sally was privileged to behold what Miss Shaw described in a fervid whisper as "the rising surge of the new flood of genius."

"Sascha" played to them, and Sally found his playing ordinary. In appearance he resembled any of those pallid, long-haired young men whom one may see playing first violin in a third-rate orchestra. He had the pasty skin, the large dark eyes, and the somewhat unwashed appearance common to them all;

but when he laid aside his bow Etta Shaw turned tear-filled eyes upon Sally, and murmured, "Isn't he *divine*?"

It was after this that the fat young man with red hair and freckled hands got up and in a small, high voice recited a poem entitled "Sunset."

"The West," he began, gazing at the chandelier whilst Etta gazed at him.

"The West
A Drain running
With
Yellow Dye.
Into it Someone has
Thrown
An orange
Burst
Squelching
Rotten
The Sun!
Out of the Gate of the East
Like the Head of a
Bald
Obese
Old Man
Fat
Hairless
Pallid
Looks the Moon."

The young man's high voice ceased, but he continued to look at the chandelier for at least a minute. Then with a start, as of one roused from a trance, he ran his limp white fingers through his limp red hair, and sat down.

"Good gracious!" said Sally. "Who is he?"

"Aubrey Cuthbert—*the* great poet. He wrote 'Dead Flies and Carrion.'"

"He would," said Sally, in tones of deep conviction. And I'm sorry to say that she so far forgot herself as to murmur, "Oh, my sainted Cousin Eliza" just under her breath.

"*Marvellous*, isn't it?" said Etta.

A purple feather brushed Sally's cheek, and the woman in white flannel spoke across her to Etta in a deep, booming voice.

"Insistent!" she said. "That is the word that comes to me. The clamorous voice, the ego that will not be denied—"she paused, and added on a yet deeper note, "you know, of course, that his aura is almost pure magenta."

"Oh, how can he, with that hair!" said Sally.

"Sssh," said Etta, and looked reproachful. The purple feathers drew away.

"He has a soul-twist," said the deep voice, and Sally just saved herself by turning a giggle into a sneeze.

Two hours later she had ceased to feel amused. The radiators had succeeded one another without a pause, and, whilst the enthusiasm of Etta and her friends appeared to remain steadily at boiling point, Sally had long ago succumbed to the cold touch of boredom. She decided that a little genius went a long way, and that, the less evident the genius, the farther did it go.

It was, therefore, with a feeling of considerable relief that she emerged with Etta into the dark and foggy street. The lamp posts had misty rainbows round them, the air was raw with a damp that might turn to frost at any moment. Sally snuffed it up with appreciation and realized how dreadfully stuffy the atmosphere of genius had been.

A Wolseley landaulette was drawn up to the curb and a chauffeur stood beside it, holding the door open. The light under the club portico showed him as a well set up man in neat, dark livery. He turned as they crossed the pavement, and Sally was startled by his extreme good looks. Etta poured out a flood of voluble directions whilst Sally took her seat; then she, too, got in, the door was shut, and the car moved off, gradually gathering pace.

Then Etta suddenly started, looked in her bag, and accused herself of being the most forgetful woman in the world.

"Telegrams," she explained, "telegrams that I ought to have sent off this morning, and they went *right* out of my head all through meeting you; and will you mind *very* much if I just stop and send them off now, for they really *ought* to go?"

Without waiting for an answer she called down the speaking tube and directed the man to stop at the nearest post office. As the car stopped, she jumped out and left Sally to a few minutes' welcome silence.

Inside the post office Etta Shaw wrote two telegrams and sent them off. Their contents would have interested Sally. The first was addressed to Mrs. Callender, The Cottage, Chark, and ran: "Detained for a few days. Do not forward letters. Meredith."

The second, over the address of which Miss Shaw hesitated for a moment, was to Bill Armitage at the War Office, and read: "Joining Fritzi. Please do not interfere in any way. Most important. Sally Meredith."

Sally was just beginning to feel comfortably sleepy when Etta returned, and her drowsiness deepened as they ran smoothly along, first between fog-bound lights, and later through the solid misty darkness. Etta talked all the time, but her voice became a mere lulling murmur. Once or twice Sally half woke up with a jerk and said, "Yes." Once she started awake, and looked with blinking eyes at a crowded street pavement where a line of stalls and barrows hugged the curb under a flare of yellow gas. She gave a sharp exclamation.

For a moment she thought that she had seen Fritzi standing there in the crowd of dingily dressed persons who were pressing round the stalls; but the whole thing was gone before she could take it in, and she sank into sleep again deeper—deeper—deeper.

Afterwards she never could decide whether it was her wakeful night and the stuffy air of Etta's club, or whether that sleep of hers had been less legitimately induced.

The car slid on, smoothly and without a check. The yellow mist changed to a white mist; and the white mist thinned away to nothingness. The full moon came up out of a bank of fog, orange red at first, but growing paler as it mounted. The sky cleared to a sapphire black set with a sharp glitter of stars. They held their own for a brief half hour, and then the moonlight flooded the whole arch of the sky and the level fields and lanes beneath it.

Sally woke up with a start. The car had stopped. The door was open, letting in the frost, and Etta Shaw was getting out. She heard her say, "Shall I wake her?" and a man's voice answered, "Not if she's really sound asleep."

Sally sat up and pushed the rug off her knees. Etta and the chauffeur were standing by the car talking. Sally looked past them and saw a high stone wall pierced by an oak door which stood ajar. This wasn't Chark—where were they, and why had they stopped? She struggled to order her thoughts, and, leaning forward, called sharply:

"Etta, where are we?"

Etta Shaw turned. Her voice sounded high and nervous.

"Such a stupid mistake," she said. "He didn't understand, and it was so foggy I never noticed which way we came out of London. This is Charnwood, my aunt's house. You'll have to stay the night with me, instead of my staying with you—" She ended as she had begun with "Such a stupid mistake!" and a light fluttering laugh. Sally felt suddenly very much annoyed. Cally would be frantic, and Bill—Bill would—well, what would Bill think? What had possessed her to sleep like that? She picked up the rug, and got out stiffly. They passed through the door in the wall, the chauffeur following. The door was shut behind them.

Etta went on talking.

"Such a *cold* night, and going to be colder. Something hot to drink, don't you think? Do you like cocoa? Oh, don't carry that rug, Lazare will take it."

The foreign name arrested Sally's attention, recalling it from vexed thoughts of Bill and Cally. She turned on the flagged path just below the door step, and looked with faint interest at the too good-looking chauffeur. His pale, regular features were distinct in the moonlight. His glance at Sally was a bold one as he came forward with his hands out to take the rug from her. Sharply annoyed at his bad manners, and at Etta's folly in engaging a man of that type, Sally looked down. She saw the chauffeur's hands palm upwards in the clear and brilliant moonlight—large hands with long, thick fingers, and, dark against the pallor of the palm, a jagged, cross-shaped scar.

"Oh," said Sally, on a little indrawn breath; and with that sound and that breath her power to move and cry went from her. The rug dropped from her hands upon the path. She tried to get her breath, to scream, to move; and as she tried, and found herself numb with the nightmare sense of helplessness, the man she stared at caught her by the arm, and the hand with the scar covered her mouth.

Chapter Eleven

IT WAS WHEN M. Lasalle was staring into the depressing depths of the Smuggler's Leap that there suddenly came upon him the New Idea. Before it came his mind was as dark as the pit below him; and then, with a little spurt of light like an igniting match, the infant idea was there. Immediately his consciousness turned to it, centred about it, and became blessedly unaware of all the tormenting thoughts which had been making his poor mind a battlefield. It now ceased to be a battlefield and became a laboratory, a place thoroughly congenial and filled with the useful and docile idea to which poor Fritzi had now for weeks been a stranger.

As with his inner eye he contemplated this blessed change, and with his inner man rejoiced over it, he became aware of the overwhelming necessity for some place of security and retirement where in solitude and peace he might nourish and mature the New Idea. He fumbled in his pockets, pulled out his handkerchief, and wiped the sweat of a past horror from his brow. The action was definitely symbolic, and M. Lasalle's thoughts were so much uplifted that the fall of his fountain pen entirely escaped his notice. Having wiped his brow, he turned from the Smuggler's Leap and walked slowly and dreamily back along the way by which he had come. Continuously he considered the twin problems which assailed him:

The Way of Escape.

The Place of Secure Retirement.

As he regained the path, a buffet of wind struck the headland and scattered heavy raindrops. By the time that he came in view of the high road the full force of the risen storm was beating upon a countryside already streaming with water. The battered trees bent and strained, a distant thunder kept up a continuous rumble, and for a moment M. Lasalle stood still, dazed with the sudden noise and stress. Between the lines of wind-bent trees which marked the road there was a patch of light. Shadows of waving branches crossed it confusedly. M. Lasalle came to the end of the path, and saw a large limousine standing in the road just at his right. The headlights turned the drenched road in front of them into a silver river. The bonnet of the car was open, and the chauffeur was burrowing into its depths.

M. Lasalle stood and looked at the handsome car, the oblivious chauffeur, and the stormy night. A voice spoke with extreme distinctness to an inner consciousness still grappling with the two problems. It said, "The Way of Escape." M. Lasalle instantly walked across the road, opened the door of the limousine, and got in. He sank upon comfortable cushions, and a feeling of peace descended on him, blotting out the storm.

After ten minutes or so the chauffeur shut the bonnet with a clang, started the engine, and took his seat. The car moved on its luxurious way. Twenty, thirty, thirty-five miles an hour, with the road running swiftly past, and the storm dying down. The rain continued. M. Lasalle sat at his ease, and watched the faint lights of villages appear and pass. After an indefinite time there were more lights, and more; then tram lines and lamp posts with great blinding arc lights. A belated tram slid by, cutting in in front of the car and stopping. The chauffeur put the brakes on hard, the car came almost to a standstill in its own length, and M. Lasalle, opening the right-hand door, stepped unobtrusively off the step into the wet road.

Chapter Twelve

SALLY DID NOT lose consciousness, but terror rushed in upon her and benumbed her every faculty. She felt herself lifted, an arm as hard as iron about her waist, the hand crushed down upon her mouth. It was worse than the most awful dream that she had ever had. To an accompaniment of twittering noises from Etta, an "Oh, do be careful!" treading on the heels of "Oh, you'll hurt her!" and "Oh, Lazare, do take care!" they crossed a hall and began to ascend a staircase. The man who carried Sally stopped half way up the stair to say "Chut!" not roughly, but with a certain intensity. The fact that Etta instantly held her tongue pierced through Sally's terror and set her mind groping.

Next moment Etta was opening a door and switching on the electric light. Sally felt herself set down. She had shut her eyes so as not to see the man's hand and wrist so horribly close, but now she opened them. She was in a room furnished as a sitting room. It had on the floor a green carpet ornamented by wreaths of faded pink roses. More rose garlands adorned the cream-coloured walls. There were two windows with rose-coloured curtains drawn across them. A settee upholstered in the same material stood between the windows. On the right was a door half open. On the left, a similar door, but shut. A small, bright fire burned on the hearth close to the right-hand door. The room was warm. Sally took a shaky step forward, leaned against the raised end of the settee, and turned to face Etta Shaw who hovered near the door by which they had entered. The man Lazare passed to the left-hand window, and stood there motionless.

Sally did not speak for two or three long, slow minutes. She looked at the comfortable, prim, everyday room, and she looked at Etta Shaw whom she had known since she was seven years old. Etta stared back at her with defiant eyes and a high colour. At last Sally said in a sort of whisper:

"Will you explain?"

She saw Etta look past her at the man for instructions, and she looked round quickly and caught Lazare's little nod.

"Now, Sally," Etta Shaw's tone started very high and trailed off.

Sally spoke again in that breath of a voice.

"What does this mean? Will you explain?"

"Now, Sally, my dear, there's nothing to be frightened about, there really isn't."

"I'm not frightened," said Sally, lying valiantly.

"And you needn't be. All that has happened is—is—" she stuck.

"Yes? I should be glad to know just what *has* happened."

"Well, you've come here on a little visit, and there's nothing to be afraid of, but—well, you see, Sally, in a matter of life and death one can't stand on ceremony, and we simply had to bring you here so as to—to—well, to reason with you."

"I see," said Sally slowly. She put out her right hand and indicated Lazare, without looking in his direction. "I've seen him before, and I expect I have talked with him. I suppose he wants to finish the argument we had then. Is that it?"

"That," said Lazare, speaking from behind her, "is it, precisely."

"And you imagine," said Sally, "that you can keep me here against my will, and that all my friends, my *real* friends, will just sit round and do nothing?"

"Tell her," said Lazare shortly.

Etta hesitated, twisted her fingers, and again looked past Sally, this time in appeal.

"Tell her," repeated Lazare, and she burst at once into nervous speech.

"We're not *cruel*—and there was no need to worry people, when you were quite safe, and with *me*, so I just sent your Mrs. Callender a telegram to say you were detained in Town for a day or two, and—and—"

"Am I to thank you for being so kind and thoughtful, Etta? Did you think I would?" Sally's voice had strengthened, and the colour was coming back into her face—"Well, you said and—and what? Go on."

"I sent *two* telegrams." Etta was between triumph and offence. "The *other* was to Major Armitage to tell him that you were joining your uncle, and asking him not to interfere. I think it's not the *first* time you've asked him that, is it, Sally, darling? I remember some years ago that you told him to mind his own business. He didn't take it very well, did he? I don't *think* he'll come and look for you after getting that telegram, do *you*?"

Triumph had the upper hand. Etta's hard, blue eyes were fairly blazing with it now, and her nervousness was gone. Sally looked at her, and her own faint flush died away. Her little face set and whitened. Her dark grey eyes, made darker by the inky rim of the iris, dwelt on Etta. She did not speak, but the ice of her contempt made the room seem cold. After a moment she turned towards the man.

"On the whole, I think I would rather you defined the position," she said, and Lazare replied easily.

"As you like, Miss Meredith. It is really a simple one. As you say we have talked before. I made you a good offer. You refused it. I make that good offer again—now—if you accept, you have only to open the red lacquer case, and I will drive you anywhere you wish. You may, after all, sleep at home tonight. If you refuse—" he paused.

"Yes—that is what really interests me," said Sally coolly—"If I refuse?"

"Then we have made certain provisions for your comfort in this hospitable house, and we hope by reasonable argument and friendly pressure to induce you to exercise a lady's privilege and change your mind." He paused and bowed. Then after a moment,

"The provisions—I will explain them. This door"—he pushed wide the one which was ajar—"it leads to a small, but, I am assured, a comfortable bedroom, and the other, the opposite one, to a bathroom. Only the room in which we now find ourselves opens onto the corridor. That one door has, as you will see, two stout bolts on the outside. The windows of all three rooms are barred, and have old-fashioned shutters of your English oak. They look over the vegetable garden behind the house. The rooms were so arranged and the windows barred to meet the requirements of an aunt of Miss Shaw's who was at one time deranged. They are very—shall I say—convenient now."

His bold and sneering look made Sally turn again to Etta Shaw. "And your aunt?" she said, and wished her voice were louder.

"I told you." Etta tossed her head a little. "I told you at the Club that Aunt Emma doesn't notice things much. She stays in bed, and thinks about old times. If you screamed the house down, she would only think it was poor Aunt Harriet, the one who used to have these rooms years ago. She lives in the past, you see."

"And your servants?" Sally saw Etta through a mist, heard her laugh as if from a long way off.

"They are not *servants*, but devoted *friends*, ready to sacrifice anything and everything to the *Cause*. You won't find anyone to help you in *this* house, Sally, my dear."

Sally put her left hand behind her until it touched the arm of the settee. She leaned hard on it, and groped with the other hand until, passing over the smooth surface of a cushion, it found and gripped the back. Then she let herself down into a sitting position and shut her eyes.

The room was full of buzzing noises. Etta talking in a rapid whisper. Then at last Lazare:

"Get her some food, not too much," and after an interval the sound of a tray being set down.

Lazare's voice again.

"Quite useless to faint, Miss Sally, we are hardhearted. You had better have some supper and go to bed. In the morning we will talk again."

"I'm not fainting," whispered Sally, and was aware of Etta saying pleadingly:

"Oh, Lazare, I don't like leaving her. Let me stay—do let me stay," and Lazare's abrupt answer:

"Foolishness. She is tough enough for two. Come away—at once, Etta."

Then the door was shut. Sally was alone.

She heard the bolts slide home. The relief, the utter relief of being alone. She sat for a moment, drinking it in. Then opened her eyes, and looked about her. They were really gone. A table had been drawn up close to the settee. There was a tray on it, an old-fashioned black tray inlaid with mother-of-pearl flowers, cocoa in a jug with a pink and gold rim, a plate of bread and butter, a cup and saucer that matched the jug. Sally abominated cocoa, but she drank all that was in the jug, and finished the bread and butter to the last crust. The plate had a pink rose in the middle of it. As she ate she picked up her courage and arranged her thoughts.

"I won't think tonight—I *won't*," she resolved. "I'll have a bath, and go to bed, and sleep. If I start thinking now, I shan't sleep."

She pushed away the table, got up, and went into the bedroom. It was really a dressing room, comfortably furnished. The narrow bed with its rose-coloured eiderdown looked alluring. A nightgown of Etta's was laid out upon it. There were a sponge and a new toothbrush on the washstand, and a clean comb and brush on the chest of drawers which did duty for a dressing table.

Sally went into the bathroom and started the hot tap. Almost boiling water made her think less furiously of Etta Shaw.

When she emerged warm, clean, attired in Etta's nightgown, she felt curiously separated from the fear and misery of half an hour before. After all, this was a civilized country—cocoa, hot baths, and the thoughtful toothbrush spelled reassurance.

Sally came into the bedroom, shut the door, and then frowned a little. There was a keyhole, but no key. In spite of the cocoa, the hot bath and the toothbrush, fear put up its head again.

"I'm a jumpy idiot," she said with emphasis. "But go to sleep without anything to fasten that door, I simply won't."

She looked about her, and next moment was moving the washstand. The back of it just fitted beneath the handle of the door, and jug and basin could be trusted to sound the alarm if anyone tried to enter. She contemplated her handiwork with a little glow of self-satisfaction. Then she switched out the light, and took a flying leap into bed. Her head touched the pillow. It was cold and smelled of lavender. The sheets smelled of lavender too. Sally began to think vaguely of a long, long lavender hedge, with its dim, spiky leaves, and its purple mist of flower. An old rhyme came tinkling into her sleepy, drifting thoughts.

"Lavender blue, lavender green, when you are King, I will be Queen."

She fell very fast asleep.

Chapter Thirteen

IT WAS MANY hours before she woke. She opened her eyes, and on the instant a sense of strangeness came upon her like a breaking wave. A moment before she had been in some friendly place of dreams; then, in a flash, this strange place, dark, but not quite dark, a kind of pink dusk, in fact.

Sally rubbed her eyes, sat up, and shook back her hair. She was remembering. The quick procession of yesterday's events rushed through her mind, and in a trice she was out of bed and at the window. It was closely shuttered, and the shutters were locked. Pull as she would, she could not open them. A chink of light showed at the shutters' edge, and Sally discovered that the darkness had been pink because what she mentally termed "another of those blessed rose-coloured curtains" hung before the window. She decided that she never wished to see pink curtains again.

She dressed rapidly, put the washstand back into its place, and emerged into the sitting room. More pink darkness, more rose-coloured curtains, more locked shutters. In the bathroom the same effect, but here produced by a rose-coloured blind. Sally switched on the light, and sat down on the pink settee.

Her watch had stopped, so she had no means of knowing what time it was, but she thought hopefully of breakfast. Last night's cocoa and bread and butter seemed a long time ago. She was hungry, but her courage had come back to her. Yesterday's terrors seemed as far away as yesterday's cocoa.

All the same, she jumped a little when the door opened and a man came in. He had a flat, rather stupid face, and little dark eyes. Without taking the least notice of Sally, he crossed to the fireplace, knelt down, produced paper and sticks, and proceeded to build and light the fire. After a moment Sally said politely:

"Good morning. Can you tell me the time?"

The man continued to take no notice.

Sally tried the same remark in French, Italian and German, with the same result.

The fire began to burn, and the man got up and went out again, turning out the light on his way. As soon as Sally heard the bolt go home, she jumped up and put it on again. After that nothing happened for half an hour. Then Etta Shaw came in, leaving the door ajar behind her. She stopped just inside the room, and said good morning in rather uncertain tones. Sally responded cheerfully.

Etta came further in, and began to talk, her manner suggesting an odd blend of the solicitous hostess and the careful jailer.

"I'm so glad you're all right," she began with a jerk, "and, oh, Sally, you *do* realize that if it were anything but a matter of life and death, and, and—service to the Cause—I mean you do realize, *don't* you? And I do hope you didn't lie awake, or feel *worried* or anything."

"Thanks," said Sally, "I slept beautifully. Are you going to open the shutters?"

"Well," said Etta, "that's just what I was going to say—about the shutters, I mean. You *will* be reasonable, won't you?"

"That depends," said Sally. "What do you call being reasonable?"

"Well, if you promise not to scream—just give your word of honour, you know—I'll open them directly."

"And if I don't promise," said Sally, "we shall just have to go on wasting your electric light, is that it?"

"It doesn't cost much," said Etta. "We make it ourselves." She spoke with perfect simplicity.

Sally burst out laughing. You couldn't go on being angry with Etta, she was such a fool.

"Well, it would be a pity to waste it anyhow. I don't mind promising for—let's see—the next two hours. I should like some breakfast before I start screaming—that is, if I'm allowed breakfast. Am I?"

Etta got very red.

"You promise not to scream, or call out, or wave things out of the window? It's only the vegetable garden, but we've got to be on the safe side."

"For two hours, yes."

"On your word of honour?"

"Oh, very well, my good Etta—yes."

Etta produced a key, and unlocked first one shutter and then the other. As she threw them back the light came in, pale, golden, exquisite.

Sally looked out and saw a turquoise sky overhead and, below, endless lines of cabbages emerging from a silver mist. There was no human habitation in sight, no smoke from any chimney, and no sound of traffic, nothing but the misty garden stretching to meet a hedgerow full of billowy elms, and beyond the elms a belt of woodland.

She turned to find Etta looking at her with tears in her eyes.

"Sally, you'll do what they want, *won't* you?" she said in a low, agitated voice.

"Do you know," said Sally, "what they want me to do?" Etta threw her a startled glance.

"They want you to open the red lacquer case."

"Yes," said Sally, nodding encouragement. "Why?"

"Because your uncle's formula is inside it."

"Yes?"

Etta Shaw threw up her hand, and her words came with a rush.

"That wicked, that abominable formula! Anyone who could invent such a thing, or dream of letting it loose on the world, is just a homicidal maniac; and if governments and laws won't restrain a person like that, and take his murderous weapon from him, why I, for one, will stick at nothing to rescue what remains of civilization from the appalling, *appalling* fate prepared for it."

"Yes, yes," said Sally. "Of course you wouldn't, and that's why you've kidnapped me?"

"Yes," said Etta, with a sort of gasp. "When one has to choose between such awful, *awful* horrors and a little discomfort to one individual, do you think one *hesitates*?"

"I'm sure you don't," said Sally. "I don't see you hesitating for a moment. Well, what next?"

"Open the case and give us the formula, and, *and*—"

"And what?"

"You shall go free at once."

Etta came closer, her hands clasping and unclasping upon one another with an awkward yet pitiful motion. That she was in deadly earnest was plain. "And the formula?"

"Is destroyed for *ever*."

Sally looked at her keenly. It *was* possible to be such a fool, for here was Etta proving it in her own person. Amazing!

"You want the formula in order to destroy it?"

"Yes, yes!"

"And M. Lazare, he wants to destroy it too?"

"Lazare is the noblest and *most* devoted of us all. I have *never* met anyone like him. Oh, Sally, wait till you really know him. We are absolutely at one in our aims and ideals— the *most* beautiful soul companionship."

"Mercy—she's in love with him!" The dismayed thought flitted through Sally's mind. Aloud she said:

"Let's stick to the formula. You think M. Lazare wants it destroyed?"

"What else?" Etta's surprise was quite genuine.

Sally crossed to the fire, stirred it with her foot, and then turned round, hands clasped behind her and a slight smile on her face.

"Then, my dear Etta, it's all so nice and easy—he has only to meddle with the case, try and force it open, stamp on it, put it in the kitchen fire—in fact, any old thing—and the formula will be destroyed all right. He heard Fritzi tell me that there was a compartment full of nitric acid which would open and flood the case if any one tried to find the spring without knowing the secret. You see it's as easy as mud. Why drag me into it at all?"

Sally suddenly changed her light tone to one of deep seriousness.

"Etta," she said, "just look the thing squarely in the face. Your friend Lazare doesn't destroy the formula because he doesn't want to destroy it. He wants to use it—he offered me a very large sum of money for the use of it. Talk about letting homicidal maniacs loose upon the world—you'll know a good deal more about it, if M. Lazare gets away with Fritzi's formula."

The angry red flushed high into Etta's face.

"He *said* you would slander him—" the words came tumbling out. "I suppose you think yourself very clever—I suppose you think you can separate us, my faith in him, with your inventions, your clever, *silly* inventions; but I tell you, Sally, that nothing could shake my faith. I *know* Lazare—his nobility, his sacrifices, his lofty soul-sense set him very high above slanders til this. And as for what you say about *destroying* the case, why you must think me very simple—very simple indeed. Why, if we destroyed the case, how could we *be sure* that the formula was really inside it? As Lazare says, we must make *certain* of the accursed thing before we destroy it. He says you may have tricked us, or your uncle may have tricked us. He says we *must* make sure, for the whole future of humanity now hangs trembling in the balance!"

Sally groaned.

"Oh, Lord!" she said. "Etta, you make my brain reel! How do you do it? It's like turning a tap, and out it comes. I don't think I *can* bear any more before breakfast." She twinkled impishly, and added: "Come off the high horse for a bit, and let's call Pax. That reminds me I made up a rhyme about you and the high horse last time you lectured me in the summer which, as you have not heard it, I will now proceed to recite." She put her head on one side, copied the red-haired poet's limp attitude, and intoned:

"There was once a Miss Shaw who said, 'How
Did I get such a very high brow?'
And they answered: 'Of course
If you ride the high horse,
It develops, we cannot say how.'"

The door banged on the last word. The bolts were rammed home. If Sally's incautious tongue had routed Etta, it had certainly not tended to ease the situation.

She tossed her head and laughed.

"Oh, well, she'll come round," she said to herself. It was not the first time she had seen Etta fling out of the room in a temper, and it did not greatly distress her. Her immediate concern was breakfast. Was there going to be any, or was there not? The question became more and more insistent.

At last, when she had almost given up hope, the automatic person who had lighted the fire came in with the black japanned tray. Without a word he set it down and went out again.

Sally nearly flew across the room. The pink- rimmed cup half full of sugarless cocoa—no jug this time to refill it from. On the pink-rimmed plate a single slice of plain, dry bread.

"Pigs!" said Sally, and ate it lingeringly. It seemed to make very little difference.

When the last crumb was gone she went and looked dejectedly out of the window, and wrinkled her brow at the cabbages. Her thoughts were not exhilarating.

"Etta's a first-class, prize fool. She always was. And I don't know that a first-class prize fool, idiotically in love with a thoroughly unscrupulous man like that Lazare creature, isn't just about as dangerous as anyone can be. No use appealing to her reason—she hasn't got any: or to her heart, because it's taken up with Lazare; or to her conscience, because that's at the beck and call of the Cause. It's a very pretty kettle of fish. Lazare gives me the creeps. I wonder if Bill will really think I sent that telegram, or whether he'll guess that there's something fishy about it."

A quite horrid feeling of loneliness sprang up in Sally. Thinking of Bill was a mistake. She ought to have known better. The picture of him, big, solid, comfortable, and so dreadfully far away was being too much for her fortitude. She brushed her hand across her eyes, and turned with a start to face Lazare who was closing the door behind him. It shut, as it had opened, without making any noise at all.

Lazare advanced with a bow.

"Good morning, Miss Sally," he said. "I am come for our little talk—I hope a friendly one, and that you will not send me away as angry as that poor Etta, whom I have met and consoled. It would be better not."

He seated himself on the raised end of the settee farthest from Sally, and indicated the opposite corner.

"Sit down, and we will talk."

"No, thanks," said Sally, her head in the air and her hands behind her back. The consciousness of tear-stained cheeks lent pride to her tones.

She saw Lazare show his teeth in a smile, and disliked him as much as she feared him. Seen in the daylight, he was older than she had thought; thirty-five or so. The regular, aristocratic features had no relief of colouring; the skin was sallow-pale; hair, brows, and lashes all of an indeterminate flaxen. The effect was almost that of a head modelled in clay. The contrast between this head, cast in a mould of so much distinction, and the ugly, plebeian hands was very noticeable. No amount of care—and very obviously much care had been lavished upon them—could redeem their coarse brutality. A little shudder ran through Sally whenever her eyes rested upon them.

Lazare watched her for a moment, and then spoke.

"Very well," he said, "but it is not my will if you stand before me as prisoner, so do not set it down against me. Come, are you going to be reasonable?"

"Not what you call reasonable, M. Lazare."

"That," said Lazare, "is a pity. Have you ever reflected, Miss Sally, how much wasted energy would be saved if people would do at the beginning what, in the end, they will certainly have to do?"

"Abstract cases don't interest me," said Sally coldly.

"Very well, we will come to the point. You are admirably direct for one of your sex, differing in that respect, if I may say so, from our dear Etta who has a great penchant for the abstract, and desires never to arrive at the point. You will open the case?"

"No," said Sally.

"Oh, but you will. I can assure you of that. It is only a question of when."

"All right," said Sally. "And when I've opened it?"

"The rest is my affair."

"Why don't you assure me that you only want the formula in order to destroy it?"

"Because, my dear Miss Sally, you would not believe me."

"Etta believes it," said Sally—"she *actually* believes it." She looked at him hard, and saw a faint stir of amusement in his face.

"She does me the honour of having a very high opinion of me," said Lazare politely. "I gather that you have tried to shake it. Believe me, my dear Miss Sally, it is waste of time. If I were not sure of that, I would so arrange that you had no further opportunity of slandering me; but as the only effect of what you say is to increase the devoted friendship with which Etta honours me, I am quite willing that you should say anything you like."

Chapter Fourteen

LAZARE STAYED for two hours. During these two hours he passed from sarcasm to threats, from polite ease to a manner of cold brutality. For the last three-quarters of an hour his conversation was limited to one sentence fired off at irregular intervals.

"Will you open the lacquer case?"

Sally remained standing by the window all the time, but she edged backwards so that she could lean against the wall. She found herself counting between the sentences—"one, two, three, four, five, six."

"*Will* you open the lacquer case?" Silence. Then—"one, two, three, four, five, six, seven, eight, nine, ten—when was it coming—eleven, twelve."

"*Will* you open the lacquer case?"

After nearly an hour of it she was only just holding on to her self-control. When she was at the last gasp Lazare got up and went out, slamming the door.

Sally felt her way to the nearest chair and sat down. She did not think at all, or want to think. She just sat and let the blessed silence soak into her. It was like water when one is very, very thirsty.

Then, the door opening and closing again, she looked up, trying to keep the sudden terror from her eyes. It was Etta with a tray—not Lazare, thank God, not Lazare.

Etta exclaimed sharply as she put the tray down.

"Oh, Sally!"

"If that's something to eat, I'm ready for it," she said, and saw the unbecoming flush mount to the roots of the faded hair.

"They—we want you to write a card first—just a few lines; and then you shall have this nice hot soup. It really *is* good; Aunt Emma has just had some."

"A card?"

"Yes, to Mrs. Callender, just to tell her you are all right, and that you don't know when you'll be back."

"I won't!" said Sally, with sudden vigour.

Etta wrung her hands.

"Oh, Sally, don't make him any angrier," she whispered. "Don't, *don't*, DON'T! I've never seen him so angry—and—and it frightens me. *Do* write the card."

Whilst Etta spoke, Sally tried to think. A little ray of hope flashed upon her.

"I won't write a card," she said, "I'll write a letter."

"But why?"

"I don't like post cards," said Sally; "never did. Perhaps I don't like acting under compulsion either. Anyhow, I'll write a letter if I write anything. I don't mind saying that I'm ready for the soup." She talked on to give herself time.

Etta fluttered nearer the door.

"I might ask him," she said waveringly. "There couldn't be any *harm* in my just *asking*; at least I don't *see* how there could be. I think I'll *just* ask him."

The last nervous sentence took her out of the room.

Sally had the cup of soup in her hand as the door closed. She drank it in great gulps, making sure of it before she began upon the slice of bread. When Etta's hand touched the handle she had only eaten half of a rather meagre slice. The other half went into the pocket of her coat.

Etta came in in a flurry.

"He says you *may* write the letter, but not to imagine that you can play any tricks." Then, as her eyes fell upon the empty tray, she gave a startled cry and looked frightened.

"Oh, what *will* he say!"

"Why should you tell him?" said Sally, and knew as she spoke that Lazare would not be told; so much was evident from Etta's look of relief.

She pushed her chair up to the table, took ink, pen and writing block from Etta, and sat ready to begin. She had her plan. It was a risk, of course, but that didn't really seem to matter now. She looked seriously at Etta, and said with a sort of careful simplicity:

"What do I put on the top of the paper?"

"London," said Etta.

"Only London. I don't suppose she'll *think* about it at all."

Sally wrote London in the right-hand top corner. "Do I put a date?"

"Yes, date it today."

Sally dated it. Then she dipped her pen, and wrote in a style carefully modelled on Cousin Eliza's letters to servants: "Mrs. Callender." Etta instantly took the sheet away and tore it up.

"Now, Sally," she said angrily, "what's the good of that? You know perfectly well you wouldn't write like that to an old servant like Mrs. Callender; nobody would."

"Cousin Eliza did."

"*You* wouldn't, so it's no use your trying to play those sort of tricks, to make her believe that there's something wrong."

"I'll write anything you like," said Sally, meekly. "Shall I say, 'Darling Mrs. Callender,' and send her my love?"

Etta tapped an impatient foot. "Write the way you always do," she said.

"All right," said Sally.

She dipped her pen, wrote the place and date again, and then, more slowly, "Dear Mrs. Callender."

Etta looked over her shoulder and nodded.

"Now put: 'I'm obliged to stay here for a day or two. I will write again when I know my plans. Don't forward any letters as I may be back any day.'"

Sally wrote with bent head, a little glow of triumph warming her as she remembered other careless scrawls which began, "Dear Cally," and were rounded off by wildly illegible initials. It would be odd indeed if Cally were not suspicious over this formal note. At least if she did not suspect, she would be seriously huffed; and in either case she would certainly talk about it to all and sundry.

She looked up as she finished writing "any day," and enquired:

"Anything else?"

"No," said Etta, "that will do. Now sign it."

Sally wrote "Sally Meredith" in her best hand, whilst Etta watched her, frowning.

"Don't you put 'Yours truly' or anything?"

"I will if you like." And Sally wrote in "Yours truly" above the signature. She addressed the envelope which Etta laid before her, and put down her pen with a dejected air which by no means corresponded with her inward feelings.

"What about some more soup?" she said. "There wasn't very much, and I've done what you asked."

"Oh, I can't, I really *can't*," said Etta, and went out quickly with the tray.

Sally finished the half slice of bread, settled herself comfortably on the settee, and went to sleep.

She woke from a dream of fighting cats, opened her eyes, rubbed them, and wondered if she were still dreaming.

A young man was standing in the middle of the room playing a minor scale on the violin. As his melancholy dark eyes met Sally's sleepy ones, she recognized the young Pole with the unpronounceable surname who had been one of the "Radiators" at Etta's Club the day before. "We're so intimate. I call him 'Sascha.'" She recalled Etta's words with a startled realisation that M. Sascha was evidently so intimate as to be up to his neck in what Sally with modern terseness described as: "this rotten show."

She blinked at him with innocent kitten eyes, and said:

"I didn't hear you come in. You are M. Sascha, are you not? I heard you play at the club." The minor scale proceeded. Interwoven with it, phrases almost totally unintelligible.

Sally was unable to decide whether it was embarrassment or an almost complete ignorance of English which produced this confusion, but confusion there certainly was. She repeated her remark in French, enquiring at the end of it whether Monsieur spoke French.

The melancholy eyes looked offended. In atrocious but fluent French M. Sascha informed her that he was an educated Pole, and that all educated Poles spoke French. Whilst he spoke he continued to play the scale.

"Then let us talk," said Sally.

She began to realise why she had dreamed about a cat fight. M. Sascha's notes were of a piercing intensity.

"You can tell me about Poland. I've never been there."

There was a momentary gleam in the violinist's eyes, but he shook his head, and began to play arpeggio at top speed.

A curious idea slid into Sally's brain. Fritzi and the story of the young violinist who was a spy. If it were Sascha? It might have been. Sally ventured a chance shot. Leaning forward, and smiling sweetly, she let her gaze rest admiringly upon the young man and enquired:

"Did you ever finish your 'Symphonie Chemique,' Monsieur?"

The effect was instantaneous. His bow halted on a discordant note, then dropped, whilst a flood of words broke from his lips.

"My Symphonie, you have heard of it? Ah, mademoiselle, what felicity! But, until you have heard it, you cannot conceive all that there is in it of inspiration and of terror. And the moment of that inspiration—wonderful! An experience of the most remarkable. See, you are sympathetic. I will recount it to you. I stand—regard me—I stand in the laboratory at midnight. It is dark. Only a single ray from an electric torch pierces the gloom, and discloses those machines by which men wrest from reluctant Nature her sublime secrets."

He began to play as he spoke.

"See, this is the motif of darkness, typifying the immense darkness of ignorance pierced by the single ray of inspiration. I look around me. I behold all these things. They repose, these forces, these terrors. They are concealed in a powder, in a liquid, in an acid that frets to be free. Listen to the motif of the picric acid. It dreams already of the bomb that is to be. See, I will play to you its dream."

Sally gazed at this unbelievable young man who glistened with earnestness. She watched his agile, dirty fingers, and listened to the dream of the picric acid which ended in a tolerable imitation of an explosion, mingled with what she imagined to be the shrieks of the exploded. As the last piercing wail died away, Sascha threw back his long dark hair, placed his right hand, still grasping the bow, over his heart and bowed to his audience. Sally delighted him by clapping. She also said bravo twice, and smiled again.

After this, half an hour passed very pleasantly. The dream of the picric acid was succeeded by love passages between the quicksilver and gold—"noblest of the elements." The quicksilver motif was really rather charming, and the passage ended, as Sascha explained, in the union of the lover and his beloved, no longer two, but one—"the perfect Amalgam." He talked all the time, and, the music having ceased to describe explosives, Sally's eyelids closed. When he embarked upon the "Sleep of the emollient oils," she too slept. It was very nice and peaceful after Lazare.

A discord waked her. Footsteps in the passage and voices—Lazare and Etta. Sascha clutched his damp brow.

"All, all have I forgotten for my Symphonie!" he panted. "I was to play scales and exercises—to practise, and every minute I was to ask: 'Will you open the lacquer case?' *Mon Dieu*, what will Lazare say?" He looked terrified. The door was beginning to open.

For the second time Sally came to the rescue.

"Why should he know? *I* shan't tell him," she said.

Etta and Lazare came in.

Chapter Fifteen

WHEN BILL ARMITAGE reached Chark and discovered that Sally had gone up to Town for the day, he experienced feelings of great irritation. Why should Sally go to Town? If she must go, why go today of all days? Mrs. Callender was not helpful, and for once she was not talkative. Like David she held her tongue, and it was pain and grief to her. Afterwards, in the society of Hannah Preston, she made up for this unnatural silence.

"The first minute I set eyes on 'im you could 'ave knocked me down with me own duster, you could. ''Aven't you seen Miss Sally?' I says, and the Major 'e looks stiff as a blank wall, and 'e says, 'No, and 'ow should I 'ave seen 'er,' 'e says. Well, Hannah." (Mrs. Callender's h's were like currants in a bread and butter pudding. Sometimes they appeared, as it were, in clumps, and sometimes she seemed to run out of them altogether.) "Well, Hannah, I looks at 'im and it come over me—why that telegram couldn't 'a been from him at all. Just like that it come over me. Bill it was signed, for I ast James and he said so. But 'ow do I know, says I, 'ow many other Bills she mightn't 'ave known? It's common enough to be called Bill, and a bit too common for real gentry is what I think about it. And like a flash I says to myself,

"Old your tongue, Ellen Callender, as none can do it better than you,' and I 'olds it. Like enough it's another young man she went off to meet, and the Major not knowing a word about it, and make mischief is a thing I never did yet, and never will do, and don't hold with neither, so there I stands, and there he stands, and 'e says: 'When will she be back?' 'e says. And I says: 'I'm sure I couldn't say, Sir.' 'Will she be late?' 'e says, and I thinks a bit and says cheerful like: 'Sure to be late, Sir, with all the shopping she 'ad to do.' And so after a bit, off he goes, and not best pleased about it. And I thinks to myself: 'Well it is for Miss Sally as she's got a considering sort of person in the house instead of one of these flighty, chattering girls.' Magpies I call 'em. 'No one can never say as 'ow I made mischief,' I says to myself, and I says the same to you, Hannah."

Mrs. Preston set her heavy face. "I don't hold with covering things up, Ellen," she said. "I don't hold with it, nohow. Speak the truth and shame the devil is my motto, and those that carries on with two young men simultaneous is asking for trouble, and trouble they'll get."

Bill got Etta Shaw's telegram about an hour after his return to Town. He had gone to his room at the War Office in a bad temper. The telegram did not sweeten it. It was mysterious, and he hated mystery.

"Joining Fritzi"—where, and why—in Heaven's *why*? And then the snub direct—"on no account interfere." That cut. Bill did not admit that it cut. He covered the wound with anger, the anger of a man who is struck by a friend. The blow fell on the old wound and roused the old resentful pain. He told himself that he washed his hands of Sally Meredith. This was the second time she had told him to mind his own business, and, by Heaven, she should not have to tell him that or anything else again.

Major Armitage wrote late, his brain busy, his face like a thunder cloud. Clerks had their heads bitten off. Altogether Etta

Shaw would have considered that her telegram had enjoyed quite a success.

Next day Bill lunched with his cousin Eleanor Farquhar. She was his favourite cousin, but she found him a none too easy guest of the monosyllabic and abstracted order.

They lunched *tête-à-tête*, a fact much regretted by Eleanor as the meal proceeded. One by one her topics of conversation were ruthlessly slaughtered by an indifferent "Yes," or "No."

Eleanor was pretty, dark, and lively. Her eyes began to sparkle behind their justly admired lashes. She sought a weapon with which to prick this monstrous indifference, and found one to her hand in the suddenly remembered glimpse of Sally. She tapped on the table with a pretty ringed hand, and said:

"Ever see anything of Sally Meredith these days, Bill?"

She had the satisfaction of seeing her cousin blush.

"Er—sometimes."

"I saw her yesterday in a taxi with a woman whose face has been worrying me ever since. I remembered her at once—Sally I mean—she hadn't changed a bit. I thought she looked awfully pretty, but I can't place the woman she was with, though I knew her face. You know how worrying it is when you cannot get hold of a name or a face. There, I almost had it then, but it's gone again—older than Sally, rather hard, an appalling hat, Reckitt's blue. Oh, Bill, I've got it; the hat did the trick. I know where I saw her last—in the dock at Bow Street with Sally—you know that *dreadful* day—the Suffrage raid; and they let Sally go, but this woman got two months or something like that, and she had on an awful blue hat then, *pure* Reckitt's, an angel's complexion wouldn't have stood it."

"Was it Etta Shaw?"

Bill's tone was indifferent, but Eleanor looked at the big hand clenched on the table and saw the knuckles whiten.

"Why, yes, it was, Bill, what's the matter?"

"Nothing," said Bill. "Sally's affairs have nothing to do with me." And he began to make violent strictures upon a new play which neither he nor Eleanor had seen. They went on talking about plays, and, when lunch was over and Bill excused himself on the score of work, his cousin Eleanor watched him go with a little amused pity in her dark eyes.

"Poor old Bill—he's still got it badly," was her comment on the situation, "but, at any rate, I made him talk."

It was on Monday that Sally walked out along the Strudwick road, and met the woman in the blue motor veil. On Tuesday she talked with Lazare in the pitch dark of a lane near Lenton Station. On Wednesday she went to town, and met Etta Shaw instead of Bill Armitage. Thursday was the day of Bill's lunch with Eleanor Farquhar, and it was on Friday that Inspector Williams rang up.

At the first sound of the clipped, laconic speech, Bill Armitage's expression changed.

"That you, Major Armitage? Inspector Williams speaking."

"Yes, what is it?" For the life of him Bill could not keep the words from hurrying.

The Inspector's voice came to him over the wires with maddening deliberation.

"Thought I'd better ring you up. Bit of a queer start down at—you know where. Young lady not back. Haven't heard from her, I suppose?"

"Yes, er, no."

There was a pause.

"I should rather like to come round and see you, if you'll be at liberty."

"What do you mean by a queer start? Yes, I'm in, come round."

There was no reply, the Inspector having rung off. He arrived presently, a wooden-faced person, very neat and well set up. He took a chair before he replied to Bill's immediately repeated question—"What do you mean by a queer start?" Then he said:

"Just got back from Chark when I rang you up. My man there wired me to come down this morning. Seems the housekeeper got a letter from the young lady this morning, and an hour afterwards it was all over the village that the letter wasn't from the young lady."

"What do you mean?" cried the astonished Bill.

"That's what *I* said to Thomas, the man down there; and all he could say was that such was the talk in the village. Well, I went up to The Cottage and saw the housekeeper, and—well, to cut a long story short, here's the letter, sir."

He took out a pocket case, extracted Sally's carefully written note, and put it into Major Armitage's eagerly outstretched hand.

"What do you make of it, sir?" he said.

Bill looked at the letter steadily.

"It's her handwriting," he said at once, "but—" he frowned and narrowed his eyes.

"Well, sir?"

"It's too tidy, formal. It looks as if she'd written it very slowly, making every letter—oh, hang it all, it's her writing, but it's not her."

The Inspector gave a slow nod.

"Just what that Mrs. Callender said, only she put it on different grounds. She said, 'It's Miss Sally's writing, but Miss Sally never wrote me a letter that began and ended like that,' and she stuck out that the young lady never wrote it. Says she always wrote to her 'Dear Cally,' and finished up with her initials."

"Then what?"

"That isn't all, sir. After a bit of pumping, she told me Miss Meredith went to town Wednesday to meet you, sir, leastways to meet someone who wired to her to come up, and signed the wire, 'Bill.' I take it you didn't wire?" Bill shook his head.

"Someone did. It was handed in at the Charing Cross Post Office at 8 a.m., sender's name and address not filled in; and the girl will get into trouble for that. Just now, when I asked you on the 'phone whether you'd heard from the young lady or not, I didn't know what to make of your answer, sir. Perhaps you wouldn't mind telling me whether you have heard from her?"

Bill pulled a drawer open, took out Etta's telegram, and handed it over without speaking.

"H'm," said Inspector Williams. "Fritzi being—?"

"M. Lasalle," said Bill, "that's what she called him."

"H'm. Well, that's not all either. Wednesday Miss Meredith got the wire telling her to come up to town, but she'd already walked to Lenton Station the evening before to meet the six-thirty. You didn't send a wire asking her to do that, did you?"

"Certainly not."

"Well, Mrs. Callender says you did; so I followed that up, and here's a copy of the wire somebody sent. Same post office, you see. Now, sir, here are three telegrams, two supposed to be from you, and one supposed to be from the young lady, the two from you being fakes. Well, sir, I just put it to you. What about it?"

Bill pushed back his chair. If Sally's telegram was a fake—but whose fake? Not a stranger's. It must be somebody who knew her pet name for old Lasalle, and who knew also just where to catch him, Bill, on the raw. Who on earth? And the answer came in his Cousin Eleanor's pretty teasing voice, "I've got it, Etta Shaw." He brought down his fist with a bang on the table, and leaning forward he burst into speech. In five minutes the Inspector was in possession of a good many miscellaneous facts and surmises regarding Miss Shaw. Her "Suffrage" history, with its one or more terms of imprisonment; her affiliation with the New Party of Peace; her faculty for attracting odd and dubious persons; her comfortable income; and her address—? No, for the life of him, Bill could not remember where she lived—with an aunt somewhere, he thought.

"And Mrs. Farquhar saw Miss Meredith with this party? On Wednesday? Is she sure it was Wednesday?"

"We'll make sure."

Bill grabbed the telephone, was fortunate in finding Eleanor at home, and began to put a series of questions to her.

"You remember seeing Sally Meredith in a taxi with Etta Shaw? What day was it? You're sure it was Wednesday? Absolutely sure? Sorry to bother you, but it's important."

Eleanor's exasperated voice rang in his ears.

"Really, Bill, you're the limit! Of course I'm sure. I'd been down to see Teddy, and was on my way to lunch with Joan. Yes, and I'm quite certain it was Etta Shaw; I always loathed her. By the way, Sally saw me and tried to get out—their taxi was stuck in a block—but the Shaw creature pulled her back. Pretty fair cheek, wasn't it? What happened then? Oh, the block gave, and they whisked out of sight. I'd like to have seen Sally; I've always liked her awfully. I say, I hope there's nothing wrong."

"Ask what Miss Meredith was wearing, sir," said the Inspector quickly.

Bill asked the question, and heard Eleanor's soft laugh.

"My dear boy, what a flattering interest! Well, if you really want to know, and as far as I could tell, Sally had on a little black velvet hat, grey fur and a dark grey coat, or a coat and skirt. I could only see half of her, so I can't tell you what her shoes and stockings were like. The hat was awfully becoming." She laughed again.

Bill rang off and repeated the substance of Mrs. Farquhar's remarks. The clothes corresponded with Mrs. Callender's description. The inspector's comment was that it was all a bit of a queer start. He supposed he'd better be getting along, and added that he expected to be able to get Miss Shaw's address without much delay; when he had it he would run down and take a look round.

As he went out he nearly fell over a clerk hurrying down the passage. The incident faded immediately from his mind. It would have interested him more if he had known that the young man who sped on his way with apologies could at once, and from memory, have supplied him with the missing address.

Chapter Sixteen

IT WAS Saturday morning.

Sally stood by the barred window, her back to the rose-coloured room that she loathed, her hands gripping one of the bars. Lazare had just left her, and she was trying to steady her shaken, trembling thoughts. For two hours he had been battering her with the one question, and at the end had gone away in a cold fury that shook Sally's self-control and left her dazed.

"You think," he said, "you think that we shall not proceed to extremities—you feel yourself sheltered by Etta—you think 'she will not let them go too far.' I tell you"—he stood in the doorway, a hand on either jamb, his light eyes hard on her—"I tell you, I am at the end. Till this evening I give you and no more. Then, if you do not open the case, you go elsewhere, where there will be no Etta, no other woman, not even that young fool Sascha who begins to be softhearted over you, no one but myself, and some others perhaps even less sentimental than I am. There are ways of making a woman do as one wishes. Believe me we shall employ them."

He stood in silence for a moment, then let his hands fall from the door posts. There was finality in the gesture. They fell heavily. The door shut. The bolts ran home.

It was then that Sally turned from the room and gripped the cold iron of the window bar. Her eyes, unseeing, stared at the sky. She did not know how the time passed. There was no time.

Only a cold and desolate fear, colder than the iron and more desolate than pain.

The last forty-eight hours had been a nightmare. She had not undressed or slept for longer than an hour or two at a time. She had been kept on a starvation ration of dry bread and weak cocoa. She had not been alone for more than ten minutes at a time. When Lazare left Etta would come with her obvious, her increasing terror, her tearful entreaties, her appeals. When she went away another woman took her place; Etta called her Nadine. She was hard-faced, dark, and silent. Her part in the household seemed to be that of nurse to old Miss Shaw. Sally feared her, and believed her to be utterly without compunction. Then Sascha would be sent into the room to practise, and at intervals to ask her the one intolerable, maddening question— "Will you open the red lacquer case?"

Sascha, it was true, was the best of the four. He could be diverted into discoursing of his art, persuaded to play his own compositions, and to ignore the fact that she promptly went to sleep. Yesterday he had brought her an illicit slice of cake.

Sally found the darkness passing from her eyes. She still held on to the bar and looked at the sky, but now she began to see that this sky was blue. There was a thin, ghostly sunshine. It showed a golden beech tree, shining in the distance like a tree on fire, and a brown tangle of hedgerow beyond the green cabbages and the purple beetroot. The ordered rows of vegetables, the colour and the light were consolations. They made a thin film of beauty and order which screened her fear, her loneliness, her aching horror of Lazare and of what he might do if she held out. She would not cry, she would not think of Bill, she would not think that they could break her down.

When she heard the door open she let go of the bar, and turned round, her head up, whistling a little lilting air. They shouldn't see that she was frightened, anyway.

Sascha came in, violin in hand. Sally went on whistling. It wasn't so difficult as when she thought it might be Lazare returning. The Pole shut the door and came forward.

"You whistle?" he said. "Lazare leaves you in such anger as I have never seen, and you can whistle? It is nothing to you?" He waved the violin at her, and his ugly French became more rapid still. "You are brave, but it is mad to be too brave—mad, Mademoiselle Sally, mad!"

He paused, took breath, and asked with a complete change of voice and manner.

"What was that air—the one you whistled? I do not know it. Like this, was it?"

He began to pick it out delicately, humming to himself—"I have it, *hein?* What is it then?"

Sally gave a shaky scrap of a laugh—

"Kitty, my love, will you marry me,
Kitty, my love, will you go?
Kitty, my love, will you marry me?
Either say yes, or say no,"

she sang in a whisper. Then she laughed again a little more steadily, and added: "And I keep on saying 'no.'"

"You are *mad*," said Sascha gravely. Then with a burst of emotion. "Behold your face white and thin, and the circles about your so beautiful eyes; and your little hands, they shake for all your braveness, your little trembling hands that I would kiss. Ah, Mademoiselle—" with amazing suddenness he was on his knees, catching her dress with the hand that already held the bow—"Ah, Mademoiselle, will you not save yourself, whilst there is time? I love you, is it not that you know it? And if I love you, can I see you destroy yourself, and for what? For an idea, a scruple, an—I know not what—"

Sally sat down and folded her hands. She looked at Sascha and saw his face work. She felt his clutch on her skirt, and she felt something vehement and passionate in him that clamoured to her to save herself.

Her eyes grew dark and intent. When her voice came—at first it would not come—it was full of a sort of faltering earnestness.

"Have you ever seen a battlefield?" she said.

This strange response to his emotion brought his eyes to her face. He remained on his knees, his violin fallen to the floor, the hand with the bow catching the hem of her dark skirt, his wide startled gaze on the little face above him, so still, so impassive. But this impassivity, as he saw, was in reality emotion behind the bars of self- control. The artist in him perceived the real Sally, and his heart began to adore this reality.

"I have. I drove for the French Red Cross. We used to go down to the firing line and bring in the wounded."

After a long pause, which he did not break, she said very low: "That's why."

"Why you will not open the case?"

Sally nodded, a child's gesture, so simple.

"Yes—more battlefields—more—" she made long breaks between the words, which came whispering across the little space between them. Sascha felt awed. Presently he would go over the scene, dramatize it, sensationalize the emotion and draw music from it. For the moment he felt simple, and very young. He bent and kissed the edge of the grey tweed skirt which he held.

Sally pulled it away sharply.

"Good gracious, don't do that!" she said. "Get up, and be sensible—and you'd better get going with your fiddle or someone will come in to see what on earth we are doing. Play something restful, there's a dear boy, and if you love me, let me go to sleep."

"If I love—when it is that I adore."

Sally smiled at him.

"Well, that's awfully nice of you," she said briskly.

His eyes reproached her. They were soulful eyes, very like those which a dog fixes upon a mistress whose cruelty refuses him cake at tea. Then with a start he searched four pockets in rapid succession, and at last produced a large slab of chocolate neatly folded in silver paper. With a deep bow he handed it to Sally who actually found that she wanted to cry.

"Sascha, you're an angel!" she said, and a bright round tear fell on the silver paper. She whisked its successor away, curled herself up on the settee, and began to eat chocolate whilst Sascha played weird harmonics, expressive, as he informed her, of a life's unalterable devotion. To these touching strains she fell asleep.

Chapter Seventeen

AT FOUR O'CLOCK that afternoon Lazare came away from the telephone with the look in his face which Etta feared more than anything else in the world.

He met her as he turned from the instrument, took her familiarly by the arm, and marched her into the dining room. He had shut the door, and she was fluttering and asking: "What is it?" when he abruptly bade her be silent for once and listen.

"Major Armitage is coming down here," he said, and, as Etta gasped and caught at his arm, he went on—

"If you're going to be useless to me, say so at once, and I go elsewhere."

"To Nadine, I suppose?" said Etta, frightened but holding on to him.

"Certainly, if I think she will be more useful."

"No, no, Lazare—why do you speak to me like that? You know I'll do *anything*."

"You will do as I say, exactly and without protest?"

She bent her head, struggling with the tears which he hated. Lazare unclasped her hand from his arm before he spoke again. Then he said:

"Major Armitage and Inspector Williams are coming down together. Something has made them suspect you—yes *you*, my Etta—and they are coming down with a search warrant. They are coming by car. We have an hour, or to be safe, since one of them is an impatient lover, three quarters of an hour. Major Armitage's car could not do it in less. There is, therefore, no need for panic."

"How do you know?" gasped Etta.

"My dear Etta, what a question! One has ears and eyes everywhere in an affair like this. 'A' collects information about Major Armitage, and 'B' shadows Inspector Williams. Both report to 'C,' whose duty it is to keep me informed. So simple. Now you have to listen. This is what you must do. You will go to Sally Meredith, and you will weep. That, my Etta, will be, for you, no difficult task."

Etta flushed, and he went on.

"You will weep, and you will say that you cannot any longer bear this state of things; your heart is torn, and you cannot bear it. See how much in character is the role which I assign to you."

"What do you *mean*?" Etta fell back a pace, looking at him strangely.

"It is most beautifully simple. Your heart is torn, you can bear it no longer, and you offer to let her go. Nadine is in your aunt's room, Sascha and I in here. You take her out by the back way, up the garden and through the gap in the hedge. In the lane there you will walk as far as the stile. Then you will tell her to get over the stile and take the footpath through the fields. Meanwhile you yourself will return to meet Major Armitage."

"You're going to let her go? Oh, thank God."

"You thank a little soon. I let her go as the cat lets the mouse to run a little way, to think itself free; and then again—the sharp claws and the glaring eyes. I think that the psychological effect will be good, quite apart from the necessity of having an empty house for Major Armitage and his inspector to search."

The high flush died out of Etta's face. She put out her hands rather aimlessly, and said in a choked voice:

"You mean to bring her back?"

"Certainly."

She burst into tears.

"I can't do it, I *can't*. I thought you *really* meant to let her go. Why don't you? Oh, Lazare, why *don't* you? We've gone far enough—too far—I can't go on, *I can't*." She began to sob bitterly.

Lazare looked at her with contempt.

"What a useless woman you are," he said. "I go to Nadine."

With that she caught at his sleeve.

"Oh, Lazare, don't ask me."

"I do not ask you, I ask Nadine."

She clung to him, weeping.

"She does not love you as I do."

"Prove it."

"How can I? I can't deceive her, *I can't*."

"Can you not? This scruple comes late. Who deceived her at all but you? Who brought her here? And who—who will pay the penalty?"

Etta shivered, partly at his tone and partly at the picture he suggested. She had not thought of herself like this. It sounded small and sordid, and she had had in mind the heroic pose.

Lazare's hands fell heavily on her shoulders.

"Look at me, Etta," he commanded, and as she looked up, still with that shiver running over her, he let his eyes dwell on her nervous shifting ones, and said: "Will you do it, Etta? For me?" He drew her suddenly nearer, and kissed her. "For The Cause?" He kissed her again.

Etta's glance kindled. Her facile enthusiasm flared up.

"Yes, yes," she said—"The Cause, and you. You are The Cause, and what I do for you is done for humanity. You were *right* to remind me."

Her colour was once more high. Lazare took her to the door, drew her, still talking, into the hall, and at the foot of the stair repeated his instructions.

Sally woke up with a start as Etta Shaw came in. Still sleepy, she heard Sascha dismissed, and seized a moment when Etta's back was turned to slip the rest of the chocolate into her pocket. "Thank goodness, I've got one," was her reflection. Then she sat up and blinked at Etta, who immediately said:

"Sally, darling, oh, Sally," and burst into a flood of tears.

"Oh, Etta, for goodness' *sake!*" said Sally, crossly. "You're as bad as that awful poem about Mary Magdalen—you know the one where it calls her eyes 'two portable and compendious oceans.' If you don't take care, you'll melt. I shall throw cold water over you if you go on."

Etta choked down a sob, came close, and whispered:

"Oh, Sally, you're in such *frightful* danger."

"Yes, I know," said Sally. "What about it?" Emotional conversations with Sally were apt to be one-sided. There was as much offence as emotion in Etta's, "Oh, Sally, but you *are.*"

"All right," said Sally, "we'll take it that I am. Don't you think that as my very oldest—er, friend, and my actual hostess, it's rather up to you to do something about it?"

"Yes, *yes*," said Etta, with another sob, "that's what I *mean*, that's why I'm *here*—as your friend, Sally. I can't bear it any longer. My heart is torn, and I can't *bear* it, and I'm going to let you go."

Sally steadied herself against this unexpected rush of hope. It was like being struck by a big wave, but she kept steady and controlled her voice.

"Good work!" she said. "It's decent of you, and I shan't forget." Her hands gripped each other. "When?" she asked.

"Now, at once. We must hurry whilst the coast is clear. Here's your coat and your fur. Your hat's on the table. I don't think you had an umbrella."

"No," said Sally, in a funny, shaky little voice, "I didn't." How exactly like Etta! Heroics one moment and umbrellas the next. Sally preferred the umbrellas.

She put on her outdoor things in silence, and then drank what she hoped would be the last cup of cocoa that she need ever taste. Hunger and the emergency alone could have got it past her lips. As it was she fixed her mind on the great fact that she was being set free and swallowed it.

Etta tiptoed along the passage, and came back.

"Quick—there's no one there. I'll go first," she said, and Sally followed her into the passage. It was getting dark, and no lights had yet been lit. The murmur of voices came from a room on their left. "Aunt Emma—quick—Nadine is there," whispered Etta, and they reached the stair head. Sally held tightly to the baluster. It was so dreadfully like a dream. The dusk, the hurry, and Etta's whispering voice. They passed a half landing with two doors, and came down a short flight into the lower hall. Etta took her by the arm, turned a corner, opened a door and they were in the empty kitchen, large, old-fashioned, with a great ingle nook and a flagged floor. The air was heavy with the smell of burned fat, garlic and unwashed dishes. The scullery was worse. They came into a stone passage, and so to a door at the end of it. The evening damp struck in as Etta unlocked and pulled it open—a blessed cold and clarity. They left the house and the ghosts of dead meals behind. It was lighter out here, and they hurried through the vegetable garden until fruit trees began to screen them from the house. Sally was dragging a little on Etta's arm as they turned into a walk between high box hedges but she kept on gallantly. The walk ended in broken woodland guarded by a rough hedge growing on a bank. Etta made for a gap, slid down into the lane beyond, and turned to give Sally a helping hand.

Sally, in the lane, leaned against the bank panting.

"All right, in a minute," she said, and when the minute had passed:

"Now where?"

"Just down the lane as far as the stile. It's only a hundred yards or so, and then you get the footpath across the fields to Upper Elvery. It's two miles. Can you manage it, do you think?"

Sally nodded fiercely. Manage it? With Lazare behind her?

They pushed on to the stile in silence, and there Etta stood still.

"I must go back. You can't miss the way if you keep to the footpath. It comes out on the Upper Elvery road two miles from here. Turn to the right when you get to the road and you'll be at the station in ten minutes."

Sally climbed over the stile and turned. Etta was just a dull blur in the shadow of the overhanging beeches. She did not move either to go, or to take the hand which Sally held out. Perhaps she did not see it.

"Good-bye, and—and thanks," said Sally.

"Why didn't you open the case, why *didn't* you?"

The words seemed to burst from Etta's lips. Sally stared. "Oh, come, Etta," she said, "don't dig that up again. You know why, or if you don't, it's because you can't take in some of the plainest speaking I've ever wasted on anyone. So long, I expect we'll meet again some day."

"It's your own *fault*," said Etta very low, and with that she turned and ran back along the lane.

Sally shrugged her shoulders, told herself that she would be able to bear up if she never saw Etta Shaw again, and set out across the fields. The dusk was passing into darkness. Hedgerows and trees were inky black against a fading dove-coloured sky. The footpath was narrow, cow-trodden and muddy, the air very cold and damp. Sally drew in great breaths of it, and it was sweeter to her than the primrose-scented air of spring. She walked, relieved from an intolerable pressure, an intolerable dread; for in her own mind she knew that what she feared most of all was, not what Lazare might do to her, but whether for any fear or pain she might weaken and give way.

She walked, released, and the dusk covered her.

Etta ran back to the house as if it were she who were pursued. She panted as she ran, and kept repeating over and over, "It's your own fault, Sally, it's your own fault. I can't *help* it, I can't *do* anything. It's your own fault, Sally, your *own* fault."

Lazare was waiting for her at the back door.

He took her by both arms and brought her into the lighted kitchen.

"She has gone across the fields?" he asked sharply, and Etta trembled and said:

"Yes."

"It will take her more than half an hour to reach the road. I can be there in ten minutes. Now, this is what you have to do. First wash your face, and you are not to weep again, or I am done with you. Then you will send Nadine down here, and you will sit and read aloud to the old lady. That will compose you. I am taking the car out at once, and I will drop Sascha in the village where he may sit at the inn until the coast is clear. When Major Armitage arrives you will be polite and surprised. You will let the inspector search the house. If you are asked where is the chauffeur and the car, he has gone into Ledlington to have a prescription made up for your aunt. I will really do that in case they make enquiries. I shall just have time. When they are gone—ten minutes later you will turn on the lights in my room and leave the blinds up. I can see that from the cross roads."

He turned to go and heard Etta's voice, plaintive and hesitating.

"You haven't—oh, Lazare, I have done it, aren't you *pleased*?"

"I shall be, when it is finished," he said harshly, and went out.

Chapter Eighteen

"THIS MUST BE the place, sir. Two miles out, and a high wall running all along by the road—"

Major Armitage brought the car to a standstill and swung round, his hand still on the steering wheel.

"Well, what's the procedure?" he asked.

"Ask if the lady is at home as if you were paying a friendly call, I should say, sir."

"No thanks, Williams. It's a beastly job, but for the Lord's sake don't make it any worse than it is. This is an official visit, and you do the talking."

"Very good, sir—it's all in the day's work as far as I'm concerned."

They got out, tried the door in the wall, and found it unlocked whereat the inspector frowned.

"Either there's nothing in it, or they're expecting us," he said, as they passed in.

There were lights in the front of the house. One room on the ground floor showed a glow behind curtains. From a bedroom above it a broad ray of warm light streamed out upon the dusk.

Bill pressed the bell, but the inspector lifted up his hand, and beat a heavy tattoo with the knocker. The sound died away, and a momentary silence was broken by the tapping of high-heeled shoes upon a stone or brick floor. An instant later the unbolted door was opened by a woman in the grey alpaca and white linen of a nurse—rather hard faced but very correct, with dark enquiring eyes. Correct—yes, that was the word—impassive too, and foreign certainly.

Bill summed up Nadine in these terms, whilst the inspector was asking for Miss Shaw, and they were being shown upstairs as far as a half landing which displayed two doors. Nadine opened the one upon the right, switching on the light as she did so, and they were left in a primly old-fashioned drawing-room. It was of good size, but so crowded with furniture as to lose all effect of size. Heavy brocaded curtains of a rose-magenta in colour hung before the two windows. An enormous ebony piano sprawled across the far end of the room, and photographic enlargements of Miss Shaw's parents adorned the patterned walls.

Major Armitage had time to observe these things, and was proceeding to condemn the room as" frowsty" when the door opened and Miss Etta Shaw came in. She had washed her face as Lazare had bidden her. She had also composed herself to the best of her ability, but she was obviously in some agitation as she came forward and enquired:

"Did you wish to see me?"

"If you are Miss Etta Shaw," said the inspector. Bill merely bowed, and wished for the thousandth time that they were through with it and on the road again.

"I am Miss Etta Shaw."

"Then I have a few questions to ask you, if you will be so good as to answer them." The inspector here dived into his pocket and produced a notebook from which, having cleared his throat, he proceeded to read.

"When, if I may ask, did you last see Miss Sally Meredith?"

Etta flushed scarlet and swung round on Bill. "Sally? You're Major Armitage, aren't you? Isn't Sally at Chark? Don't tell me there's anything wrong."

"One minute, Miss Shaw"—the inspector's tone was dry—"I asked you a question, and I'll be obliged if you'll answer it."

"But I don't know what you *mean*. What does he mean?" and she again addressed herself to Bill.

"I asked you, Miss Shaw, when you last saw Miss Sally Meredith."

Etta had a moment of indecision. Then in the nick of time she remembered the meeting with Eleanor Farquhar, and said with an air of offence.

"I don't know why you ask me that, but of course I have no possible objection to answering any question. I met Miss Meredith by chance on Wednesday last, and she lunched with me at my Club."

"When did she leave?"

"With me at about half-past four or five o'clock. I had my car outside, and I drove her to the Piccadilly Tube Station and dropped her there."

"You'd be prepared to swear to that."

"Of course." Etta stared at him with hard blue eyes. "And now, perhaps you'll tell me why you ask me all this, and what Major Armitage has to do with this—this inquisition? Have you gone into the Police, Major Armitage?"

She gave her high laugh, and Bill felt his old antagonism rise until it almost choked him. The woman rang false, and if she had injured Sally, if she had moved a finger to injure his little Sally, his little darling Sally! Thoughts moved in him, coming up like bubbles from a great depth, rising as the bubbles rise in boiling water, impelled by a furious heat below. The indifference, and the coldness, and the quarrel with Sally were pierced through by these hot, stinging thoughts. He looked gravely at Etta Shaw and did not say a word, whilst the inspector, wooden and imperturbable, continued his questions.

"What does the household consist of? How many servants? Their names? Nationalities? Length of service?"

"H'm—all foreigners," was his sole comment, as Etta with each reply became more obviously worried and upon the defensive. As he closed the notebook he said: "And you dropped Miss Meredith at the Piccadilly Tube at five o'clock?"

"Yes, I told you so."

"H'm," a pause, then sharply, "Then how do you account for the fact that she was seen driving with you through Ledlington nearly an hour later?"

Etta turned scarlet. If she had been less angry she might have broken down, but the inspector's manner had fretted her temper to breaking point. She stared at him furiously.

"I can't account for things that didn't happen."

"You assert that you were alone in the car when it came through Ledlington."

Etta's restless brain was working quickly enough. It had been dark—too dark for anyone to have more than an impression about the inmates of a closed car. It must have been the policeman at the level crossing in Ledlington who had thought that there were two people in the car. Impossible that he could be sure, *impossible*.

"Of course," she said, so calmly that the inspector thrust the notebook into his pocket and remarked that, if Miss Shaw were ready, he would like just to go over the house.

"You've got a warrant?"

He showed it to her, and she led the way to the door.

"Upstairs first, please."

They mounted the stairs in silence. At the top Etta opened the first door on the right.

"My aunt's room," she said stiffly, and they looked in upon a scene which she felt to be extremely reassuring.

Old Miss Shaw was sitting up in bed with an embroidered cashmere shawl about her plump shoulders. The room was full of the comfortable glow of firelight and of shaded electric lamps. The light fell softly on the old lady's pink cheeks and eyes of china blue. Her silver hair was surmounted by an old-fashioned cap adorned with frilled rosettes of narrow lace and lavender ribbon. An enormous white Persian cat lay at full length upon the pink eiderdown that covered her feet. A kitten of the same family, very young and fluffy, was arching its back and gazing with bolting eyes at Alfred, the elder of Miss Shaw's two beloved canaries, at that moment perched upon his mistress's outstretched finger. Marmaduke, the younger and more timid of the birds, had retreated to the open door of his cage which stood, as it always stood, upon a special table at the bedside.

By the fire sat Nadine sewing. In effect, a most reassuring scene.

Bill was conscious of hot embarrassment, and even the inspector coughed and became aware of his heavy boots.

"A man to see to the electric light, Aunt Emma," said Miss Shaw, going up to the bed and speaking gently.

Bill frowned. The words came so glibly. Did one lie like that without practice? Suspicion was hot in him in spite of the old lady and her cap.

"That door beyond?" said the inspector gruffly.

"A dressing room. Nadine will show it to you." Etta's tone was indifferent, but the inspector did his duty and tramped across the soft pink carpet with its white rose garlands to inspect a dressing room which certainly did not contain Sally Meredith. Meanwhile old Miss Shaw had turned her head. The china-blue eyes dwelt vaguely on Bill, and presently she said in a sweet, fluttering voice:

"Do I know you, my dear?"

Bill came a step or two nearer, and said:

"My name is Armitage, Miss Shaw. What a beautiful cat."

The old lady beamed at him.

"Clarence, do you hear that?" she said. "The gentleman says you are beautiful; and he's a good pussy, too, which is better than being handsome." She nodded gravely, and then added in a confidential whisper—"He understands *everything*, every *word*. We mustn't make him vain."

They left the room feeling that Miss Etta Shaw had scored. She herself had a slight air of conscious triumph as she passed before them up the passage and threw open a door upon the left.

"These were my Aunt Harriet's rooms. She was not herself for some time, and we had to have these bars put up. I use the sitting room occasionally."

"Now, why," thought Major Armitage as he stood in the doorway—"why so much explanation?" and at the same time he was aware of the unreasonableness of this thought. He did not follow the inspector into the bedroom and bathroom, but walked idly to the right-hand window, standing, had he but known it, where Sally had stood so often. His feeling for her, newly realized, had, as he himself would have phrased it, knocked him off his balance. He was conscious of her as he had never been conscious of her before, not even in the old days when he had held her in his arms and felt himself between her and the world. It was the other way round now. It was Sally who was between him and the world. She was between him and everything, so near, and so dreadfully, dreadfully dear. He turned from the window, and, with the instinct to move and do something, walked to the settee and moved one of the cushions. It was crooked, and he had the straight eye of the games-playing man. A tiny edge of white showed where the back of the settee met the seat. Half mechanically he picked up a small white handkerchief, and immediately came broad awake. Four inches square, made of veined linen. How many times had he teased Sally about her handkerchiefs.

He called, "Williams!" sharply, and held out his big hand with the ridiculous thing on the palm.

The inspector took it, turned it over.

"No mark, sir," he said.

"It's Miss Meredith's, I swear it is."

Etta raised an angry voice.

"Really, Major Armitage, what next? Half the women I know use these handkerchiefs. What *nonsense!*"

Inspector Williams shrugged his shoulders. "Let's get on," he said without emotion. He passed into the corridor, but Bill touched Etta on the arm and held her back for a moment.

"Miss Shaw, you're angry, and perhaps have a right to be angry," he said rather gruffly. "I won't say you haven't, but if you do know anything about Sally—Miss Shaw, it's a rotten game, I mean Sally's so *damned* plucky, you know."

He broke off, oppressed with the sense of failure to say what was in his mind to say, and of failure, utter failure to move this woman with the hard flushed face and angry eyes.

"I don't know what you *mean*. I think you're mad," said Etta Shaw.

The search went forward. They passed from room to room, and, having finished with the house to its last cellar, they tramped through the dark garden, inspected the empty garage, and peered into glass houses and potting sheds. In the end they drove away carrying with them the little linen handkerchief and the memory of Etta's face. At the cross roads Bill drew up.

"What do you make of it, Williams?" he said, and the inspector said he didn't make very much of it anyway. The man at Ledlington *thought* that there were two ladies in the car. He recognized Miss Shaw, and thought that there was someone with her. You *think* you've found Miss Meredith's handkerchief. There's a deal too much thinking about the whole thing."

He was silent for a moment, and then said:

"You don't like Miss Shaw, if I may say so, sir; and naturally that makes you think worse of her than you would on the evidence alone. I don't like her either, but—well, facts are what we want, and, if you'll be so good as to drive me into Ledlington, I'll see if I can't check some of her statements. I want to know if the chauffeur really went in there to get a prescription made up, and one or two things like that. I'll poke around, and come up by train if you want to get back."

"All right."

But, as they parted in Ledlington, Bill had a word to say.

"Evidence or no evidence, that woman's a wrong 'un," he said. "Take it from me, Williams, she's a wrong 'un through and through, and I'm dead sure she knows something—dead sure of it." The conviction grew as he drove alone, mile after mile of dark wet road slipping away behind the car. Lonely roads at first, then houses, lights, and the intersecting tram lines, and the packed life of outlying London. He was driving slowly along a crowded thoroughfare, now waiting his turn in a block, now edging ahead of some lumbering drag, when, there on the dirty pavement under the flare of the crude electric light which advertised a cinema, he caught sight of a face he knew. It was a dreamy face under an old felt hat. The round blue eyes looked directly at him. Bill Armitage uttered a wordless exclamation, ran his car in to the side of the road, pulled up, and jumped out, all in the space of a minute. He came up with the dawdling figure a couple of yards from where he had stopped the car. The man had his back to him. Bill, breathless with excitement, laid a gentle hand on his shoulder:

"M. Lasalle!" he said.

Chapter Nineteen

LAZARE HAD MADE good time into Ledlington and back. He took the Upper Elvery road, and as he drew up under the hedge, just short of where the footpath across the fields ended in an old-fashioned stile, he reckoned that he had ten minutes to spare, even if Sally made better time than he thought possible.

He meant to wait for her in the road, but on second thoughts considered that their little explanation had better take place in some less exposed place. He therefore switched off his lights, crossed the stile, moved a pace or two to the right, and leaning against the trunk of an elm, became, in his dark livery, invisible among the shadows. He felt, as he waited, no ennui, but the rising excitement of the gambler who awaits the fall of some decisive card. He had played boldly in letting Sally go. The sudden threat had prompted some sudden counterstroke, and he had taken the risk and played boldly and high. Now, with the issue still uncertain, he counted all the risks and knew that there was not one which he had not foreknown and hazarded with cool acceptance. Sally might turn back. She might suspect Etta, and do anything but follow her instructions. She might meet someone. In fine, there were risks, and he took them with his eyes open. What, he wondered, was passing at the house. Etta— to have to use a woman like that! What a fatality, and yet no one else would serve. Please the saints she would not do anything of a folly too outrageous. He shrugged his shoulders over Etta Shaw. What a woman! Her folly, her gullibility, her exigeance! If she had the beauty of Helen of Troy in one hand and ten millions of francs in the other, one would be still well quit of her. Thank heaven, the affair would soon be finished. His thoughts began to busy themselves with the future.

Sally came slowly through the darkness. She could no longer see her way. She felt the muddy path under her feet and trudged on. If she stepped on grass, she stopped and felt for the mud again. A mist had risen and hung a few feet above the fields. She had the feeling that she was wading in some cold, impalpable stream, between shores that hid strange dreams. A night bird called harshly and was silent again, and from far overhead she heard the beat of its wings.

To float like that with warm wings that beat upon the darkness and bore one home! Sally lifted each foot in turn, and as she set it down she went on saying: "I must, I *must*, I MUST."

Because of that insistence she went on walking. It would have been so easy to stop lifting her feet, to stop thinking, to lie down in that cold stream of mist and let it cover her whilst she slept.

Lazare heard her come slowly, slowly, and he moved to the very edge of the dense shadow and waited for her there. She did not see the stile or know that it was there until she struck her knee against one of the wooden bars. Then she cried out—such a faint little cry and immediately Lazare had hold of her, his right arm about her shoulders pinioning her, and his left choking the little faint cry almost before it was uttered.

Sally felt nothing. The shock was too great, and she too near the end of her tether. She did not faint, but the capacity to feel any emotion was gone. She was aware only of external things, that Lazare's arm was like an iron bar about her shoulders, that it was difficult to breathe with his hand over her mouth, that the hand itself smelled of petrol and tobacco. These impressions came calmly into her consciousness and were suspended there. They produced no effect. They did not seem to concern her at all. The iron bar about her shoulders—no, she knew that it wasn't an iron bar, she knew, of course, what it really was—Lazare's arm. It tightened. He was going to lift her over the stile, and then suddenly the lifting movement stopped. They stood linked together listening. A hum that became louder, much louder, a faint glow that turned to glaring whiteness, and with a roar and clatter a large motor van came banging down the road. Sally felt herself half lifted, half dragged behind the elm trunk against which Lazare had leaned. She felt this still in that queer surface way, and knew, if she could scream or do anything to attract attention, that here were help and safety. The glare and the grinding noise went by. She had not moved or even tried to scream. She knew that she had lost her chance, and the knowledge did not move her at all.

Lazare waited until the noise had died in the distance. Then he proceeded to gag Sally very neatly, using a folded linen handkerchief and a woollen muffler. He also tied her wrists and ankles with strips of cloth. Then he lifted her over the stile and set her down in the corner of the car, after which he lit his lamps and drove slowly down the road until a cross lane enabled him to turn.

As he ran back along the way that he had come, a solitary cyclist passed them. Sally saw him, as it were, spring out of the darkness into the white circle made by their headlights; she saw his heavy, good-natured face, the loud check upon his tweed cap, and then the darkness had him again.

The young man, for his part, saw a face at the window of a passing car; just the top of a pale oval and two eyes, the rest lost in a muffler. He saw this and thought no more of it. There was, indeed, nothing in it to give him food for thought. Sally shut her eyes, and became less and less aware of the darkness, the movement, and of these impressions which still rested vaguely upon the surface of her mind.

Lazare drove briskly for about half an hour, choosing unfrequented by-ways. At the end of half an hour he turned and drove back, slowing down at the four-crossway just above Charnwood. He looked back into the car where Sally sat motionless, and then across the trees to where lights showed in the lonely house. One high, uncurtained window blazed against the sheer dark. He gave a satisfied nod and drove on.

The door in the wall was ajar. Etta met them on the threshold.

"Lazare, Lazare he's come, he's here," she whispered, and as Lazare pressed on up the stair, she followed, making desperate attempts to attract attention. He took no notice until he had laid Sally down on the rose-coloured settee in old Miss Harriet's sitting room. Then he turned an impatient face.

"What is it? Here, help me to get this off," and he bent over Sally, unfastening the muffler and removing the gag.

"He's here!"

"Who is here?"

"Le Noir!"

Lazare's hands stopped moving. He said: "So," in an expressionless voice, then, "Where?"

"In the dining room. He wants to see you."

"Naturally."

He folded up the muffler and rose to his feet. "Untie her. And you'd better give her some soup. Then stay here with her until I send for you." He went out, and Etta cut the strips of cloth from Sally's wrists and ankles, put a cushion under her head, and went across the passage to send Nadine for the soup.

When she returned Sally's eyes were open. They looked at her, at first without any expression at all. They reminded Etta for these few minutes of the eyes of one of Aunt Emma's kittens, for they held neither knowledge nor fear but only a clear wonder. The look changed very gradually. Etta wished that Sally would look away or shut her eyes. She was thankful when Nadine came with the cup of hot soup. Sally drank it very slowly. When it was finished her eyes came back to Etta's face, and she said in a soft, bewildered voice:

"Why?"

Etta looked away.

"Why did you?"

"You had better not *talk*, Sally."

The eyes began to accuse her. She could not evade them.

"You did—didn't you? Why?"

"I don't know what you mean."

"Oh, yes you do; but after all what does it matter?"

Sally put her head down on the cushions and shut her eyes. It didn't matter. Nothing mattered very much. Time went on. Then suddenly Etta's tears falling hot upon her hand, and Etta's voice choked with sobs:

"Sally, you'll do what they want you to. Oh, you *must*. I know you don't trust me now, but, Sally, you *must*. They mean to make you. They'll do awful things, and you'll *have* to give way in the end."

Something pierced Sally's numb indifference. She would have to give way in the end. That was fear. That thought itself was fear. She turned wild eyes on Etta Shaw, and then, as words of appeal trembled on her lips, the door was opened and Lazare came in.

"You are to come down," he said, speaking roughly. "Can you walk?"

Sally got to her feet, holding to Etta's arm. As she walked she let go of it, and by dint of clutching the baluster she came down the stair.

In the hall she paused. Lazare opened the dining-room door.

"In here," he said, and they passed in, Etta first, then Sally, and last of all Lazare. He shut the door, and, going over to the table, sat down. Etta guided Sally to a chair and took one beside her. The chandelier, fully lit, hung down above the dining table and was reflected from its polished surface. In the middle of the table, rose red against the dark mahogany, was the lacquer case. Sally saw it, and for a moment could see nothing else. When at last she lifted her eyes from it she was aware of Etta on her right and Lazare upon her left. Beyond Etta, Nadine, and on the farther side of Lazare, Sascha, and immediately opposite, sitting alone at the head of the table, a lean man with long hands hidden by black kid gloves, and a face hidden by a black mask that covered him from brow to chin. Above the mask a black skull cap such as priests wear or Harlequin in the masquerade. The gloved hands were folded upon the table.

"This, Miss Meredith," said Lazare, "is M. Le Noir. He has come to see the affair finished. The lacquer case is, as you see, before you upon the table. You will now open it."

Sally did not reply. She was counting the fishes and the roses on the case. There were three fishes and six roses. It was the third fish that one pressed, the third fish and the sixth rose. It would be very easily done.

"You will open it, and you will play no tricks. If you bungle and spoil the paper, you may be very sure that we shall kill you. You are too intelligent not to see that, I am sure. If you give us the paper you are compromised sufficiently, and we can let you go with safety to ourselves; but, unless you are compromised, we can never let you go. I am sure you see that. Now you will open the case?"

He took it up as he spoke, and laid it before her. Sally looked away from it. She looked at Sascha, but his eyes were downcast and his dark young face sullen. He suffered, but he was afraid. Sally stopped looking at him.

"Open it," said Lazare in a commanding voice. He tapped the table, paused, and, bending to Sally's ear, he whispered a single sentence, a single threat.

Those around the table heard no word of what he said, but the surface quiet and indifference of the whole circle was violently broken.

Sally screamed once, not loudly, but on a dry, hoarse note. The sound brought Sascha to his feet trembling like a startled animal, his hands gripping the table, his dark eyes wide and blank.

Lazare said: "Sit down, you fool!" his voice a dead monotone, and the boy dropped back into his chair, still holding to the table edge.

Nadine looked scornful. Etta's mouth fell open, giving her a vacant look. Le Noir did not move. Eyes, hands, and mask—all remained like a black picture painted on a background of dense shadow. Sally did not scream again. She shivered from head to foot and woke up. The dazed indifference which had shut her in went with a crash like ice that gives to a sudden thaw. She did not feel cold or tired or weak any more, but strong, vital, and intensely conscious. No more drifting with the stream of encompassing thought, no more quiescence. She was suddenly shocked broad awake into an intense consciousness of her danger and of a courage that rose to meet it. She sprang to her feet and cried in a clear, ringing voice:

"What fools you are—what utter fools! Don't you see when you're beaten? Don't you understand that nothing, *nothing* will make me give you that formula!"

The eyes in the black picture that was Le Noir shifted a point. Their gaze had been upon Sally. They shifted to the right and rested on Lazare. They conveyed without words a faintly ironic impression as who should say: "Is this the girl broken down—at the yielding point?"

Lazare stared back, cold and deadly. Into the momentary hush came the loud pealing of the front door bell.

Chapter Twenty

THERE WAS NOT MUCH that was admirable about Lazare, but he possessed the coolness and courage that dominate an emergency and pass without conscious effort into rapid and effective action.

Before Sally could scream his hand was on her mouth, and whilst he held her, struggling this time like a wild thing trapped, he spoke in his usual tone of command.

"It is probably the inspector—I ought to have expected it. Sascha, you will take Le Noir out by the back way? Wait with him in the shed until I send you word. Etta, you will help me to get her upstairs. They are not likely to search again, but be prepared. Take the lacquer case, Nadine, and put it in the old lady's room in a drawer; they will not look for it among her caps, I think. After that you will open the door. If it is the inspector or Major Armitage, Miss Shaw is engaged. If he asks for the chauffeur, show him in here, and come and tell me."

Sally had stopped struggling as soon as she found that it was not possible to wrench herself free. Instead she let herself go limp all over and hung a dead weight upon Lazare's arm. That horrible gag again—but no use to struggle, better let them think she had given in or fainted. The thoughts flashed through her mind, and it remained clear, receptive, ready to seize upon any chance.

The bell was ringing a second heavy peal as they carried her through the hall, Lazare going at a steady pace, Etta shaking, trembling, in a dumb terror, but fearing Lazare more than she feared the law. They took her into the old room. Then Lazare said: "The bathroom. Open the door and set the taps going. Splash and make a noise. Lock yourself in with her until I come. Do you understand? I'll kill you if you blunder, you foolish woman."

All so gently spoken. Etta nodded, speechless. They laid Sally on the black and white linoleum floor, and Lazare went out. Etta's shivering fingers were already on the taps. The water flowed with a pleasant gurgle. The little room began to fill with steam. Etta shot the bolt, and sitting down on the edge of the bath she began to cry quite silently, her face working, her hands twisting upon each other with a horrible, writhing movement. Sally's wide, clear eyes watched her. She felt pity. To be like that—how dreadful! Etta made her think of a battered, rudderless ship driven here and there but always nearer and nearer to the rocks. It was a horrid thing to see.

Downstairs Nadine had opened the door. Inspector Williams stood upon the threshold. A hireling bicycle leaned heavily against a bush of Euonymus at his left hand.

"Good evening," he said. "You take a long time to answer bells in this house, don't you?"

Nadine smiled gravely.

"I kept you waiting?" she said in the good English that yet had such a foreign sound to the inspector's ears. "I am sorry. I was with my old lady, and I could not leave in a hurry. She does not like hurry."

This was a long speech for Nadine, but the inspector was not to know that. He thought her a pleasant young woman, and not ill looking, for a foreigner. Trim too, and neat waisted, in that grey and white uniform.

"Well," he said, "I thought I'd like to see that chauffeur of yours. I missed him in Ledlington, so I took a bike and came along here after him. I see he's in, as the car is standing outside."

"Oh, yes, sir. Will you come in? I will tell him, and send him to you. He is in the kitchen, I think."

Nadine smiled again. Sally had never seen her smile; but she could smile at a man and with a very good effect. Her eyes told the inspector that he was a fine figure of a man. Her smile displayed some very beautiful white teeth. Inspector Williams walked into the dining room, and sat down in the chair lately vacated by M. Le Noir. He admired the polished table, and the admirable set of Adams chairs which surrounded it. He had a brother in the antique furniture line and fancied his smattering of knowledge. When Lazare came in he looked up sharply and saw a respectful-mannered chauffeur who came to a halt just inside the door and bade him a polite good evening.

"Ah—the chauffeur?"

"Yes, sir."

The notebook came out again. When the elastic band had been slipped off and the right place found, the inspector was ready. He did not exactly dawdle, but he certainly made no haste. In his experience, a witness was never the worse for a little anticipation. It made them nervous, and if there were any cats in bags, it, so to speak, loosened the string that shut the bag.

"You drove Miss Shaw down from London on Wednesday last?"

"Yes, sir."

"Where did you pick her up?"

"At the Club, sir."

"At what hour?"

"About a quarter to five, I should say."

"She was alone?"

"No, sir."

"Who was with her?"

"Another lady, a young lady, sir."

"Did you know her?"

"No, sir."

"Miss Shaw did not mention her name?"

"Not that I remember."

"How was she dressed?"

Lazare appeared to be thinking.

"I could not say, something dark, and fur round her neck. It was foggy, and getting late."

"Well, it doesn't matter. You drove the two ladies down here?"

"No. sir."

"Come, come, you were seen driving them through Ledlington; you were seen by more than one person."

"It may be. I drove Miss Shaw through Ledlington on our way home. The other lady we dropped at the Piccadilly Tube Station before we left London."

"At what time?"

"Five o'clock, or perhaps a few minutes after."

The inspector heaved an inward sigh. Duty had urged this second visit, impelled the hire of a bicycle, and brought him on a fool's errand. The man sounded all right, well mannered, well set up. Couldn't help being a foreigner; nothing else against him. He shut the notebook, got up, nodded affably to Nadine in the hall, and heard the door close behind him with feelings of satisfaction. He lifted the bicycle out of the Euonymus bush, passed through the gate, mounted his hireling, and rode briskly in the direction of Ledlington.

Lazare permitted himself to smile. He glanced at the clock and stood with folded arms, waiting until five minutes had ticked themselves away. Then he crossed the hall, opened the door that led to the back premises, and called "Gregor!" Instantly the silent man who kindled the fires and did most of the work of the house came to meet him. Lazare spoke to him in a rapid undertone, and, turning away, walked slowly up the stairs. He stopped at Miss Shaw's door and knocked. When Nadine opened it he said in a low voice:

"It's all right. He's gone. Come downstairs. We must talk things over."

"Nadine," said old Miss Shaw from the bed, "you are letting in the draught upon Alfred." The soft voice was reproachful. "Shut the door, my dear. Alfred hates draughts, and so do I."

Nadine came out into the passage.

"What a life!" she said. "When will the affair be finished? I have enough of it, my dear Lazare; and that I tell you frankly."

"Come down and we will talk it over. I have sent for Le Noir to come back. It is safe enough now."

He laid his hand on her shoulder in a sort of caress, and for a moment she lifted her fine eyes and smiled that slow smile of hers. Then she moved back a pace, and said—

"Etta, does she come down?"

"Certainly."

"My friend, I do not find that very clever of you. If it is necessary to proceed to extremities," she shrugged her shoulders, "you think she will be of use, your Etta?"

"It is you who are not clever, Nadine. If we proceed to extremities, it is above all things necessary that at every step Etta should be involved. Otherwise," he made a gesture with one of those ugly hands—"I have a little imagination, my dear, and I see Miss Etta Shaw very comfortable in the witness box whilst you and I are in the dock. Therefore, every step that we take, our dear Etta takes it too. I go to fetch her."

Nadine looked down as if considering. Then suddenly, fiercely, raised her eyes to his: "Our—dear—Etta," she said, with a pause between each word. "She is not dear to me, but she is dear to you. You make love to her, you kiss her. Am I blind? Or do you think I am as stupid as she is?"

"Not stupid," said Lazare lightly. "Oh, no, my dear Nadine, not stupid—only jealous." Nadine laid her hand on his breast.

"Jealous—of Etta?" she laughed. "*Mon ami*, you flatter yourself, but you do not flatter me."

"It is true all the same."

Nadine shook her head. Then with a sudden rush of anger, she said:

"Why do you make love to her?"

"Because I choose," said Lazare. He laughed, and added, "Come, Nadine, do you think that even that dear Etta would believe all that we have told her if she were not just a little just a little blinded by passion? She and her New Party of Peace! Do you really think she would believe that you, and I and Le Noir are all consumed with a desire for peace, peace," he laughed hardly, "if it were not that a woman in love will believe anything?"

"Ah, *par exemple*, Lazare, do you think that I believe what you say to me about another woman? Perhaps I reflect that you say the same thing of me. Perhaps I am not in love?"

Her eyes mocked him. He bent forward to kiss her, but she drew back.

"Not this time, my friend. Go to your Etta, for consolation."

Chapter Twenty-One

"M. LASALLE," said Major Armitage.

Fritzi turned, with Bill's hand on his arm and the sound of Bill's voice in his ears. A look of surprise was succeeded by one of friendly recognition, which in its turn slowly gave place to an expression of undoubted dismay.

"Major Armitage!" he said. And then, spreading out both his plump hands, "Alas, you have found me."

"We thought you were dead," said Bill briefly.

M. Lasalle looked shocked.

"How could I be dead? Where, my dear friend, was my corpse?"

"In the Smuggler's Leap," said Bill, a little grimly. "You see, we found your fountain pen there, and your footmarks on the edge. And Miss Meredith told us how worried you'd been. And of course we thought—"

M. Lasalle looked, for him, severe.

"You thought—what did you think?"

"We thought that you had committed suicide."

Fritzi's blue eyes expressed the uttermost reproach and horror.

"I! A suicide?" he gasped. "And my religious sentiments, and my moral principles, and my devotion to science, what of them? Suicide? Am I, then, an ingrate to throw back to the *Bon Dieu* his gift, to say to him, 'You have given me a brain, and a heart, and an intelligence. You have given me health, and a sufficiency of money. And all these things I throw back, I will none of them'? Suicide! Believe me, my friend, that is a very singular idea."

"Sally didn't believe it," said Bill, partly to stem the flood of M. Lasalle's reproaches and partly to introduce Sally's name.

Fritzi beamed.

"Sally is intelligent," he said. "She would never believe such a thing, never."

Bill took M. Lasalle by the arm and drew him onto the curb beside the car.

"I want to talk to you," he said. "Where are you living?"

M. Lasalle hesitated. He had the air of a child who desires to conceal something.

"My friend," he said, "where I live, it is, shall I say, a matter of confidence? With your permission I will merely describe it as a place of retirement. I had need of such a place, and one was provided."

"I want to talk to you," said Bill. "We can't talk here."

M. Lasalle considered.

"This road, it is true, is noisy," he said. "Yet it is amongst these thronging crowds that I can think so well. I come out, I plunge into this moving stream of persons all intent upon their own business, and I find that my ideas flow on undisturbed. But, as you say, for conversation it is not so well. You shall drive me in your car to a more retired street. There we can talk."

Bill felt a consuming impatience, but M. Lasalle appeared serenely unaware of the fact. He kept up a continuous flow of conversation to which it is to be feared Bill paid but perfunctory attention. He heard the story of Fritzi's midnight walk, of his misery and despair, of the coming of the New Idea, and of the way of escape afforded by the opportune motor and its oblivious chauffeur.

"Figure to yourself," said M. Lasalle with extreme rapidity. "To this day he does not know that he was to me a good angel!"

Bill turned out of the thoroughfare into a side street, without commenting upon this statement, and after a slight dramatic pause, Fritzi proceeded to describe vaguely, but with enthusiasm, the New Idea.

"A food for infants, beneficent and nourishing beyond all others. My friend, is not that an idea? To feed, to invigorate the coming race—that is better than to destroy. You say to me that there are already a hundred foods and each one claims that it has these qualities, but to that I reply, Mine is beyond them all— It is truly novel, truly wonderful—It is better than nature. Ah! Is not that a triumph?"

Bill said nothing. He drove the car in silence. Two more turnings and they were in an ill-lit, dingy street, empty from end to end. Here he drew up, and turned upon his companion with a purposeful air.

"Now, M. Lasalle, we will talk," he said. "This is what I want to say to you."

M. Lasalle interrupted him.

"My friend," he said reproachfully, "do I not talk? Have I ceased to talk since we met? It is, in effect, a long time since I have talked so much."

"I don't mean that sort of talk." Bill's tone was dogged. "I want you to listen to me."

"Very well, I am all attention."

"Well, Monsieur, after you disappeared, Sally told us—"

"Ah!" interjected M. Lasalle, "you call her Sally?"

Bill began to feel sympathetically towards persons who slew benevolent uncles and buried them in lonely woods.

"Yes," he said briefly, "what I'm trying to say is this: Sally told us that you were very much troubled about your invention."

"Ah!" said M. Lasalle, "it does not matter now. You have an excellent and sympathetic heart, but indeed, my friend, I am no longer troubled about the matter. It is gone into the past. It is for me no more; and, instead, my whole mind, my energies, my intelligence, they are occupied with a new idea, its inception, its development. It is in order to mature this idea undisturbed that I am in a place of retirement."

"M. Lasalle, will you listen to me?" said Bill loudly.

"But, my friend, of course." In the dusk M. Lasalle was seen to wave his hands with an inviting gesture.

"Sally said that before you disappeared you had been bothered with people trying to get hold of your formula. I want to know if that's a fact."

"But yes, it was certainly a fact." He used the past tense as one who speaks of remote events.

"Will you tell me who they were?"

M. Lasalle hesitated, threw out his hands.

"To what purpose? The affair is in the past."

"I'm afraid it isn't. I'm afraid I must press for an answer. Who were those people who approached you?"

Fritzi became agitated.

"Monsieur, I cannot tell you. It is an affair of confidence. They approach me in confidence. They rely on my honour. I refuse their offers, but I pledge myself to secrecy. It is true that I have cause to complain of their conduct. They spy upon me. They will not take my answer. They even threaten. But yet I feel that I did give my pledge. It is an affair of my honour, and I beg that you will not press it."

"I do press it," said Bill, stubbornly. "The men are criminals. You say they threatened you. I know they threatened Sally. How can you hesitate?"

Fritzi became yet more perturbed.

"Ah, my friend, you are young. You are of the age that judges rashly and condemns without thought. These men, I regard them in a sense with pity. They are without moral principle, it is true, and it makes them to be pitied that it is so with them. Of them some have perhaps suffered and been oppressed. Of one it is true, I know. See, I will recount to you his history without the name, that would be a breach of confidence. Figure to yourself a boy, superbly handsome, gifted, and of a high spirit, the son—illegitimate, it is true—of a man of highest rank and immense wealth. He is educated as an heir, spoiled, flattered, caressed—and at sixteen his father dies. The will that was to have provided for him, it is not made. He is cast on the world. He is of no society, he is neither noble nor peasant. He has from his father his handsome face and his proud spirit, and from his peasant mother the class rancour that eats the heart, and the ugly common hands of which he is so ashamed. I tell you when he saw me look at his hands, he turned as white as death. In that moment I pitied him. Can I wonder that he has the desire to pull down, to destroy? Truly to understand all is to forgive—"

Bill strove for patience.

"M. Lasalle, the matter is serious. I ask you for names and facts, not for philosophical discourses."

"But, my friend, I am bound, and the affair, as I say, is in the past."

"I wish to heaven it were. M. Lasalle, you've got to pay attention! The affair is very far from being in the past. The formula has been stolen, and Sally has disappeared."

"Mon Dieu!" said M. Lasalle. "What is that you say?"

Bill said it again rather louder than before.

"Oh, la, la, la, la, la," said M. Lasalle. Then with sudden vigour: "Impossible!"

"What is impossible?" said Bill. "Do you mean that the formula isn't stolen, or that Sally hasn't disappeared?"

"My friend," said M. Lasalle, most unfairly, "calm yourself. Tell me what has occurred. Why do you say that the formula is stolen?"

It was too dark to see Fritzi's face, but his voice held an odd inflection.

Bill groaned inwardly. The whole thing was like a nightmare. Why should he be holding an apparently endless conversation with a lost uncle in a dark street that smells of dustbins?

"Because," he began, and then, as if suddenly enlightened, "Oh, I say, do you mean that it isn't—that you took it with you? Because, if you did, it would mean—"

The idea almost knocked him off his balance. Why, it would mean that Sally was all right. It would mean—He caught Fritzi by the arm, and almost shouted, "Sally, is Sally with you? She said—I mean the telegram said so, only we thought it was a fake. Is she, is she? Oh, for the Lord's sake, do say something."

"My young friend," began M. Lasalle. Then he paused, coughed, and said uncertainly, "Sally? What is all this about Sally and telegrams? With me? But, no, my friend, how should she be?"

"Then it *was* a fake," groaned Bill, and relinquished his hold upon M. Lasalle's arm.

"Go on about the formula," he said. "You are sure you didn't take it with you?"

"Of course I am sure. I left a letter for Sally, and in it I told her that the red lacquer case was in the bookshelf. I told her behind which book she would find it, and all the decision of whether to use or to destroy it I left in her hands. They are small, Sally's hands, but of the most capable."

"She looked in the place you said. The red lacquer case was gone."

"Impossible! You are sure?"

"It was gone, and now Sally's gone too."

"La—la—la—and when did Sally go?"

"On Wednesday!" and Bill groaned out the story of the woman in the blue motor veil who had, as he put it, come bothering Sally on Monday, and how she had gone up to town on the Wednesday and disappeared. He told of the faked telegrams and of his fruitless search for Sally, and at the end Fritzi took off his hat and ran his fingers through his hair.

"But it was on Wednesday that I saw Sally," he remarked, and felt Bill grip his arm again.

"When? Where did you see her?"

"In the road over there, near to where you met me. I had gone out to take the air, to think, to dream; and all of a sudden like a flash I saw Sally."

"Where?"

"In a car. It went slowly because of much traffic, and the light of a street lamp it shone in right upon Sally's face. I think she had been asleep. She blinked and looked at me, and I think to myself, 'Aha, now you are caught.' And then the car moves on and they are gone."

"Which way was it going?"

"How can I say? It came from London, however."

"What time was it?" The words hurried from Bill's lips.

"My friend, when I work the time is nothing to me. How do I know?"

"But the street lamps were lighted. It must have been after dark."

"Yes, yes."

"Have you no idea what time it was?"

"My friend, none."

"What sort of car was it?"

"It was a car."

"Yes, so you said; but what make?"

"I do not know. To me they are all alike."

"Was it a Wolseley?"

"My friend, I tell you I do not know the one car from another. I hear them spoken of, a Ford, a Wolseley, it is all the same to me."

Bill's jaw dropped. That there should exist a human being whose intelligence was so low as not to be able to distinguish a Ford from a Wolseley, simply staggered him.

"Oh, I say!" he said.

"Yes?" M. Lasalle was all polite attention. "What is that you say?"

Bill said nothing. He was speechless. He began to put in some rapid thinking. Old Lasalle was a washout, absolutely. No use wasting more time on him. But he had seen Sally, it was obvious that he had seen Sally; and in spite of his vagueness it was also quite obvious that he had seen her driving in the Ledlington direction after dark, and at a point at least five miles distant from Piccadilly. So much for Etta's evidence.

He experienced an instant and overwhelming desire to get back to Ledlington, to find the inspector if possible, but anyhow to get back to Ledlington. He felt furiously incensed with M. Lasalle. What business had he to lay Sally open to these risks? Why couldn't he settle his own affairs with his own conscience? Am I now not even to know a Rolls-Royce from an omnibus! He had at that moment no use for inventors, absolutely none at all.

"My friend," said M. Lasalle at this auspicious juncture, "you appear to me to be troubled. If it is about Sally, I beg of you not to be uneasy. For me, I am persuaded that if Sally has gone away, it is for some very good reason. Reflect! You think that *I* am dead. Am I, therefore, dead? Not at all. I have merely retired myself that I may have some peace. In my judgment it is so with Sally. She has retired herself. She plays you a trick. Presently she will laugh at you."

At this moment Bill lost his temper so thoroughly that his subsequent recollection of the terms in which he expressed himself was rather vague. It is, however, certain that he was extremely rude to the astonished M. Lasalle, that their parting was of a very abrupt nature, and that, a little later on, three policemen called upon him without success to moderate the speed at which he was driving in the direction of Ledlington.

M. Lasalle, for his part, resumed his interrupted walk. As he wandered slowly and meditatively amongst the crowds that hurried, pushed, and jostled, his thoughts resumed their philosophic calm.

"That is a worthy young man, of a rash and impulsive temper, but worthy. That he loves Sally is apparent even to me, who am not observant in such matters. It is also his excuse. By this time, he doubtless regrets his hasty words and his discourteous departure."

He continued to walk, gazing dreamily at the passers-by. Presently a strange little smile covered his face.

"The red lacquer case—the formula," he murmured. "I wonder—very much—I wonder."

Chapter Twenty-Two

SALLY LAY QUITE STILL. The linoleum was rather cold. The air in the little bathroom was heavy with steam. The sound of running water and the sound of Etta's voice went on continuously.

Etta had not moved. She sat on the edge of the bath, twisting her hands and talking in a low monotone that was not at all like her usual voice.

"Sally, I can't help it. You know that I can't help it, don't you? I don't know what to do, I don't indeed. If I could help it, I *would*. Lazare says—and I must believe him—you do see that, don't you? If I didn't believe what he says, everything would go. You must see that, Sally. You couldn't expect me to let everything go like that. Sally, don't look at me like that. I'm doing it all for the Cause, for the Cause and for Lazare, and what is one individual when the whole cause of humanity is at stake? I have to think of that. You must see that I have to think of that; you must, Sally, you must."

It was the same thing over and over, always coming back to that appeal to Sally, until Sally herself was sick with pity and knew that for nothing in the world would she have changed places with Etta Shaw.

The water went on running. Etta's voice went on. Then footsteps, a loud, insistent knocking on the door, Lazare's impatient voice:

"It is I. Open the door."

Etta shivered, drew the bolt with a jerk, and let him in. He stood on the threshold, threw Sally a glance that noted her unchanged position, and said: "She has not tried to move?"

Etta shook her head.

He knelt down and removed the gag. Sally relaxed every muscle. She lay there, her eyes closed, her mouth fallen a little open. Lazare shook her, gripping her shoulder roughly.

"Here, none of that," he said. "Get up."

But when she neither stirred nor answered he picked her up, stood for a moment to bid Etta "stop that confounded water running," and then set Sally down on the settee in the sitting room.

"We don't want her just now. She'll come round fast enough when we do. Etta, it is you we want. Nadine has gone down. We must come to a decision, and how can we do that without you?"

He put his arm around her as he spoke, felt that she was trembling, and spoke soothingly to her as they went out. As soon as Sally heard the click of the bolt she opened her eyes and sat up.

The voices died away. The footsteps died away. Sally's hearing, like all her other faculties, was at its most acute. It was as if her consciousness was flooded by an intense light in which every thought stood clear and every perception was heightened. She was aware that a crisis was approaching, and that the danger in which she stood was real and imminent, but she was not actually afraid. The emotion that had been fear seemed to have changed, and to stimulate instead of depressing. Something in her tingled at the thought of Lazare and his threat; her head came up, and her jaw set firmly. She knew that she would never open the case for them, never give them the formula. The terror lest she should give in had passed, and with its passing she was strong.

Sally had a simple faith that if one did right one was protected, and that if one did wrong one was punished. She believed this quite firmly as a child believes it. The conviction that it would be wicked to give the formula to Lazare presented itself to her in this ingenuous manner and brought with it the certainty that help would come. She began to cast about in her thought for any possible avenue by which this help might reach her.

Nadine had gone down. Lazare and Etta were going down. They were going to come to a decision about her, Sally. They would all be downstairs. Sally had in her mind the picture of an empty passage with a door on the right and, a couple of yards further on, another door on the left. The door on the right her door, the door on the left the door of old Miss Shaw's room. If—Sally's heart began to beat—if she could only make the old lady hear. She remembered what Etta had said about her aunt— "She doesn't get out of bed, but of course there's no reason why she shouldn't." No reason why she shouldn't—and a terribly insistent hope that she might, if she were to hear Sally calling.

As the thought took shape Sally was at the door, her mouth pressed to the crack. She called "Miss Shaw! Miss Shaw!" She went on calling.

Old Miss Shaw was sitting up in bed. Nadine had left her comfortably propped up with pillows. The room was pleasantly warm. The fire burned clearly. Miss Shaw was talking to Marmaduke who had come out of his cage and was sitting timidly on a little sugar-loaf peak that she had made for him with a fold of the embroidered linen sheet.

"Foolish, my dear, foolish," she was saying. "I have told you so very often that Gwendoline will not hurt you."

She stroked the head of the white kitten which lay beside her fast asleep, a shred of rose-leaf tongue caught in its milk teeth, its blue eyes only half closed.

"Gwendoline is young, and you should make allowances for youth and high spirits as Alfred does."

She put out her finger, and Marmaduke said, "Tweet" rather nervously, and retreated to his cage.

"Fie!" said old Miss Shaw. "Fie!"

It was at this point that she thought she heard someone call her name. She listened intently, and she heard it again: "Miss Shaw! Miss Shaw!" It seemed as though the large white cat heard it too, for he got up, stretched himself, and jumped down from the bed.

"Did you hear it, Clarence?" said Miss Shaw. "Did you hear someone calling me? Now that is very singular. I don't know when it happened before, and I don't know who it can be, my dear."

Clarence walked to the door, sat down before it, and uttered the loud, harsh mew of a pure-bred Persian. The voice kept on calling. Clarence turned his head, cast a glance of the utmost reproach at his perturbed mistress, and mewed again.

Old Miss Shaw moved Gwendoline very gently to the bottom of the bed. After that she closed the door of the canaries' cage. Then she folded back the bedclothes, and cast a guilty look around. Clarence mewed for the third time.

"There is someone calling me," said old Miss Shaw. "Who can it be? It cannot be Etta or Nadine, for they do not know that I get out of bed when I am alone. Who can it be?"

She pushed the bedclothes still further down, put her feet out of bed, and sat looking at the door and listening.

"Miss Shaw! Miss Shaw!"

Someone was certainly calling her. The voice sounded as if it came from Harriet's room. Who could possibly be in Harriet's room? It couldn't be Harriet. Oh, no, it couldn't be Harriet. Harriet would not call her Miss Shaw. She would say "Emmy dearest." Old Miss Shaw's eyes filled with tears. Who could possibly be in Harriet's room? She stood up, holding to the bedpost, and then walked slowly to the door. Her feet were encased in bed socks of pink lamb's wool so that she did not feel the need of slippers.

Clarence mewed for the fourth time. He also looked at her angrily and patted the door with a white furry paw. The minute that it was open he stalked majestically into the passage. The old lady followed him.

There *was* someone in Harriet's room.

"Miss Shaw! Miss Shaw!"

Miss Shaw came slowly toward the sound. The passage was cold. She looked over her shoulder at the warm glow which shone from the open door of her room. The passage was dark. She hated the cold and the dark, but she would just see who was in Harriet's room before she went back to her warm bed. Afterwards she would ask Nadine for a hot-water bottle, without telling her that she had been out of bed—that would never do, no, that would certainly never do; they would scold her if they knew.

She reached the door, rested her left hand on the jamb, and with her right tapped upon the nearest panel, making the faintest of faint sounds, and listening tremulously for a response.

Sally, leaning against the inner side of the door, had heard each stage of the old lady's approach, the click of the latch, Clarence's mew, the shuffle of Miss Shaw's feet in the woolly bed socks; each of these sounds was more beautiful to her than music.

When that mere whisper of a tap brushed the far side of the panel against which she leaned, Sally's sharply indrawn breath answered it. Her voice would not come for a moment, and she heard Miss Shaw give a little whimpering cry.

"Oh, dear. Oh, dear," and then—"Is there anyone there?"

"Yes, yes," breathed Sally, trying to keep the thread of sound steady and controlled.

She heard Miss Shaw's hand slide on the panel. She heard her give a deep sigh.

"Oh, who is it?"

Sally got her voice clear.

"I'm locked in. Will you undo the bolt, dear Miss Shaw?"

"The bolt?"

The hand slid and fumbled again, touched the bolt, and fell away.

"It's so cold."

"Please, *please*, Miss Shaw. Open the bolt. Let me out."

Once more that slow groping, but this time the bolt moved, creaked a little, and slid back.

Sally's hands gripped each other.

"There's another bolt lower down. Will you open it? Please open it."

"My dear, I think—I think I should be going back to bed. The passage strikes a little cold."

"Just the one bolt, dear, *dear* Miss Shaw, just the one bolt. Then I'll help you into bed. That will be much better."

Clarence was rubbing and purring about his mistress's ankles. She felt sufficiently encouraged to bend a little and push back the second bolt.

Next moment the door was open. Sally and Miss Shaw stood looking at each other, with Clarence purring between them.

"I'll—take—you—back—to—your—room. Sally had to force the words, but they came.

But Miss Shaw shuffled past her into the room.

"Harriet's room," she said. "Such a pretty room. We always liked pink, Harriet and I. A gentleman who was an admirer of mine when I was a young girl once told me that I reminded him of a pink rosebud. I thought that very pretty. He was a fine, tall man, but he had false teeth. Alfred, my eldest canary, is called after him. I had a good many admirers, my dear, but I never married—I never married." She paused, stopped looking aimlessly about the room, and, fixing her china-blue eyes on Sally, she said:

"I'm afraid I am rather forgetful, my dear. Do I know your name?"

"My name is Sally. Dear Miss Shaw, won't you come back to bed? It is much too cold for you here."

"All in good time," said Miss Shaw. "There is no hurry. Young people are so impatient, and you know that it is a fault and should be overcome. You wouldn't think it, my dear, but when I was a girl I had a sadly impatient temper. It cost me the affections of a very worthy young man to whom I was at one time engaged. He had the most beautiful ginger whiskers, and his name was Marmaduke. I have called a young canary after him: he is at present of a timid disposition, but I am in hopes that that will pass."

Sally took the old lady firmly by the arm.

"Come back to bed," she said. Bending forward, "Supposing somebody were to come!"

"Ah, yes, yes. Very well thought of, my dear, and, as you say, it is cold."

She let Sally lead her to the door, and watched her fasten the bolts again.

"But why do you do that, my dear?" she asked.

Sally did not answer. She piloted Miss Shaw safely into her own room, deposited her in her bed, and tucked her up. Gwendoline had not waked up; she lay in an extremely engaging attitude, her head pillowed upon her paw, breathing regularly. Alfred and Marmaduke sat side by side on their perch, with golden feathers all fluffed out.

"And now my pillows," said Miss Shaw. "There are five, my dear, and I should like you to shake them all thoroughly. It does make such a difference. Yes, Clarence, you may come up too, but don't tread on Gwendoline. No, my dear, that pillow goes next to the bolster, and then this little one fits into my back. Now the square one, and the two with the frilled pillow cases on the top. Harriet embroidered the monograms, E. and H. entwined; E. for Emma, and H. for Harriet, my dear."

"I must go," said Sally, desperately.

"One moment—or rather, why must you go? People keep going away today, Etta and Nadine, and that very large, pleasant young man who said his name was Armitage. He reminded me a little of Clarence, not the cat, of course, my dear, but my cousin Clarence who went to Australia in the year '63 and was never heard of again. Or was it South Africa?"

"Did you say Armitage?" said Sally, breathing quickly.

"No, no," said Miss Shaw, "it was he who said Armitage. He stood there just inside the door, looking quite immense, and I said to him, 'Do I know you, my dear?' and he said, 'My name is Armitage.' And then he admired Clarence and stroked his head."

"When?" said Sally, "when?"

"Just after tea," said Miss Shaw placidly. "Nadine had taken away the tray, and the man came to see to the electric light, though I didn't know that there was anything wrong with it."

Sally's heart beat violently. Bill was looking for her! Bill had been here! Then, *that* was why they had let her go. It was a cruel trick to get her out of the way; and Bill had come and gone, and had not found her. Just for a moment her heart failed her a little; and then she was strong again.

"I must go," she said. "Dear Miss Shaw, don't tell anyone you've seen me. You don't want them to know you got out of bed, do you?"

Miss Shaw shook her head with astonishing vigour. Then she took Sally's hand and pressed it.

"Come again soon, my dear. And before you go, if you would fetch me a clean pocket handkerchief from the chest of drawers over there; the left-hand top drawer, and the handkerchiefs are on the right-hand side of it, marked with my initials."

Then Sally remembered. It was just as if Lazare were standing in the room, the sound of his voice came so plainly to her ears. She heard it again as she had heard it when he bade Nadine take the red lacquer case into the old lady's room and hide it there. "They won't look for it under her caps," he had said.

Sally caught the old lady's hand in both of hers. "Where do you keep your caps?" she panted.

A mildly puzzled expression came into Miss Shaw's blue eyes. "My dear, I asked you for a handkerchief, not a cap," she said.

Sally dropped the hand and ran across the room to where the chest of drawers stood facing the door. The top of it was covered with photographs in frames, each standing by itself upon a little crochet mat.

Sally began to open the drawers with trembling hands. The top drawer had linen in it, and the next black silken garments that crackled and smelt of camphor. The caps were in the bottom drawer. There were dozens of them, all made on the same formal pattern, with rosettes of lace and net, and quillings of pale coloured ribbon. Some had blue ribbon, and some pink, and some lavender. There was one with cherry-coloured rosettes. As Sally turned them over, Miss Shaw's fluttering voice continued to remind her that the handkerchiefs were in the left-hand top drawer and on the right-hand side of the drawer.

The red lacquer case was wrapped in a fold of white net inside the cap with the cherry-coloured rosettes. Sally unfolded the net with light, shaking fingers, and saw it. She held it. She looked at it. There were the three fishes and the six roses. It was really the red lacquer case. She held it in her hand.

What next? Where was she to go to now? Every second mattered now. Instantly, and before an answering thought could shape itself, there came the sound of running feet. Someone coming up the stairs, running quickly and lightly, with the sound of a high-heel tapping.

Sally spun round, the hand with the lacquer case behind her. Miss Shaw's eyes were round with dismay, her puckered mouth opened with an "Oh!" of frightened breath.

No time to get away. No time to pass the stairhead unseen. No chance at all really, but a desperate one that must be taken. As these thoughts came, Sally had the dressing-room door open, was on the threshold, her eyes imploring those vague blue ones that watched her from the bed.

"Don't tell. They *mustn't* know," she breathed, and closed the door with her left hand. The right still held the red lacquer case. She leaned against the shut door. The room was in total darkness. She heard the running feet cross the threshold of Miss Shaw's room, and stood rigid, listening, listening. She heard Miss Shaw say "Nadine," and waited for what would come next. The footsteps came quickly across the room. Sally would not move a finger. If Nadine were to open the door she would find her. She was coming straight towards it. She was going to open it. "Ah!" Sally took a long, long breath, the footsteps stopped short. She heard the jerk of the bottom drawer; she heard it catch as it had caught just now when she herself had opened it; and she knew that Nadine had come to get the lacquer case. And the case was not there. It was here, in Sally's hand. She could feel the little raised roses as she held it. She thrust the case deep into the pocket of her coat. The drawer creaked, there was a swish of skirts, and Nadine's voice hard, insistent.

"Who has been to this drawer?"

Old Miss Shaw could see what Sally could not see. She looked at Nadine with the red patch on either cheek, the blazing suspicion in her eyes, and she began to tremble and to whimper softly, taking little distressed breaths and fidgeting with the sheet.

"Who has been to this drawer?" demanded Nadine, coming a quick step nearer. "Have you been out of bed? Have you been to the drawer? Tell me at once, *at once!*"

Miss Shaw began to cry. The tears rose singly and, overflowing, rolled down her smooth pink cheeks one by one. She made no effort to wipe them away.

"No, no, oh, dear me, no," she said, and then said it again, and then a third time.

"Who has been in here? Tell me at once. Tell me who has been to the drawer."

"No, no, oh, dear me, no, no," wept Miss Shaw, and then, in a piteous voice, "If you would give me a pocket handkerchief, my dear. They are in the left-hand top drawer, and on the right-hand side of the drawer, marked with my initial."

Nadine raised her hand, took the old lady by the shoulder, and said:

"Who—has—been here?" She spoke low and furiously. Miss Shaw broke into wailing sobs.

"No, no, oh, no. Oh dear me, no," she gasped, and Nadine, suddenly releasing her, sprang for the door. She left it wide open behind her. Sally heard the sound of her flying feet, the tap of the high-heeled shoes as she whirled downstairs. The canaries fluttered and twittered. Miss Shaw wept on.

There was just this one minute. Nadine had gone to Lazare with the news, and in a minute they would be here again, skilled and desperate searchers. Before Nadine had reached the stairhead Sally was out of the dressing room. She put her finger on her lips, ran to the farther door, and passed like a flash from warmth and light, rose shades and pink wreathed carpet, into the visible dusk of the passage, with its odd air, the walls which looked black, and the narrow strip of crimson felt which lay on its polished boards like a dark streak.

All the light there was came from the stairhead on the left and from Miss Shaw's open door behind her. The light from the stairs was no more than twilight, reflected from the chandelier in the hall below. Sally heard the dining-room door flung open, caught the blurred sound of voices, and ran on tiptoe as far as the top of the stairs. For one breathless moment she leaned over the smooth rail, and wondered if it were possible, just barely possible, to reach the halfway landing; but immediately the vague noises from below rose in a sharp crescendo, a chair fell with a crash, and, even as Sally drew back shuddering, the hall was full of people and voices. On the other side of the stairhead a second passage showed. She did not know where it led to, but she ran for the darkness and the shelter, ran with her hands stretched out before her, groping along the wall, the fingers of her right hand slipping on the shiny wall paper. There was a clatter of footsteps and a hum of voices behind her, coming nearer. Her hand touched wood, the jamb of a door. She felt for the handle, turned it, and slipped into a dark and unknown room. The door opened outwards, the handle on the side nearest the stairs. Sally left a crevice open and stood there with the dark all round her, looking through the narrow crack. She could see the landing, vague in twilight, and three figures at the top of the stairs. Then, with startling suddenness, the whole scene sprang into light as Lazare depressed the electric switch.

He stood on the top step, his hand raised and touching the wall, Nadine beside him, and Etta on the step below. They were all talking at once. Sascha and Le Noir were nowhere to be seen. The passage into which Miss Shaw's room opened was now lighted from end to end. Lazare stood for a second, his eyes searching it. They dwelt upon the door of Miss Harriet's room, and Sally thanked heaven that she had remembered to fasten the bolts. Then the lifted hand dropped, Etta passed in front of Nadine, and they all went along the two yards of passage and through the open door of Miss Shaw's room.

Chapter Twenty-Three

Miss Shaw was still sitting exactly as Nadine had left her, the large, slow tears rolling over her pink cheeks and making a damp path on the fine embroidered shawl she wore.

Etta came to her, kissed her, patted the trembling hands, and spoke soothingly, whilst Nadine and Lazare stood just inside the door and watched, Nadine's foot tapping impatiently, Lazare quiet and controlled.

"Aunt Emma," said Etta, "dear Aunt Emma, do tell me, did you get out of bed just now? Did you, dear?"

"No, no, oh, dear me, no," sobbed Miss Shaw. "I don't know, my dear, I don't know."

"Now, Aunt Emma, don't be afraid. There's no harm if you did get out. Just tell me, did you open your cap drawer and take my—my card case out of it? It was red—a flat case, about so big. Did you take it out of your cap drawer?"

Miss Shaw stopped sobbing and sniffed.

"She tumbled my caps," she said, her mild blue eyes looking reproachfully at Nadine. "She tumbled them; and you know how particular I am about my caps." She sniffed again. "My dear, if you would get me a clean pocket handkerchief. They are in the left-hand top drawer, marked with my initial."

Sally, looking through the crack of the door, had seen Etta go into Miss Shaw's room, had seen Lazare and Nadine follow her. They left the door open behind them. Already she knew what she must do, what she must try to do; knew also how small a chance she had of succeeding. She must get down the stairs now, at once, whilst they were in Miss Shaw's room. She had quite a clear picture of what would happen in a minute. Etta would make Miss Shaw talk, they would find out that she, Sally, was missing, and the house would be searched from garret to cellar. If she could get downstairs and out of the house before they missed her, there was a slender chance, otherwise none at all. But to leave this dark room and go out into the light, to pass so close to that open door and risk the stairs. All these thoughts passed through her mind with unbelievable rapidity. They were there as Etta disappeared into her aunt's room, and when Lazare and Nadine followed her and passed from sight, Sally had already taken her decision, was already pushing the door open. To come out into the unshaded light of the landing was like taking a plunge into ice-cold water. Sally did not give herself time to think. She ran quickly, lightly, out of the dark passage on to the stairhead and down the stairs. As she passed the corner she heard Miss Shaw sniff and say: "If you would get me a pocket handkerchief, my dear." There were eight steps and a turn, six more and the half-landing with the drawing room opening on to it.

Sally reached the turn on noiseless, flying feet, caught the stair rail to steady herself as she swung round, and came down on the second step of the short half-flight. Here she checked for a second, listening. Above her the voices went on. She looked down through the bannisters and bit deep into her lip. Someone was on the stair coming up from the hall, not running or seeming to be in a hurry, but walking heavily with bent head and hanging hands. Sally looked down petrified, unable to run on or to go back, unable to move at all. As if drawn by her gaze the bent head lifted, a dark, startled face looked up. Sascha's eyes met Sally's.

Agonized anxiety, agonized protest, that is what each read in the other's eyes. Sally checked a sob and ran down the four remaining steps. As she reached the half-landing Sascha threw out his arm as if to bar the stairway to her, and she heard a man's footsteps cross the hall below. At the same time Etta cried out in the room above, a sharp, startled cry.

There was no going on, there was no going back.

The drawing-room door was not a yard away. Sally opened it, ran in, and, when she would have closed it behind her, found Sascha on the threshold. He came in quickly, pushed the door to; and they stood in the dark, breathing hard, and heard a step go past and up to the flight beyond. Then Sally breathed his name and felt him quiver, they were standing so close together.

"Help me," she said, "Sascha, Sascha!"

Her groping hand found his wrist and clung to it, and the pressure pleaded as her whispering voice had pleaded. Sascha shuddered from head to foot and was silent. The hand that lay against Sally's was as cold as ice. Then, like a person in a dream, he put out the other hand and turned on the light.

The three globes in the central chandelier flashed into brilliance, making the room a dazzle of garish magenta. The heavy curtains across the windows, the upholstered furniture, seemed to rush into sight. Sally almost screamed. It was so sudden.

Her hand dropped from Sascha's wrist, she fell back a pace. And then he was close to her, whispering in her ear, agitated and incoherent:

"Sally, if they find you, you are lost. I can do nothing, and I suffer. You say 'Help me.' No one can help you unless you do as they say."

"Put out the lights," said Sally.

"No, no, it is the only chance. You say 'Save me,' I will do my possible. If the room is dark, they suspect at once; but if there is light, if I practise here, it may be—see, my violin, there on the piano. I must play, but my hand shakes."

"Yes, yes, I see. Play quickly."

As she spoke a door slammed violently upstairs. Sally darted across the room, parted the rose- magenta curtains, and, letting them fall together behind her, she threw up the window with desperate hands. It creaked and moved stiffly. She leaned out. A long-drawn wail from Sascha's violin seemed to fill the room behind her.

It was Le Noir who had gone upstairs. He did not hurry himself but came at an even pace to the stairhead and looked along the lighted passage. The door of Miss Harriet's room was standing wide open, and from within came the sound of voices. He walked slowly past Miss Shaw's room, glancing in as he passed, and came to the other door.

Lazare came to meet him, deadly pale.

"She's gone," he said.

Le Noir surveyed the scene: Nadine, with that unaccustomed patch of red high on the cheek bone; Etta, limp and tearful; Lazare's extraordinary pallor; trailing from a chair, Sally's grey fur; and, fallen on the ground near the settee, her little black velvet hat.

"How?" he asked.

It was Nadine who answered him, her voice shrill with rage.

"It was the old woman. She must have got out of bed and let her out. So much for this fool who says she cannot walk, she never gets out of bed." She glared at Etta as she spoke, and said, "Fool!" again viciously.

Etta sobbed, and Lazare spoke.

"She's taken the case," he said.

Le Noir put a hand on his arm, moved a pace or two aside, and spoke in such a manner that no word reached anyone except Lazare. Then he turned and went back by the way that he had come without hurry. In the hall he glanced at the clock before taking the back way out of the house. He crossed the garden and the patch of woodland, found the gap in the hedge, and climbed down into the lane.

A small two-seater car stood there close in under the trees.

Le Noir took off his skull-cap mask and gloves, assuming in their stead goggles and a fur coat. Then he drove away. The address at which he subsequently arrived would very much have interested Inspector Williams. Lazare, left behind, took command of the situation. He turned first to Etta.

"Find Gregor. Tell him not to leave the foot of the stairs. Send Sascha here. She cannot have got down. There was not time." And as she made haste to obey, he spoke to Nadine.

"You and I must search the house room by room. Lock each door and take the key. She must be found. She is not where we left her, she is not in these rooms. Take the other passage whilst I go to the drawing room. If you call, I shall hear."

"If I get my hands on her!" said Nadine fiercely, and they hurried out.

In the drawing room Sally leaned from the window, straining to see, stretching out her hands and feeling along the ledge and below it. The window ledge was wide. She leaned right out. There was ivy growing on the house, and something with a thick woody stem, wistaria as the guessed. She crawled out onto the ledge, felt for the woody stem where it bent and came up on the far side of the window. Holding on to it with her left hand, she knelt on the ledge, her right hand on the sill. Kneeling like this, she looked into the room and called low but insistently.

"Sascha, come here! Don't stop playing, but come, quick."

The light struck in between the curtains as he parted them and showed her outside on the ledge leaning on one hand.

"Shut the window, shut it," she whispered, and he dropped on one knee and caught her hand.

"Sally—beloved—you kill yourself. I am to see your death?"

"I hope not. Oh, for goodness gracious sake, do what you're told, my dear boy. Shut the window, shut it!"

They both heard Etta run down the stairs and, close on that, a heavier tread, Lazare's.

Sascha choked on a sob and pulled the window down.

The glass was between them, between him and his beloved, a wall of separation through which he could see her dimly. His heart was full of tears and useless pain.

"Latch it," said Sally through the glass, and he obeyed, and, turning, pushed through the curtains and heard them fall to behind him with a soft thud. He stooped for the bow that he had dropped, lifted his violin into position, and began to play the air of the Liebestod.

The heavy step was at the door; Lazare was on the threshold, cold fury in his eyes.

"Is this a time to play?" he said, and came striding into the room.

Sascha fell back before him.

"What is it?" he stammered.

"She's gone. She's taken the case and gone. That's all, and, if you don't hanker after prison life, you'll turn to and find her before she gets clear away and brings the police down on us. If you've any sentiment in the matter, just think what your hands will be like after picking oakum for five years or so. It will be good-bye to that cursed fiddle of yours, anyway."

"Five years!" gasped Sascha. "Prison!" His voice failed.

"Abduction is a pretty serious affair if one is caught. Pull yourself together, we'll find her, we must find her. How long have you been in here? Are these windows all fastened?"

Lazare parted the curtains, letting the light shine upon the catch of the nearer window. Seeing that it was latched, he was passing to the farther one when there came to them from outside a tearing sound followed by a thud.

With an oath Lazare sprang to the door and made down the stairs at top speed, calling upon Sascha to follow him.

Sally had not waited for Lazare to burst into the room. As soon as she saw Sascha's hand go up to latch the window, she gripped the thick but rather loosely hanging wistaria stalk in one hand, the close-growing ivy with the other, and, feeling with her toes for any slight foothold, swung herself gingerly off the window sill. Eight years before she had been the bright particular star of her school gymnasium, but she was sadly out of practice, and the wistaria stem felt horrifyingly loose and brittle. She shifted her grip carefully, and came down a foot or two. She reckoned that the window was not more than twelve or fourteen feet above the ground, fifteen at the outside. The ivy held well, and she gained confidence and let herself down another five or six feet, scared by the rustle of the leaves and the sound of the voices in the room above. And then, all of a sudden, the ivy stem which she was gripping tore away from the wall, her foot slipped from its precarious hold, and she fell outwards and backwards, hardly repressing a cry. The distance was nothing, the ground below a newly dug bed in which bulbs had just been planted. Sally was shaken and frightened but not hurt, and the fright and the shaken feeling were due not only to the fall, but to the sound which followed it. As she lay huddled up on the moist earth and gasped for breath, she heard Lazare's oath and the rush of feet, and in a moment she was scrambling up and running somehow, anyhow, away from the house.

It was dark, but not pitch dark; trees, bushes and walls were blacker than the general gloom. Sally's feet found a path, and she ran for her life. She saw vague shapes of trees, and a dense mass which she believed to be the box hedge by way of which Etta had brought her through the woodland belt to the lane. She was thankful that she had her coat on, and that both coat and skirt were of dark grey woven stuff that would neither rustle nor show up in the dark. As she passed the trees and came to the walk between the high bare hedges, she heard the noise of pursuit break out behind her, and, looking over her shoulder, saw the flash of an electric torch.

She gained the path, and after a yard or two it turned. The hedge would hide her now until they, too, reached the turn.

She ran her fastest, trying to remember how the path went and whether there were turnings in it. She thought there were turnings, but was not sure. Oh, why hadn't she noticed more when she and Etta passed this way?

Ah, there was a turning now, leading off to the right. She passed it by a yard or two, and then stopped short, shaken by a new terror. She could hear Lazare behind, running and calling, and in front, coming towards her down the narrow way between the hedges someone else, walking quickly with the firm tread of an active man.

She stopped dead, spun round, ran back, and dived down the turning that led away to the right.

Chapter Twenty-Four

Major Armitage had driven through Ledlington at a scandalous pace just about the time that Inspector Williams was returning Lazare's polite good night. He whizzed past the inspector in a dark lane, without a guess at his identity, and with no more than the casual reflection that bicyclists were the curse of the country road.

At the four-cross way above Charnwood he halted to consider a plan of campaign. A deep inward conviction that Sally was in danger, and that he had turned his back on her, had sent him tearing back upon his tracks. He had thought only of getting back at any cost and in the shortest possible time. Now he realised that a plan was necessary, and set about making one.

The front-door approach to Charnwood having been tried, and not having proved a striking success, some less obvious method commended itself to his mind. Upon three sides and part of the fourth side the house and garden were surrounded by a high wall. This he had noticed when he and the inspector searched the grounds. But a belt of woodland ran along the back of the property, protected by a high thorn hedge which met the stone wall again lower down, and Bill distinctly remembered that at one point there was a gap in the hedge. He remembered it because he had stood there in the gap for a moment and looked down into the lane below. He did not know how narrowly he had missed seeing Le Noir's car cunningly drawn in under the trees a few yards up the lane; but he remembered the gap and the lane, and it occurred to him, as it had occurred to Le Noir, that it would be a handy place to leave a car, and a convenient one at which to enter the Charnwood property without advertising his arrival. He could then reconnoitre the neighbourhood of the house, and be guided by what he observed there. This settled, he drove slowly along the ridge above Charnwood looking for the lane which he reckoned should run into the main road somewhere within the next quarter of a mile. He had no difficulty in finding it, for, as he felt his way, looking all the while to the right, a bright glare pierced the trees, throwing the branches into ebony relief, and with a grinding of gears a small car pushed up the last steep that merged the lane into the highroad. It turned the corner, slid past him in a blinding dazzle, and was gone. M. Le Noir was on his way to town in a hurry.

Bill Armitage dropped down the lane until he sighted the gap in the Charnwood hedge, drew up under overhanging trees, and, shedding his driving coat and gloves, proceeded to climb the bank, and to make an unlawful entry upon the property of Miss Emma Shaw.

This did not trouble him at all. He felt exhilarated because the same instinct which had driven him back to this spot now told him that he had not come in vain. Sally seemed to be very close to him, and she seemed to be needing him, calling to him, trusting him. If, in these circumstances, a man in love is not moved to warm exhilaration, he must indeed be slow and dull of spirit. Bill strolled through the woodland very much as if it belonged to him and not to old Miss Shaw at all. He did not at the moment care a fig for old Miss Shaw or for anyone but Sally and himself. He walked, in fact, the Fields of High Romance, and in these Fields of High Romance there are never more than two who walk and are agreed: the Knight and his Lady. The Shadowy Dragons, the dreams and dangers are but so many opportunities for the Knight to display his knightly valour; they are not real, or to be feared. Bill strode across the woodland and entered a gravelled path that ran between high box hedges.

When Sally ran, therefore, it was from Bill that she ran. A dozen more flying steps and she would have run right into his arms, but those steps were never taken. Instead she fled panic-stricken down the dark right-hand turning, and Bill, absorbed in his thoughts of her, never even knew that she had been within his reach. He strode on in the mood for adventure.

Lazare had not sighted Sally, but Sascha had, for, when Lazare rushed downstairs, Sascha darted to the window, appalled by the thought that Sally had fallen, and perhaps been terribly injured. As he stood peering out he saw a dark figure scramble up and run in the direction of the box hedge. Sally, then, was neither killed nor injured, and she was making for the gap in the hedge. Lazare would catch her. She had no chance. Lazare would certainly make for the gap, since only by the gap could Sally possibly escape. Sally had no chance at all against Lazare. He would overtake her or cut her off. She would be brought back, and he, Sascha, would have to stand by and see her tortured or worse. He could not bear it. There were things that one could not bear—one could not. He choked, and hurried after Lazare, stumbling on the stairs because his eyes were hot and misty with tears. The hall door stood wide open. At the foot of the stairs, Gregor, impassive and silent with folded arms. Sascha pushed past him and ran out and round the house. He could hear Lazare ahead of him, making for the gap. He could see the beam of light from the torch in Lazare's hand. It shifted from side to side, swinging to and fro as he ran, lighting vividly now a leafless bough, now a bush full of berries, now a space of newly turned earth.

Sascha ran, and thought of what five years in prison would be like, and his hands. His heart failed him, and he checked and almost stopped. His hands would grow like Lazare's hands, ugly, and thick, and coarse; and they would never make music any more. He would never play again. They would kill his music. Five years! But Lazare would torture Sally. She was so brave she would not open the case just for threats. They would torture her, and worse. Five years—his music—Sally—prison—and his music fell away into the shadowed background of his mind. There remained Sally, only Sally, Sally whom he loved and who would never, never care for him, Sally whom Lazare would torture, only Sally.

He lifted up his voice and called hoarsely:

"Lazare, Lazare, Lazare!"

The beam of light rested, falling across two high black pillars with a lane between them, leafy pillars, each leaf picked out by the intense white glare, the entrance to the box walk. Lazare halted just as he was about to enter the path, half turned, and called back over his shoulder:

"What is it?"

"Lazare—here—this way—I saw her," panted Sascha, and Lazare turned, the beam of light slipping from the high bare walls, coming nearer, flashing into Sascha's eyes. He threw up his arms to shield them, and Lazare was by his side.

"You saw her?"

"Yes, from the window."

"Which way did she go?"

"Round the house, to the front."

"You are sure?"

"Yes, yes, I saw her. She ran, I saw her."

Lazare made for the house.

"Nadine, take a torch and follow the wall up the hill, I will beat down towards the lane. Send Gregor to guard the gap. You had better stay in the hall, and remember, if you play false, prison may have what is left of you, but you'll reckon with me first."

"I saw her," gasped Sascha, and between terror and relief saw Lazare swing off to the left and disappear round the side of the house.

He himself made no haste. He stopped and tied a shoe lace, came slowly to within a yard or two of the front door, where he began to run, and arrived in the hall with every appearance of having run himself out of breath.

He delivered his messages, saw Nadine and Gregor depart, and sat down on the bottom step of the stairs, a prey to panic.

Chapter Twenty-Five

THE UNCONSCIOUS BILL meanwhile pursued his way. The dense box hedges deadened sound and let no light come through. If Lazare had passed the turn of the path, Bill would have both heard and seen him. As it was, he heard nothing. The stillness of the early evening had given place to gusts of wind that promised rain. Sascha's voice did not carry any distance, and Major Armitage presently emerged from between the tall box pillars and made his way quietly in the direction of the house. There were lights to be seen in it. The landing window flared uncurtained, and a long streak lower down on the left marked the position of the window out of which Sally had climbed. Bill reached the back of the house and turned to the right. There were the barred windows just above him now, old Miss Harriet's room, the bedroom and bathroom. There was no light in any of them. He stood listening, but could hear no sound, then walked the length of the house and turned the corner. A solitary window showed unlighted on the second floor. It faced up the hill towards the four-cross way, and was, if Bill had but known it, the window of Miss Shaw's dressing room. He stood and looked at the window thoughtfully. It seemed to be open at the top. He thought it was open, but he was not quite sure. He went on looking until he could have sworn that it was open, that a dark bar crossed it at a place where no bar would be unless the top half of the window were pulled down for six inches or so.

Bill was meditating a burglarious entry into the house of a blameless old lady. He was, in fact, making out the details in an admirably methodical manner. He was also, though of this he was, of course, unaware, about to fulfil a life-long dream. The dream was Miss Emma Shaw's, and the first step towards its fulfilment was taken when Bill advanced to the foot of the wall and laid his hand upon the stem of a very fine pear tree which was trained against it.

The pear tree was of the same age as Miss Shaw, and from the age of ten years had been regarded by her with something of romantic terror, she having then overheard a housemaid remark that, if ever she saw a ladder put ready for a burglar, it was "That there dratted tree."

"Murdered in our beds we shall be, and never know it till it's done," she had added, and the words sank deep into little Emma Shaw's receptive mind and stayed there. Many and many a time did she dream of a masked man climbing up, branch by branch, until he reached the dressing room window. Sometimes the pear tree was white with heavy scented blossom; sometimes it hung thick with the little ugly pears that tasted so sweet; sometimes it was a bare, leafless skeleton; but always it remained in Emma's mind as a ladder, a burglar's ladder.

"If the house belonged to me, I would cut it down," she would say, and her sister Harriet would frown and reply:

"You should not say such things, Emma. It was planted by our dear papa."

"If the house belonged to me." For five years now the house had belonged to Emma Shaw, but she would as soon have cut off one of her own plump legs, as a single branch of the "Burglar's Ladder."

Harriet had loved it. Dear papa had planted it. It was sacred.

Bill Armitage found it uncommonly convenient. It was as easy as walking upstairs. Had it grown against the drawing room window, Sally would have come safe to ground without the tumble that betrayed her to Lazare. Bill simply walked up it and arrived upon the window sill ingenuously astonished at finding burglary so childish an affair. The window was open at the top. He pushed the upper half down, and then, putting his arm over the top, pulled up both panes, until he could crawl under them.

The room seemed very dark indeed, dark with the unrelieved gloom of a small place shut in by walls. He groped his way with great caution, and was brought to a halt by a chair which creaked faintly as he touched it.

A burglar cannot have a good conscience. Conscience played him false. When the chair creaked he grew cold all down his spine, and had a vision of headlines in the daily press, "Major Burgles Country House—Full Details."

His feet and hands seemed to swell to an immense size and to become very heavy, as, with infinite precaution, he edged forward an inch at a time until one of those out-sized hands brushed the panel of a door. He found the handle and stood irresolute for a full minute. Then he turned it, and was horror-struck at perceiving a streak of light shine brightly through the opening door. At the same time old Miss Shaw's voice said pleasantly, "Come in, my dear." Almost without knowing it, Bill went in.

Miss Shaw gazed at him across the cage which contained Alfred and Marmaduke, and opened her mouth to scream. It became quite round, but the sound that should have issued from it did not come. Even in his embarrassment Bill realized that it was exactly like watching somebody scream on a film. As the thought came and went, the round open mouth relaxed, the pink face took on first a puzzled, and then a smiling look of recognition.

"Armitage," said Miss Shaw, still fluttering a little. "Armitage was the name, not a burglar. You startled me just a little, my dear, because I have always expected a burglar to come in through that dressing room window. Nadine ought to keep the door locked. I have told her so, but she is really forgetful. Felt round all the hinges and down the sides may keep out a draught, as I tell her, but it won't keep out thieves." She nodded emphatically and fixed her blue eyes upon his face, their gaze mildly opaque, like that at the white kitten.

"Armitage was the name?" she inquired. Bill admitted it.

"Yes, yes, and it was my dear cousin Clarence of whom you reminded me. He was much attached to me when I was young, very much attached; but my dear mamma did not regard the attachment with favour. You see he was a cousin for one thing, and he was not in a position to contemplate matrimony—not at all in a position to contemplate it—even if I may say so from a distance; so he went to Australia, and, my dear, we never heard of him again; but you resemble him very strongly indeed, you really do. It affects me, even after so many years, my dear Mr. Armitage."

"Major Armitage," said Bill, in some confusion. The situation was a little beyond him. A burglarious entrance in quest of Sally was one thing, an old lady's bedroom with an old lady in tears because he, Bill, recalled a lost romance of her youth, was quite another. Miss Shaw was dabbing her eyes with the edge of the sheet.

"No one will give me a handkerchief," she said, with a small but plaintive sniff. "My dear, if you wouldn't mind. They are in the left-hand little drawer of the chest of drawers, on the right- hand side of the drawer, marked with my initial. My dear Harriet marked them. I did hers and she did mine; but my dearest Harriet was always the most proficient with her needle."

Bill opened the drawer, which smelled of lavender, took the top handkerchief from a neatly folded pile, and presented it to Miss Shaw, who immediately stopped crying, and thanked him sweetly.

"They do come and go so," she explained, gazing at him with a confidence which he felt to be touching. "Etta and Nadine, and the man who came to see to the electric light, and the chauffeur—a man whose manners are deplorable, and the other young lady whose name I forget, they *will* come and go. They just come and go."

Bill started.

"The one whose name you forget—was it Sally, *was* it, Miss Shaw?"

"Sally—yes—yes—why, yes, Sally—that was it. She was in Harriet's room with the door bolted on the outside, such a singular thing when you come to think of it, two bolts both fastened on the outside of the door, my dear; and if I had not heard her calling me, why she might, be there now."

Miss Shaw had an air of triumph.

"You let her out?"

"I got out of bed, and Clarence mewed. Did I tell you that I had called him after you? No, no, I mean, of course, that I called him after my dear cousin whom you so very strongly resemble. He mewed—my dear pussy, I mean—and I got out of bed. You won't tell anyone, will you?"

"No, never; I promise. You let her out?"

Miss Shaw nodded, folding her hands upon the embroidered shawl.

"It was Sally?" asked Bill, trying to keep the eagerness out of his voice.

"She said so. I said, 'Who are you, my dear,' and she said, 'I'm Sally.' I remember very well because one of the gentlemen who admired me when I was young used to sing a very pleasing song about 'Sally in an Alley.' No one sings it now, but the air was very pleasing, and I remember he always said at the close, 'But it should be pretty Emma.' My name is Emma, you see, my dear, and he admired me a good deal."

"Where is Sally?" said Bill.

Miss Shaw looked at him doubtfully.

"They all want to know that," she said. "Strange, isn't it? Etta went on asking me that until I felt quite bewildered—my niece, Etta, you know, poor James's daughter, but perhaps you didn't know my brother James. He was a fellow of the Royal Zoological Society, and the only one of us with a tendency to red in his hair. He came between Harriet and myself in the family. We never cared much for his wife, though she was very well connected, a Tidworth-Wadlington, of the younger branch."

By main force Bill edged in with a desperate question: "Where is Sally? Do you know? It's *frightfully* important, Miss Shaw."

"She told me not to tell," whispered Miss Shaw, fidgeting with the bedspread. It had a fringed edge. She became intent on plaiting the fringe.

"She wouldn't mind your telling me, she wouldn't *really*. I want to help her. Where is she?"

The old lady threw him an odd half-timid glance.

"You bear so *very* strong a resemblance to dear Clarence," she murmured, "even the voice. My dear, are you attached to this young lady?"

"To Sally? Of *course* I am. Please, Miss Shaw, where is she?"

"Of course, of course, Sally is a pretty name, but it has gone out of fashion a little."

"Where *is* she, Miss Shaw, where *is* she?"

"But, my dear, I don't *know*," said old Miss Shaw.

Chapter Twenty-Six

WHEN SALLY TURNED and ran from Bill's advancing footsteps, panic came on her. She no longer groped her way or tried to run warily: she no longer thought or planned. With a wildly beating heart she fled blindly into the darkness and saw it full of floating sparks of fire. She did not know that the box hedges on either side had ceased, or feel that her feet were now upon rough grass. She went faster and faster, her pace increased by the downward slope of the ground, until suddenly, with a splash, she was ankle deep in ice-cold water, and the shock of it brought her to a standstill, trembling and panting.

A gust of wind blew hard and damp against her face. It seemed to blow away those floating sparks. Panic died down. She stood quite still, with the water about her ankles, and listened intently. There was no sound of pursuit. She could see no following light. Very gently she stepped back out of the water and up onto the rising ground that bordered it. She was on the edge of a fair-sized piece of water. The faint glimmer of it answered the cloudy dusk of the night sky above. All round a blackness that spoke of shrubs and trees.

Sally turned to the left and made for the deep shadow there. She must hide, and then presently, perhaps, she could make her way back to the gap and get away by the lane. When she came close to the bushes she found that they were rhododendrons, grown wild and hanging in branching masses over the water. She moved along, looking for an opening and presently found one. She had to push aside some jutting sprays, and then found, to her surprise, that she was in a narrow pathway which appeared to skirt the lake. The overgrown shrubs had once, no doubt, been neatly kept and clipped, but now they straggled everywhere, sending up young shoots under foot and arching densely overhead. It was dreadfully dark, and very wet under foot. The only gleams of light came from the water on her right, wherever there was a gap, or a thinning of the rhododendron wall. Sally began to feel cold and desolate. This was a horrible black maze, and she was hungry, and her feet were wet, and she wanted Bill, oh, most dreadfully she wanted Bill. She came to a standstill where a birch tree rose, airy and slender, from the mass of evergreens, and, flinging her arms about its trunk, she began to cry silently, but with great bitterness.

Meanwhile, Bill Armitage had emerged from Miss Shaw's room, and advanced cautiously to the top of the stairs. He was tolerably sure that Sally was not in the house. She must have been found by now unless she had managed to escape into the grounds. The house was deadly still. No footsteps coming and going, no voices. He went cautiously down the stairs as far as the turn, and looked over the balustrade. He could hear the ticking of the tall clock which stood in the corner of the hall just out of sight, and he could see the chandelier hanging from the ceiling with all three of its globes alight. He was just going to take another step or two when the sound of a groan struck upon his ears. It seemed to come from the hall. After a moment it was repeated. Bill moved carefully, shifting his position until he could see the foot of the stairs, and there, on the last step, sat a young man with his head in his hands, groaning. From the strong draught which was blowing up the well of the stairs, Bill concluded that the front door must be wide open. As Miss Shaw would, doubtless, have said, a very singular situation. How to connect the groaning young man and the open hall door at all helpfully with Sally, was not immediately clear. It occurred to Bill, however, that, exit by the door being barred, he had better once more make use of the dressing-room window, and he began to go upstairs again, taking two steps at a time.

On the top step he turned his head and saw Etta Shaw standing just where the left-hand passage came out upon the stairhead. Light streamed from an open door a yard or two behind her, and she came forward quickly, almost running, dabbing her eyes with a bright blue handkerchief and sobbing as she came.

She did not see Bill until she almost ran into him, and the second's grace gave him time to get his balance. Even as she recoiled with a little gasp of surprise, he said very gravely, "Hush, I want a few words with you," and led the way, with a composure which he was far from feeling, down the other passage and into Miss Harriet's room.

As he went he wondered if she would scream and give the alarm, but when he switched on the light and closed the door he found that she had followed him, and was waiting in obvious terror for what he had to say.

What she expected, he did not know. What he said was:

"Where is Sally?"

She turned pale, then red again.

"I don't know, I don't know," she whispered, looking at him with frightened eyes.

"Your answers were not at all satisfactory. I have returned in order to make further enquiries. I suppose you know that there are very heavy penalties for kidnapping and that sort of thing. I ask you again: Where is Sally?"

"I don't know, I don't. Oh, Major Armitage, I really don't know, I can't go on like this. I *can't*. I told Sally that I couldn't, and I *can't*."

"Sally has been here, then?" said Bill sternly.

"No, no, I don't know what I'm saying, and I don't, I *don't* know where she is. Oh. let me go, let me go."

"Control yourself, please. I don't wish to keep you. I think you had better go to your aunt. Sit down and pull yourself together, and then go to her. Don't let her see you like this."

"Where are you going?" said Etta, as he opened the door. "What are you going to do? Major Armitage, what are you going to do?"

"Find Sally," said Bill grimly, and shut the door on her. He had never disliked anyone so much in all his life.

His passage through Miss Shaw's room was of the briefest. The old lady, who was trying to coax Marmaduke from his perch, had hardly time to look up, the canaries hardly time to flutter, before the dressing-room door had closed upon him.

Old Miss Shaw went on looking at the door through which he had vanished, for some time. Then she turned back to her birds, with a deep sigh.

"Very singular, very singular indeed," she observed, and Alfred and Marmaduke twittered their agreement.

It was with considerable relief that Bill found himself out of doors again. The house was too much for him. He felt quite definitely that he could not cope any further with the groaning young man, or with Etta, or with Miss Shaw. He felt he had had enough of canaries, and cats, and sentimental reminiscences. Being out of doors again felt very good indeed.

He made his way to the front of the house, and perceived in the distance the flash of a torch away on the left and down the hill. The high wall lay between him and the road, and a belt of shrubs followed it, cypress-like shapes that made a gloom and gave out aromatic odours as he brushed past them. A furlong or two beyond the house and the shrubs were on either side with a narrow gravel path between them. All the trees and bushes were wild and ill-kept, and as Bill moved cautiously along the path he kept his hands out before him, and fended off more than one straying branch which would otherwise have caught him across the face. He lost the light which he had seen, and blundered on in the dark which became deeper as the ground sloped downwards and overshadowing trees grew thicker and wilder.

At last even the glimpse of deep lead-coloured sky was gone, and the branches covered everything with an interwoven roof. It was like moving in a tunnel, a tunnel that was low, and narrow, and wet under foot. Bill wondered where on earth the pathway was taking him. Touch and hearing were his only guide, and under his groping touch elusive leaves withdrew, whilst his ears seemed full of odd whispering noises and of the sound of his own feet slipping and squelching in the muddy slime.

Then suddenly the light again. A flash like the flicker of a bird's wing, gone in a breath and leaving an even, inky black behind. He stood still and counted ten. Then again the quick flickering light, but this time he was expecting it, and his eye caught the flicker of water, and saw that his path lay along the edge of some large pond or lake. The flash came from the water's edge about fifty yards away, and between it and him he had a glimpse of a black waterway that was bounded on every side by the dark. He listened intently, and heard the lapping and the even flow of the water, the passing gust of a wind with fine rain in it, the rustle and movement of leaf on glossy leaf, and faintly behind these sounds the impact of feet, moving as his own had done, in wet and boggy ground. The sound was so faint that he could not be sure that it was not fancy that made him suppose he heard it. Then it ceased, and again the light flashed out, much more to the right now, and making for a full half minute a lane of brightness that moved steadily up, down, and sideways before it disappeared. In that half minute Bill heard a new sound, a little gasping sound that made him take his own breath quickly. It was very faint, very weak, but it came to him through all the voices of the night and cried to him; and as he heard it he saw.

A yard or two from where he stood the path ran sharply in to the right, and then out again a hairpin bend. The water followed it. The bank, crumbling and irregular, fell away on the near side. On the far side, high, overhanging the water, and held up by branching roots, an entangled covert of rhododendron made a wall that topped the bank.

And under the bank stood Sally. The ray of light passed between shadowing boughs, and Bill saw her. His heart leapt. He saw her. The ray of light passed on. He had seen her, and in his mind he saw her still, standing close in under the bank, almost knee deep in water, bareheaded, the short, bright hair draggled, dishevelled, the little white face piteous beyond words, the eyes blank with terror. His Sally, his little, little Sally. They had brought her to this! What had they done to her? She was so damned plucky, and they had brought her to this! A blazing fury of rage took him stumbling forward. He half spoke her name, and then his foot caught in a loop of root, and he came down heavily in a bog of mud and slime. As he fell he heard the sound of someone running. It came from behind him.

Chapter Twenty-Seven

WHEN ETTA SHAW was left alone in Miss Harriet's room she sat quite still for a moment, with a frightened look on her face, her hands tightly clasped in front of her. Then suddenly she seemed to wake into restless activity. With a start she jumped up, opened the door, found the passage empty, and came along it and down the stairs with a rush that shocked Sascha to his feet. He stood looking after her, tear-stained and woebegone, as she ran through the hall and straight out of the open front door. The light from the low-hung chandelier streamed out, showing the unwhitened step and the flagged path beyond. Tiny growing things had pushed between the flags. They cast little blue-black shadows upon the rough grey stones.

Etta's wild rush brought her to the edge of the light and then she stopped, sobbing and panting. When a figure stepped out of the darkness, she called out on a thin, high note, and got back a "Silence, fool!" from Nadine, at which she choked and was quiet. Nadine's voice, low as it was, held so much cutting contempt that it froze her words and sobs. She stood and stared until Nadine shook her by the shoulder.

"What is it? Why do you run out—cry out? Has anything happened?"

"He has come back."

Etta whispered the words.

"Who has come back? Le Noir? Does Lazare know?"

Etta shook her head.

"No, no, not Le Noir."

"Who then? Quick! Who has come back? *Ciel*, woman, if I had a knife you should feel the point! Who has come back?"

"Major Armitage—and I think—"

"You think? Where is he?"

"I don't know—I don't know."

Nadine's grip tightened on the quivering shoulder.

"You've seen him?"

"Yes."

"Talked to him?"

"Yes, yes."

"What did he want? How did he get in?"

"I don't know, He said he wasn't satisfied, and then he left me in Aunt Harriet's room, and went—"

"Where?" The word was jerked at Etta.

"I don't know—I don't *know*."

"You never do, fool!"

Nadine swung her to one side and began to run down the hill towards the lake. She had seen the flash of Lazare's torch, and the first thing to do was to warn him that Major Armitage had returned. She switched on her own torch as she ran, and, shifting it to her left hand, drew from the pocket of bar nurse's apron a small automatic pistol.

Bill Armitage, a little dazed and still shaken by a gust of fury, heard the sound of her running feet, the tap tap of them on the gravel, changing to a sucking sound where the bog began. Then, as he scrambled to his knees, slipping and grasping at branches that betrayed him, the footsteps ceased, something pressed cold against the back of his neck, and a deep, cool voice said quietly:

"Hands up, Major Armitage, or I fire."

Bill's rage overpowered him. He kicked out violently in the direction of the voice, and promptly fell face downwards in the mud. The pistol pressed hard upon his neck. The voice said viciously, "If you *move* you're dead," and then, rising a tone or two, called on a resonant, carrying note, "Lazare! Lazare!"

Sally had not seen Bill. The ray of light which rested on her had not reached him. She had not seen him, but she had heard his footsteps on one side of her, knew Lazare to be coming up on the other, and felt herself hemmed in, past hope of escape. When he slipped and fell she shuddered all over and bit deep into her lip to stop herself from screaming. She must not scream. She must stay quite, quite still, and perhaps they would not find her. She stood holding on to a slimy root, the water up to her knees and icy cold, her woven skirt sopping wet, her hands wet and so dreadfully, dreadfully cold; and standing like that, all in the dark, she saw the flicker of Nadine's torch, and heard her say Bill's name.

Bill! It was Bill!

She had been so terrified of that heavy tread, and it was Bill all the time. Everything seemed to shake. Nadine's voice came from very far away.

"If you *move*, you're dead."

She was speaking to Bill. She was armed and Bill was not, and he had slipped and fallen in that horrible mud. Sally tried to think but she seemed capable only of holding on tightly to the slippery root. She tried to let go of it, to move, to do something, but her fingers remained rigidly closed. And then Nadine called out, and Lazare came running along the path, his torch sending a dancing beam before him, his voice answering Nadine.

"What is it? Where are you?"

"Here, I've got Major Armitage. Quick, my friend!"

They spoke French. Sally heard Lazare pass her, his tread sounding almost above her head as he came round the hairpin bend. Then there was the confused sound of some sort of struggle, and Lazare saying low and viciously:

"Do you *want* to be shot? What a fool you are, Major Armitage."

Sally trembled from head to foot. It was so dark. The light came and went. There were bushes between her and these three on the path beyond. What was happening? She could hear Bill's voice now, half choked. What were they doing to him? And then Lazare spoke, coining forward a little and pitching his voice so that it would carry without being loud.

"Miss Sally, are you there?"

No answer. Sally could just see him now, a dark figure at the water's edge. He swung his torch in a half circle, and called again:

"I know you're here. What a lot of trouble you give! It is most unwise of you. I have seen footprints, so you see I know that you are here. If you do not immediately come out, we shall shoot Major Armitage. I don't think anyone will look for him in the lake. Do you hear, Miss Sally?"

No answer. The torch swept round and back again. It was strange to see green leaf and pale folded bud spring into view as the beam touched the darkness. Strange to see the little rippled waves each with its tiny shadow. If Lazare had taken three steps to the right, the light would have reached Sally; but a bush screened her and the light stopped short.

"Miss Sally, if you don't come out you will be sorry."

Bill Armitage, lying like a trussed fowl in the middle of the boggy path, strained at his bonds and strained in vain. They had stuffed some woollen abomination into his mouth, his hands were strapped behind his back, and his ankles tied together. If only Sally would not listen. If only she would stay hidden. It was the one chance, the only possible chance for either of them.

"Miss Sally, for the last time, will you come out? If you do not—" He swung round.

"Nadine, are you ready? Very well. I will count slowly up to ten. If by that time she does not answer, you will shoot. It will make very little noise."

He paused. Then, "I will begin to count now, Miss Sally. One—two—three—four."

He counted evenly, without haste. Sally heard him as if in a dream. It was not a nice dream. She wanted to wake up, but the dream held her.

"Five—six—seven—eight—nine—" When Lazare said six, Sally began to try to move, but she could not. She began to try to call out, but she could not make a sound. She stood rigid, and heard him slacken pace a little on seven—eight—and nine—and then, with a gasp that seemed to be wrenched from her, she called aloud, and her voice was like a child's cry in the night.

"Stop. Stop—I'm here!"

Lazare drew a breath of relief. His bluff had not been called. In these matters one could always count on a woman in love. The rest would be easy now.

He stepped to the right, swung his torch, and saw Sally standing under the bank, her eyes wide upon him, her lips still quivering.

"Come across."

In his bonds Bill writhed at the tone of authority. They were done now. At the mercy of this merciless devil. Sally shook her head, only just moving it.

"I can't."

"Come across."

"I can't let go." Her teeth chattered on the words.

Bill heard Lazare swear, and, with ears unnaturally strained, caught every sound that followed, the heavy tread, the breaking of twigs, the water dripping from Sally's drenched skirt as Lazare dragged her roughly up the bank, her sobbing breath and broken, "No, no, I can walk, I can," as he lifted her; and with every sound the sense of his own helplessness became more unendurable. Lazare came to a halt beside him, looked down at him for a moment, and stirred him with his foot as one would a sleeping dog. There was no violence in the movement. Bill could imagine a smile on the man's lace; he had reason to be pleased with himself.

He spoke to Nadine.

"Take the whistle out of my breast pocket and blow three longs and one short. Gregor will hear it and come. We need him."

Nadine took the whistle. Her hand touched Sally, who sagged helplessly against Lazare's shoulder.

"Bah!" she said, and flicked her lightly on the cheek. Then she laughed, and blew the whistle.

The sharp, bright sound seemed to pierce the darkness like a flame.

They stood and waited for Gregor.

Chapter Twenty-Eight

GREGOR CAME to them, guided by the flash of the torches. He showed no surprise, but stood stolidly a yard away from the odd group and waited for his orders, as no doubt he would have waited in a burning house or on a sinking ship. Lazare spoke to him in Russian.

"Have you anything to report?"

And for the first time Sally heard the man speak.

"There is a car in the lane," he said.

"Where?"

"Under the trees above the gap."

"It is not Le Noir's car?"

"No."

"You are sure?"

"Yes."

Lazare touched Bill with his foot again.

"So *that's* how you came, my friend," he said: "Well, it's easier to get in than out again." Then he turned back again to Gregor.

"Untie his feet. He can walk to the house. You will hold his arm and guide him, and Nadine will come behind with the pistol. It's time we were out of this. I will go first."

As Bill Armitage tramped back up the sloping path maddening thoughts rushed through his mind. A wild desire to make a dash for it, a realisation of the hopelessness of such an attempt, Sally's nearness, her piteous plight, a raging contempt for the ease with which he had fallen into a trap. These thoughts and others as uncheerful bore him wretched company.

As they came up the flagged path to the open door they could see that Etta Shaw was pacing the lighted hall within. Once, and then again she crossed the doorway, moving with quick, aimless steps; and as she passed her lips moved, and her voice sounded monotonously. Sascha stood at the stair foot, his right arm thrown about the newel post and his face hidden.

As Lazare came into the hall Etta veered, cried out, and stood staring.

"Open the dining-room door," Lazare ordered. "The lights, put on the lights. Do you expect me to see in the dark?"

He lowered Sally into the armchair at the foot of the table, and she huddled in it, her eyes closed. Etta looked away from her, moving nervously until Lazare was between her and that pitiful figure. With averted eyes, and in a low, hurried voice she said:

"There's been a telephone call."

Lazare held up his hand, went quickly to the door and. shut it, leaving Bill in the hall with Nadine and Gregor. Then, as he turned:

"Who rang up?"

Etta whispered the answer.

"Le Noir."

"What did he want?"

Etta moved again. Her back was to Sally now; it was easier to speak. From where she first stood she could see, not Sally's face, but one of her hands lying palm upwards on the drenched woollen skirt. She did not like to see Sally's hand; it was easier to speak when she could not see it.

"He wanted—oh, I don't know—I think he wanted to know what happened after he left."

"He was ringing from London?"

"I—I think so."

"Well, what did you say?"

"I—I said you were out. I didn't know what to say; I was afraid. I said I thought he had better ring up again. I said—"

Lazare swore.

"*You* said? Who cares what you said? What did he say, Le Noir?"

"He said—he said—oh, Lazare, you frighten me; don't look at me like that—*don't*. Oh, he said he would ring up—at least, I think—"

Her voice trailed away and ceased, and sharp across its last vague murmur there came the ring of the telephone bell.

Lazare made a stride towards the instrument, then turned, flung the door wide open, and called to Nadine.

"Here, give your pistol to Gregor and come and take this call. I think I know who it is, but it's better to be on the safe side. Gregor, if he moves, shoot at once."

Bill stood quite still. His rage was under control, his mind busy, searching desperately for something, anything, which might be turned to advantage. Nadine passed into the dining room and shut the door. As she touched Lazare in passing he said very low: "It's probably Le Noir. Just make sure, and then I'll speak to him."

Sally had not moved within, but the sound of the telephone bell had roused her. Her mind was clear. Only it was such a terrible effort to move, to think, to do anything. For herself she only wanted to slip away into oblivion. She no longer cared what happened to her. But there was Bill. The thought of Bill hurt so much that she knew she must go on trying, go on keeping awake. When Lazare flung open the door into the hall, she looked and saw him standing there, all his great strength useless, his hands locked behind him, his face above the gag a mask of mud, his eyes—

It was the look in his eyes that she could not bear. It wrung her heart. The power of thought and action returned to her in a hot tide of pity and love, and, as Nadine took down the receiver, she raised herself a little, gripping the arms of the chair, and cried out very high and sharp:

"Help! Help! Help!"

Nadine was very quick. Her hand covered the mouthpiece as the second cry rang out, and next instant she had hung the receiver up. Sally saw her swing round, saw Lazare's face of fury, and slipped sideways from her chair in a heap.

She was in the hall after that, dimly conscious of angry voices, of someone shaking her roughly, and from very far away Sascha's voice: "*Mon Dieu*, what have you done to her?"

Then another interval of vagueness, and thought began to stir.

Bill would think they had hurt her. It was horrible for Bill. She must let him know that she was all right. Then hard on that thought another, she must go on pretending to be unconscious. They must gain time, they simply must. She had screamed twice before Nadine smothered the sound, and if anyone had heard the cry—the thought became tangled. It was so slender a chance. It was practically no chance at all. What was the good of counting on it and trying to spin things out? It only made it harder. Why not force the issue and get it all over? What did it matter, anyway?

Something in Sally that was very tough and unconquerable woke up and pushed back these thoughts. It was always worth while to fight, to hang on, to take the hopeless odds and do your best with them. It was never worth while to give in.

Sally came back again to the idea of gaining time. That was the only hope, she must make time for help to reach them, and she set herself to the task with a little secret sense of exhilaration.

For a while she had only to lie still. There were hurrying footsteps, a coming and going. Then someone held a cup of hot soup to her lips, and Lazare said: "She's no use to us like this. You've *got* to get her going again. Half an hour will finish it then, and we'll be off."

Sally made that soup last a very long time. It wasn't easy, because she wanted it so badly. It was hot, and she was so very cold, but she took it in infinitesimal sips, and was thankful enough to have it.

As she came to the end of it she heard Lazare tell Nadine to go back to the telephone. "Ring up the exchange and find out where that call came from. It must have been Le Noir, but it's too important to leave to chance. If anyone else heard her scream—"

"Oh, it was Le Noir," said Nadine composedly. "Who else could it have been?"

She went through the open door into the dining room, and, as she spoke, Sally's heart beat. Nadine's voice came and went. Nadine came back.

"It was Le Noir all right," she said. "The call was from London—'a foreign gentleman,' the girl at the exchange said. So you see it is all right. He will ring again presently, I expect."

Sally fought despair, fought it inch by inch, and forced it back. She would go on just the same. She would go on to the very end, and beyond it. She set her teeth, and was ready for Lazare when he came over to her.

"Now, Miss Sally," he said. "Don't you think you have given enough trouble, and don't you think we treat you very well? Only this I suggest, that you do not try our patience too far, that would be foolish."

She looked up at him as if she did not understand. They had laid her at the foot of the stairs and propped her up with cushions. Her gaze rested blankly on him. She said nothing.

He took her by both wrists and, pulling her up, held her there at arm's length facing him.

"Now we come to business. Understand me. If you faint again we shall bring you round with a red-hot iron. It is a fine restorative. But you will not faint; I think you have enough sense for that. You will come into the dining room, and you will open the case which, as you see, Nadine has taken from your pocket."

Sally looked him straight in the eyes.

"I won't do anything until I have talked to Major Armitage. I want to talk to him. I won't do anything unless you let him speak to me."

"And if we let you?" Lazare's eyes searched her face.

"I will tell you when we have talked."

"And why should we allow this interview?"

"Because," said Sally, "I won't do anything at all without it. I don't really care much either way. I don't care what you do, or what I do. You've pushed me too far, and I don't *care*. It's just as you like."

She wavered on her feet, and he let go her hands, and saw her grope her way back to the pile of cushions and sink down there. He went over to Nadine, and they spoke together in Russian- After a minute he addressed Bill.

"Very well, we will let you have this interview. Major Armitage, I think you are really an intelligent man when you are not blinded by passion as you were just now. There are two points which I would commend to your intelligence." He came quite close and spoke in a low voice inaudible to the others. "In the first place, if Miss Sally does not open the case, this is what we shall do to her." His voice sank lower still, but Bill could hear every word, and what he heard bit into his consciousness with a burning agony. The words, the unendurable words flowed quietly and evenly from Lazare's lips, and Bill could not shut his ears or silence the lips with a blow.

"That," said Lazare, "is our programme in case of any little feminine obstinacy. Ladies like to be pressed, and to say 'No,' before they say 'Yes.' Well, that is our programme, and the first of the two points which I commend to you. The other is this, it is for you to take advantage of this interview which we are allowing you to have—it is really very good of us, you know— use your influence with Miss Sally, get her to open the case, and I assure you we will be extremely kind to you both. Now will you follow me upstairs? I don't think I will trust you in a room without bars." He turned back to the stair foot. "Allow me, Miss Sally." He picked her up and led the way. Bill followed. Gregor brought up the rear. At a word from Lazare he went off to the left at the top of the stairs, afterwards appearing in Miss Harriet's room with a pair of handcuffs in his hand.

Lazare put Sally down, bade Gregor hold Major Armitage's arms at the elbow, and proceeded very deftly to untie the rope with which Bill's wrists had been tied. Almost with the same movement he slipped on the handcuffs, and then, still in the same composed manner, removed the gag and the bandage that secured it.

Gregor busied himself with closing and locking the shutters in all three rooms. It was all very unhurried and businesslike.

"Now, Major Armitage," said Lazare. "You have your chance. I advise you to employ it to advantage. It will not be offered to you again." He went towards the door, and on the threshold turned for a last word: "Of course, if you like, you can make a noise—call, shout, bang on the shutters, *par exemple*—but I really do not advise such a course of action. Gregor will be outside the door with a pistol. If there is a sound, he will simply walk in and shoot, so I do not advise it. And now I will leave you to your interview."

He went out. Gregor followed. The door was shut. The bolts went home with a click. Bill and Sally were alone.

Chapter Twenty-Nine

MAJOR ARMITAGE'S CAR tore by in the darkness Inspector Williams was very much annoyed. He did not know whose car it was. His attempt to catch sight of the number failed, and his indignation was still hot when he rode into Ledlington.

He got off his bicycle, and spoke to the first policeman he met.

"Did a two-seater pass you here about ten minutes ago? I couldn't see the make or get the number, but he nearly did me in about a mile down the road. He must have been doing forty."

"There was a Hillman went out of here at a fair bat. I took the number."

"That would be him."

The policeman pulled out a notebook, wet his fingers, turned three pages laboriously, and read out a number which, as the inspector himself afterwards stated, brought him up with a round turn.

"Read it again," he said. And then: "You're sure of that?"

"Took it down as he went past. I tried to stop him and he took no more notice than if I'd been a-kissing my 'and. Dangerous driving, I says and took his number."

Inspector Williams stood in the highroad, a most astonished man. The number was that of Major Armitage's car. What had happened to take that car back to Charnwood at a tearing, law-breaking pace?

He began to walk along, wheeling his bicycle. Major Armitage should have been dining in London by now, but obviously something had occurred to alter his plans and send him in a furious hurry back along the road which he had just traversed. The more the inspector thought about it, the less he liked it. It was an odd case all through; practically no evidence, but the feeling of something fishy at every turn. "Like the smell of gas when you can't make out where it's coming from," he said to himself. "One minute it's there, and the next it isn't, and, do what you will, you can't find the leak. That's what it reminds me of."

He walked along very thoughtfully for a while, but turned in to the "King's Arms" where he ate cold beef and pickles and continued to think.

About half an hour later he entered the police station and, after a short conversation with the local inspector, went to the telephone and looked up Miss Shaw's number. It was in his mind that he would like to speak to Miss Etta Shaw. He gave the number to the exchange and waited, not very sure of what he was going to say.

There was a pause. The hum of the traffic came in from the street outside. Then came the little dick that told of the receiver being taken off at the other end, and immediately upon that, thin and faint, a woman's voice—a scream of "Help! Help!!" The second word, the second scream, was cut short. Someone at the other end had been concerned to cut it short. Another click, and the receiver was in its place again.

Inspector Williams lost no time. He called the exchange and began to give rapid orders.

"This is the police station. If the number that has just cut me off rings you and asks who was calling, you will say that it was a London call, and that the gentleman who spoke seemed to be a foreigner. You quite understand? It's a police matter."

The girl at the exchange experienced a delightful thrill.

Inspector Williams rang off, and turned back into the room, his usually wooden face full of anxiety.

"What's up?" said the local inspector.

"I don't know. There was a woman screaming at the other end. I must go back at once, and it's not a job I want to tackle alone. How many men can you give me?"

"Well, I don't know."

The local inspector was the embodiment of solid worth. One felt at a glance that it was worth and not brains that had made an inspector of him. His name was Mosspuddle, and irreverent constables spoke of him as Old Mossy Face.

"I don't know," he said slowly. "There's Jones just coming off his beat, and Bolster just a-going on his, and Webbing ought to be here, and—let me see." He continued to think aloud until he arrived at the conclusion that four men might be available. Eventually the four proved to be three.

Inspector Williams stood by, chafing inwardly. He could not get the sound of those faint screams out of his ears.

It was with immense relief that he stepped into the car which he had ordered, saw his reinforcements bundle in after him, one man in front by the driver, and for the third time that day set out towards Charnwood. He hoped very much that they would not be too late.

They ran down from the crossways, going slow and without lights, and drew up a couple of hundred yards short of the house. The door in the wall was shut and barred. It was not part of the inspector's plan to ring the bell. He gave a low-voiced order, and one stout constable made a back, and one by one the others scrambled over the wall. The inspector came last, and helped to haul the stout Bolster up. When they were all over there was a moment's uncertainty.

"Better go round to the back, one of you—yes, you. Webbing. The path runs round the house. Keep on the grass and go quietly."

Webbing went, and for a brief space the inspector watched the house. The upper window was lighted and a faint gleam came from windows on the ground floor which he knew to be the shuttered windows of the dining room in which he had interviewed Lazare. The hall door of solid oak was shut and showed nothing. As he waited for the moment of indecision to pass, the hall door was suddenly, violently flung open, showing the lighted space within, a man's figure stood out for an instant against the glowing background, Sascha's hands were pressed to his head, he halted for just a second, and then came stumbling down the step and away from the house, and as he came he groaned aloud:

"Sally, Sally! Oh, *mon Dieu*, Sally! They kill her!"

The moment of indecision was past. Inspector Williams ran up the path and into the hall, followed by the Ledlington constables. As they crossed the threshold there came from the room on the left the sound of voices, the sound of running feet, two shots in rapid succession followed by a crash and a loud and piercing scream.

Chapter Thirty

LAZARE WENT OUT, the bolts ran home, Bill and Sally were alone.

All the time that Lazare and Gregor were in the room Sally did not raise her eyes or look at Bill, but when they were gone she looked up and tried to smile, tried hard, and very nearly burst out crying instead. Bill stood before the burnt-out fire, his handcuffed hands behind him, his head a little sunk forward, and his face plastered with mud.

Between them stretched the rose-wreathed carpet, wet and dirty from all those trampling feet. The water dripped from Sally's skirt and made a dark stain upon the roses.

Sally got up, holding on to her chair.

"Your poor face—all that mud," she said in a little shaken voice. "Oh, my poor dear," and she went with slow, difficult steps to the bathroom, soaked the end of a bath towel in water and came back again.

Bill moved to meet her.

"You must bend down," she said, "you are so high up," and then she began to wash the mud away and to put the dishevelled hair back from his forehead. Her hands were trembling a little. All their movements were weak and gentle. Bill felt the soft hands touch his face, and wondered how much more he could bear without breaking down.

He said her name and choked on it, and she dropped the towel in a heap, and put up her face to be kissed, just as a child might have done; and when he stooped and she felt his tears hot on her cheek, her arms went round his neck and clung there.

"Sally—Sally darling—oh, my darling little Sally."

Bill went on saying it over and over, and then in a sort of rage: "What have they done to you? What have they *done*?" Sally rubbed her head against his shoulder.

"Nothing, absolutely nothing. I'm as right as rain. It's you, you poor old thing. Did I get all the mud out of your eyes?"

"You're sure—sure they haven't hurt you? Why are you such a ghost then?"

"Hungry," said Sally, laconically. "They wouldn't let me sleep, and they fed me on odd cups of cocoa, but they didn't hurt me. I'm really quite all right." She did manage to smile this time, and Bill would have found it easier if she had cried.

He said quickly, "Why did you scream—downstairs?"

"The telephone bell rang. I thought someone might hear—the girl at the exchange, or the person who was calling. I thought it was just a chance—and there aren't too many chances, are there, Bill?"

She looked at him steadily, and he looked away. "It's a tight place, Sally," he said, and Sally nodded.

"I know. That's why I made up my mind to try to see you like this. I wanted to say things, and I wanted to know if you cared. You do, don't you?"

"Sally, you know—Sally darling."

"Yes, I know. I think I got to know when I was shut up here with nothing to do but think. I used to think about you a lot—and—and want you, Bill, and I used to wonder if you cared, and sometimes I felt sure you did because of the way you looked at me that last day at Chark, and sometimes I used to think you'd marry a fat girl who took eights in shoes."

"Why on earth should I?"

"I don't know. I used to decide that you would. I think I did it to choke myself off. You see, Bill—no, bend your head a little so that I can whisper—you see when we were engaged I didn't really care. I think I wasn't old enough. But as soon as we weren't engaged, and you'd gone away dreadfully angry and hurt, I began to miss you. You see you'd always been there, so when you weren't there any longer I missed you. And then I began to think what a little fool I'd been, and then I began to care—really, you know, like you cared for me. It was a frightfully good punishment."

"You poor child, I didn't want you to be punished. Why didn't you tell me, darling, why on earth?"

"As if I would. Why I should never, never, never have told you if—if—well, if I didn't think we were pretty well up against it. We are, aren't we?"

"I'm afraid so. Of course there's a chance."

"It's very small. That was Le Noir calling. He was here this afternoon when they were trying to make me open the case. He made off when the inspector came back."

"Williams came back?"

"Yes, on a bicycle. He banged on the door and frightened them into fits, but they bundled me up here, and Le Noir got away, and then they let him in. He wanted to see Lazare. He only stayed a few minutes, so I suppose he was satisfied. Le Noir made off. He was ringing up to know what happened after he left. Bill, what are we to do?"

"I don't know, Sally."

He did not avoid her eyes this time. They looked steadily at each other. There was no need for words. It was Bill who spoke at last.

"When I came upstairs," he said, "I thought I must urge you to open the case. I didn't think I could do anything else. I meant to tell you that it was the only thing to do, and to say that it would be all right, they'd never get out of England with the secret, we'd be sure to get them first. That was my first impulse."

"Well?" said Sally. She had her hand on his shoulder. "Well?" she said, and gave him a little half-impatient pat.

"If that's what you were going to say, why didn't you say it?"

"Because," said Bill, slowly, "I remembered the look in that man's eyes. What d'you call him?"

"Lazare."

"Yes, when he said, 'If you open the case we will be very kind to you both,' his eyes gave him away. When I had time to think, I felt quite sure, absolutely sure, that if you opened the case we might have ten minutes to live, or we might have less. We certainly shouldn't have more."

Sally's hand tightened on his coat. She gave that familiar little nod of hers.

"Yes, I think so too," she said.

"You see," said Bill, "they'd be bound to get rid of us, absolutely. They couldn't keep us here, and they couldn't turn us loose, so it's fairly obvious that we'd have to go. The only possible chance is to play for time. Something might happen."

"Yes," said Sally, "that's it. That's what I kept saying to myself downstairs. It's the one and only chance we've got."

"Spin the show out, pretend to make terms—anything. You see I might be traced here. It's not too likely, but I came through

Ledlington such a fearful lick that I expect half the police there have my number. And look here, Sally, are these people all equally up to their necks in this? Isn't there a chance of any of 'em weakening? What about Etta Shaw?"

"Wash out," said Sally briefly. "She's crazy about Lazare, and scared stiff into the bargain. Sascha's a better chance. He let me go out of the drawing-room window. He says he's in love with me, but I'm afraid his passionate fear of Lazare will come out on the top every time. He hasn't any backbone, poor boy. He'd weep, and put me into a symphony, but it's no good thinking he'd have the nerve to go back on Lazare, because he hasn't got it in him. No, it's no use counting on anyone here. We've just got to stick it out. If the worst comes to the worst, horrors I mean, I expect Lazare threatened them, didn't he?"

"Yes, he did."

"Well, don't bother about that, old boy. If the worst comes to the worst, I shall pretend I've given in. They'll give me the case to open and I shall wrench the spring and release the acid. Then the formula at least would be safe out of their hands, and I think they would just shoot us without any fuss."

Sally's voice was just the very faintest whisper close at his ear. He turned his head with a groan, and they kissed, a long strange kiss that might be the last. The room was so still that the song of old Miss Shaw's canaries came to them through the bolted door. The high trilling sweetness rose up and up as the two birds vied with each other. Across it came the sound of footsteps, the sound of bolts withdrawn. Sally went quietly back to her chair.

The door opened.

Chapter Thirty-One

It was Gregor who came in. He did not speak, but motioned with his hand, and they walked past him into the passage.

Lazare was waiting at the head of the stairs, but before they came to him the door of Miss Shaw's room was opened and Nadine came out. The canaries had stopped singing. Sally looked past Nadine, and saw that someone had covered the cage with a green silk handkerchief.

Nadine had put on a clean apron. The fresh starch crackled as she walked. From behind her came Miss Shaw's voice:

"There is such a draught, Nadine, why do you not shut the door? I am always telling you how much Alfred dislikes a draught. Shut the door, my dear."

Nadine shut it, and they all went down the stairs.

Sally thought how strange it was, that glimpse into the comfortable room, he old lady's blue eyes, the white kitten, the birds in their safe cage, the very eiderdown with its effect of soft comfort, all these things were in such strange contradiction of her plight and Bill's. There was a nice old lady upstairs in a cap and a woolly shawl, and she and Bill were going down a horrible dark slope at the bottom of which lurked unimaginable horror.

They crossed the hall, and came into the dining room. Etta was on her knees by the hearth, making up the fire. She did not turn her head or look round when they came in. Of Sascha there was no sign.

Sally went to the chair in which she had sat before. The case lay on the table under the light. It was just like a dream in which the same thing happens again and again. It seemed to her as if Miss Harriet's room with its rose-coloured curtains and this polished table with the red lacquer case lying on it were objects reflected endlessly by a series of mirrors. She looked on and on, and could see no end to them. It made her feel rather giddy.

She saw Bill guided to a chair at the other end of the table, and thought it odd that he should occupy Le Noir's place. Gregor stood on one side of him with a pistol in his hand, and beyond Gregor she could see that Etta Shaw had risen to her feet and was moving towards the service door in the corner of the room. Lazare saw it, too. He had remained standing, and swung round now, saying sharply:

"What are you doing? Where are you going?"

"I don't know—I thought—"

"You are not required to think. Come here." For a moment she actually hesitated, but as he made a movement she started, came over to the table, and dropped into a chair.

Lazare sat down by Sally. Nadine remained standing on the other side of her, one hand just resting on the edge of the table.

"Well, Miss Sally?" said Lazare.

She folded her hands in her lap, and looked down. "What do you want?" she said.

"Is it possible that you are in any doubt? I think not." He put out his hand and drew the case a little nearer. "Wonderful craftsmen the Chinese, are they not? Those fishes are really swimming. I wonder which of them hides the spring, but I shall not have to wonder long. You will now open the case."

Sally put one hand to her head.

"And if I've forgotten how to open it?" she said.

"It would be most unfortunate—for you, and for Major Armitage. It would, in fact, be a disaster. I really advise you as a friend, Miss Sally, not to have forgotten."

"It's a long time ago," said Sally very low. "I only opened it once—I may have forgotten."

"Then you will make it your business to remember." He laid his hand on hers as he spoke. It lay there hard and heavy as a piece of wood, the ugly fingers spread out. It covered Sally's little hand and weighed upon it.

With a sharp movement of repulsion she swung round in her chair, leaning back upon the further arm of it and facing him.

"M. Lazare," she said panting a little, "tell me honestly—why do you want that formula? What are you going to do with it? I must know that—I must—"

On the last word she pulled her hand away with a jerk, standing back from him. Lazare made a slight gesture towards Etta.

"My dear Miss Sally, what a question! Has our good Etta ever for one moment ceased to assure you that our sole and only motive is—oh, come, Miss Sally, I think that you must know it all by heart—the good of humanity, the blessings of universal peace threatened by this new and abominable development of militarism. Surely the exalted nature of my sentiments and the purity of my motives are sufficiently established."

Sally glanced at Etta, and saw the colour rise in her cheeks. She looked away again quickly. It was dreadful. Etta was dreadful. Even in this extremity she felt sorry for Etta Shaw, with her desperate clutch on the ideals which were failing her. She turned back to Lazare frowning:

"Do you really think me a fool?" she said. "I don't believe you do. I want the truth, not all that sham stuff. I think you know very well that it never took me in for an instant, and, if you are as clever as I think you are, you will realise that it will pay you better to tell me the truth. I won't move a finger without it, anyway."

Bill sat stiffly at the opposite end of the table. He had not much hope, but he was not going to neglect the smallest chance. Out of the tail of his eye he measured the distance between himself and Gregor. He sat looking at Sally, and Lazare, and the red case, and the shining reflection of the chandelier like an island of light upon a dark sea; and all the time he made a plan—a desperate plan, but better than none at all.

He saw an unpleasant look cross Lazare's face as Sally spoke, and heard him say in the low voice which meant rage: "You will, and you won't? Do you think you have any choice?"

"You would do better to tell me the truth," said Sally wearily.

He stared at her with those light eyes of his full of gloomy anger.

"The truth?" he said. "Well, why not? Only there is this, no one can tell all the truth, because it is only when two understand each other that there can be truth between them. Between you and me—never—never. Are you so banal as not to know that? I think you know it. There is between us too strong an antipathy for there to be any truth from me to you. You may think what you please, Miss Sally. Think that I am a revolutionary and that I see in this formula the means to a World Revolution. Think that I am an anti-revolutionary with a great military power at my back. Think that I am a man who owes society and the human race a grudge, and in each of these thoughts you may find the truth you want. Think at least this, that I will have the formula if it means a hundred lives like yours. That is a little melodramatic, is it not? You see I am a peasant; and your peasant is all crude melodrama in an affair of this nature. The other side of me, the side that comes from a princely house, laughs at the peasant and despises him. If I could have been all prince I would have ruled Russia and the world." His voice sank low. "I may yet," he said, and fell into silence.

Etta's trembling voice broke upon it. At first it was only a low mutter, but it kept rising and gathering volume. She leaned towards Lazare with outstretched hands that trembled too. Her words came fast.

"What are you saying? You mustn't say such things. What do you mean? What do you *mean*? What are you talking about? Lazare, Lazare, *Lazare!*"

Without turning, he struck her across the face with the back of his hand. It was more an impatient gesture than a blow, but

Etta Shaw gave a very bitter cry and dropped her face upon her outstretched arms.

It was her cry that Sascha heard. It reached him in the study on the other side of the hall where he was pacing up and down in an agony of fear. When he heard it he shuddered as if it were he who had been struck.

The cry was not repeated, but the silence—the silence was more dreadful than any sound. He stood for a long while, or what seemed to him to be a long while, on the threshold of the study, and could hear nothing. In the end he crossed the hall with a slow, dragging step, and leaned against the jamb of the dining-room door, his forehead pressed to the panel.

When Etta screamed Nadine laughed. Sally's anger boiled over. She spoke sweetly to Lazare.

"You were quite right," she said. "You are certainly half a peasant. I am at last able to believe something that you say."

Bill Armitage leaned forward in his place. He spoke for the first time.

"Isn't all this rather irrelevant?" he said, and, at the sound of his voice, the hands which Lazare had clenched relaxed and his eyes left Sally's. A tense moment passed.

"It is rather," said Lazare. "I propose that we come to business. If you have anything *relevant* to say"—he stressed the word—"I shall be very much interested to hear it, Major Armitage."

"Well, I should like to know what terms you are proposing. If Miss Meredith opens the case—I don't say she will, but if she does, what are you prepared to offer? You will probably admit that the case is her property and that she has a certain claim to a *quid pro quo.*"

"That is so." Lazare's voice was smooth again. "Well I won't say that our original offer to her stands in its entirety, because the position—well, it has changed a little, has it not? But, in these altered circumstances, what I propose is, I think, sufficiently generous."

He put his hand into his pocket, drew out a key, and flung it upon the table beside the lacquer case. It made a little ringing sound.

"As soon as Miss Sally has opened the case she shall have that key which, as you probably guess, unlocks the pair of handcuffs you are wearing; and you and she will be free to go anywhere you like. We shall treat you as honourable persons, and merely ask for an undertaking that you will not communicate with the police or make any effort to trace us for the very moderate space of twelve hours. After that, my dear Major Armitage, your Scotland Yard may be as busy as it likes, it will not incommode us at all."

"Thanks," said Bill. His tone was dry. "It's such a generous offer that I think I should like to talk it over with Miss Meredith. You haven't any objection, I suppose?"

"I'm afraid I have." His voice rang suddenly hard. "Let us understand each other. You have had your interview. You have had my terms. You talk of a *quid pro quo*; I want mine. I am not a safe person to play with or to insult. Miss Sally was unwise just now. She will now open the case, or, if you prefer it, the programme of which I spoke will begin."

He took the red lacquer case from the table and put it down immediately in front of Sally.

"Now, Miss Sally," he said, and took her by the arm.

It was then that Sally's sensitive ears caught the first sounds from outside. She did not know what she had heard, but she knew that she had heard something. All of her seemed to listen, and it was more with impatience than with fear that she heard Lazare say:

"You don't answer. You had better answer, Miss Sally." And then, "You won't? Very well then."

His hand tightened on her arm. He got up, pulling her roughly to her feet.

Sally came back to a sense of her surroundings. At the other end of the table Bill Armitage waited with every muscle tense.

"Open the case," said Lazare in a tone of fury. "Open it! Open it at once!" He stopped short on the last word and drew in his breath sharply, catching at his self-control, and Sally heard again what she had heard before, and this time knew it for what it was, the sound of feet moving on the grass outside, cautiously, quietly. She spoke quickly because she was afraid that Lazare would hear it, too.

"I won't! I won't! I'll never open it." He jerked her arm.

"Oh, yes, you will. I'm going to tie you up to your chair and let you watch what we are going to do to Major Armitage. You'll open it fast enough. Nadine, the rope."

Sally cried out wildly at that, struggling to free her arm, to pull away from him.

Nadine laughed again.

It was Sally's voice and Nadine's laugh which sent Sascha stumbling out into the night. It was Sally's voice and Nadine's laugh which drove Bill Armitage to make his reckless throw.

With a sudden spring he was on his feet, and as he sprang he shot his right foot out backwards, hooked Gregor's legs from under him. and charged headlong down upon Lazare with an inarticulate roar. After that everything seemed to happen at once. As Gregor fell he fired, his hand obeying him just a fraction too late to be of any use; Lazare, releasing Sally, swung to his left, met the whole of Bill's charging weight, and came down with a crash; Etta Shaw lifted her head from her hands and screamed terribly; Nadine had her hand in her pocket, her pistol half out, when a man shouted in the hall—it was Jones, the Welshman, who shouted—and there was a rush of feet towards the door. Nadine sprang to it, locked it, reached for the switch of the electric light, and called out in Russian, "The police! Quick, Lazare!"

Gregor was already up. Lazare rolled from under Bill, and scrambled to his knees. As he ran, Nadine's hand moved sharply down. The light went out.

Sally, standing between her chair and the table, saw the light fail. The darkness fell like a curtain. Her eyes were fixed upon the lacquer case and the shining key.

The light was gone and the dark was full of noise. The last thing that she saw was the lacquer case, the centre fish, and the rose below it glowing as if they were alive. Her hand went out, closed on the case, withdrew itself. She stepped back, pushing over her chair so that it fell. Men were beating on the door, shouting. She went on stepping back, taking one step at a time. The noise was dreadful.

Back and back and back, until her free hand touched the velvet curtains that screened the shuttered windows. The door burst inwards with a loud cracking sound, a broken panel splintering. Bill called out. He called "Sally! Sally!" but she could not answer. The light went on suddenly. Inspector Williams with his hand on the switch saw Etta Shaw sitting back in her chair staring at him, her eyes unnaturally blue in a dead-white face, her hands held up as if to ward off a blow. He looked past her, and was aware of Major Armitage struggling to his feet, his hands behind his back and handcuffed, and in the window Miss Sally Meredith clutching the brown velvet curtain with one hand, and holding to her breast with the other the red lacquer case. Otherwise the room was empty.

The inspector was the first man into the room. As he switched the light on, the two constables pushed across the threshold, and the door, which had been swinging crazily on a single hinge, fell crashing to the floor. It was Jones, the little Welshman, who made straight for the service door. Bolster followed him.

Bill Armitage gave a great shout of "Good man, Williams! Good man!" Etta Shaw's lips moved, but no sound came from them. The key of the handcuffs lay on the empty table. Bill came plunging forward. "Here, man, unlock these damned things for Lord's sake. That's the key. Where's Sally? Where's Sally, I say?" and then as he swung round to let the inspector get at his wrists, he faced the windows and saw her. She had not stirred. The light showed how white she was. Her eyes looked as if they did not see. The handcuffs dropped with a clatter. Bolster called from the service door, "This way, sir," and Inspector Williams was off hotfoot, with a word flung over his shoulder to Major Armitage: "Take charge here, sir, will you? I can't afford to leave a man."

"There are three of them, all armed," Bill called after him, and he called back: "Thank you, sir," and was gone.

The house seemed full of the sound of trampling feet.

Constable Webbing, meanwhile, had been making his way round the house according to his instructions. He arrived at the back door, in fact, at the same moment that the inspector and the other constables burst into the dining room. The door at which he found himself was locked. He walked a pace or two, and reflected that this was a rum sort of start, and that his young lady, at this moment waiting for him outside the New Cinema, would be what he called "fair worked up."

He had begun to wonder how long it would take him to make his peace when the door behind him was suddenly wrenched open, several persons rushed out, and he felt himself tripped up and knocked sprawling into the gutter. As he picked himself up he heard, from within the house, shouts and a sound of splintering wood. He at once blew his whistle and set off across the garden in pursuit of the people who had knocked him down.

It was Nadine who had thought of Bill Armitage's car, and it was Nadine who had thought of locking the kitchen door behind them to delay pursuit. She ran beside Lazare in the darkness, her hand in her apron pocket clenched on the automatic pistol.

None of the three had spoken after Nadine's one quick whisper, "Armitage's car in the lane! Our only chance!" They ran in silence, and heard the constable's heavy tread behind them, and the piercing sound of his whistle, blown at intervals as he ran.

As they turned into the path between the high box hedges the whistle was answered from nearer the house, and they strained forward, running for their lives. They came through the woodland, and dropped down over the gap whilst the pursuers were still entangled in the unfamiliar windings of the path.

Lazare's eye searched the darkness for the car and found it. He spoke then for the first time in a sharp whisper.

"Nadine, get in," he said. "Gregor, hold them up." He seized the crank handle as he spoke and swung it frantically. There was no response. Again he swung it, and again, but the cold engine would not budge.

The sound of voices and of running feet came from beyond the hedge. Gregor's pistol spoke.

"Lazare," Nadine called from the seat, "there's a self-starter. The slope is steep."

Lazare straightened himself, called out rapidly in Russian to Gregor and jumped in beside Nadine. She released the hand brake. The car began to move with its own weight. Gregor fired again twice, leapt down the gap, and came to them running, panting. The car was sliding forward, slowly at first, but gathering momentum as the slope grew sharper. Gregor jumped for the step, and held to the side of the car. Their pace increased. The gap was behind them. The voices were behind them.

Nadine's foot rose and fell on the self-starter. Lazare switched on the lights. The engine half started, stopped, burred, checked, and finally got running some fifty yards down the lane.

Inspector Williams stood in the mud and heard the hum of the car die away in the distance. He was a man of few words. He knew when he was beaten.

He turned in silence and climbed the gap again.

"Back to the house!" he said.

When the inspector had released Bill Armitage, and the sound of trampling feet had died away, Sally let go of the curtain and began to cry. She looked at Bill, saw him coming to her, and ran into his arms, her voice breaking on his name, her whole body shaking with sobs. His arms closed hard about her, his head bent to hers. His voice, almost as unsteady as her own, whispered incoherent words of love and comfort. Presently Sally moved a little, looked up, and said in a shaky whisper:

"Bill—we're *alive*. It's over. Oh, Bill, hold on to me, don't let me go."

"I won't *ever* let you go," said Bill firmly. "You're not fit to look after yourself. Oh, Sally, you little *mug*, what made you trust people like this? How could you?"

"I didn't," said Sally. "I didn't—and I'm not a mug—and oh, Bill, what does it matter anyway? It's over, it's all over. We've waked up, and we're alive, and we've got each other. Oh, Bill, what does anything in the world matter when you've got me and I've got you, and it's over, it's all over?"

Bill said nothing. He had Sally in his arms safe and his own again, and he had no words. What were words, anyhow? She was his little Sally and he had her safe.

Sally went on speaking in the same whispering, trembling voice.

"I was so afraid that I should give in, Bill. You don't know how afraid I was. It's so awful to be afraid of being a coward." Bill almost shook her.

"You little mug," he said. "You couldn't be a coward if you tried. You're the pluckiest—" his voice failed him and he kissed her fiercely.

"I'm not—not really—and—oh, Bill, take this horrible case, it's running into me. I don't ever, ever, ever want to see red lacquer again. Put the beastly thing in your pocket, and don't, don't let us even think of it again."

"I want to get out of this," said Bill, "I want to get you away. I wish to goodness Williams would come back. I hope they caught them. I'd like to have a hand in it, but I suppose I can't very well leave the house."

"You can't leave me," said Sally, firmly. "I'm through Bill—all in. If Lazare came back I'd just crumple up like wet tissue paper, and I simply won't be left alone in this abominable house, I won't."

It was at this juncture that they became aware of Etta Shaw.

She was leaning back in her chair and looking at them with an expression that wrung Sally's tender heart. Her voice went on monotonously saying Lazare's name over and over again, and then: "He left me here. He went away and left me here. He went with Nadine. He left me. Lazare, Lazare, Lazare."

Sally sat down beside her and took her hand.

Inspector Williams threw them an odd look as he came in through the service door.

"They've got away with your car, sir," he said to Bill. "But we'll get 'em all right. They can't possibly go far. The men are going 'round the place outside. I've got to get busy with the telephone."

"You'll want the number of my car," said Bill.

"Got it," said the inspector. "Hullo, exchange! Hullo!"

He was very busy for ten minutes at the end of which he hung up the receiver and turned his attention to Etta Shaw. Before he could address her, however, there came in through the front door Constable Webbing propelling before him the unresisting and dejected Sascha, whose whole appearance was one of misery and terror. When, however, his eye lit upon Sally he exclaimed in a loud voice, "She lives then!" tore himself from Webbing's grip and, throwing himself on the floor by Sally's side, proceeded to cover the hem of her muddy skirt with impassioned kisses.

Constable Webbing was left staring a yard inside the door.

"Where did you find him?" said the inspector.

"Down by the pond, sir, a-threatening to suicide himself; and when I tells 'im as it's against the law, and that anything he says will be used in evidence against him, he does nothing but say: 'She's dead! She's dead!!' or it might be 'She's killed!' for a change, until he fair made my flesh creep. He may be foreign, or he may be balmy; I don't really know which is worst."

"All right, Webbing, you may wait outside," said the inspector.

"Now, young man, get up, will you. You're annoying Miss Meredith, and I want to ask you some questions."

Sascha got up, looked wildly round him, and folded his arms across his breast.

"I know nothing," he said, "nothing."

"Very well," said the inspector, "just remember, that anything you say may be used in evidence against you. You, too, Miss Shaw. To begin with—"

Sally interrupted him. She still held Etta Shaw's hand, and as she leaned forward and addressed the inspector, she pressed it warningly.

"I don't want there to be any mistake, Inspector," she said. "I should like just to make my own position clear if you don't mind. I came here as Miss Shaw's friend and guest—I have known her for twenty years. I stayed because I found she was being terrorised by unscrupulous foreign servants. They had entirely got the upper hand, and I am sure they are very dangerous criminals. Miss Shaw has been completely deceived, as she now realises. I want to make it quite clear that I have nothing against her. And as for M. Sascha—" Sally cast a sweet and somewhat tremulous smile in his direction.

"Have you any charge to make against him?" said the inspector hopefully.

"Oh *no*." Sally achieved an air of ingenuous surprise, "Certainly not. We've been the greatest friends, and when things began to look nasty he helped me to escape. I can't be grateful enough to him. You *will* remember that he's a friend of mine, won't you?"

"H'm," said the inspector. "And these people who are missing—it's the chauffeur and the maid—I've got their descriptions—who's the third?"

"A man called Gregor who did the housework. He's a Russian; I don't think he knows any English."

"Yes, yes, I saw him this afternoon."

"Look here, Williams," said Major Armitage, "Miss Meredith's had enough of this. I want to get her away, and you can ask her any questions you like when she's rested. I'll call up Ledlington and get a car. I'm going to take her to my cousin, Mrs. Farquhar. I want to call her up, too. Meanwhile, I don't suppose you realise that Miss Meredith is half starved. They've been keeping her short of food and sleep. Do you think one of your men could get hold of something whilst I'm telephoning? There's probably plenty in the house."

The inspector drew Bill aside.

"I must hold these two," he said. "I've asked them to send out a woman to look after the old lady. What about the lacquer case?"

"I've got it," said Bill.

"Not damaged?"

"I don't think so."

An hour later Sally, warmed and fed, was saying good-bye to old Miss Shaw.

"And you will come and stay with Etta again soon, my dear?" said the old lady.

Sally wondered whether she would ever set foot in Charnwood again. Aloud she said:

"May I pat Clarence? What a lovely cat he is."

Then she kissed Miss Shaw's soft cheek, and went out quickly.

After that there was darkness, and a smooth- running car, warm rugs, and Bill s arm about her. Long before the lights of Ledlington went flashing past them, Sally was very fast asleep, with her head on Bill's shoulder.

Chapter Thirty-Two

SALLY SLEPT LONG and heavily. She did not waken when the car drew up, or when Bill carried her up a flight of stairs. She did not do more than open her eyes once or twice when Eleanor Farquhar and her maid were getting her to bed, and once there, she sank into a dreamless rest that closed over her like the waters of a great deep.

When at last she opened her eyes again, it was afternoon. The room seemed full of golden mist. Eleanor was sitting on the end of the bed and smiling. Sally blinked, smiled sleepily, and said: "Hullo—" The sound of her own voice brought her broad awake.

The golden mist was the low sunlight slanting in through curtains of orange net. The beam fell across Eleanor in a delightful russet gown.

Sally sat up. "Oh, my dear, how nice it is to see you, and what an angel you are not to have pink curtains. I don't know how I got here a bit. I just went to sleep."

"Bill brought you. He's raging to see you, by the way, but you've got to eat something first."

"I'm starving," said Sally earnestly. "He can rage and rage. I want a real square meal—and, Eleanor *darling*, *not* cocoa unless you want me to scream."

Bill waited in Eleanor's drawing room with more patience than might have been expected. If he raged, he did so inwardly. He even smiled once or twice as if his thoughts were pleasant ones. When Sally came in he held her very tight for a moment, and then laughed and told her she was the world's champion sleeper.

"I haven't had enough yet," she complained. "Eleanor said you were getting dangerous and she was afraid you'd wreck her room, or I'd have gone off again after breakfast—no, tea. Bill, it's fearful to get so behind with meals that you don't know whether you are having lunch or dinner." Then, with a sudden change of manner—"Tell me what's been happening. Have they caught them? Have they found your car?"

"They've found the car all right," said Bill slowly.

"Where?"

"Left by the roadside about five miles from Charnwood."

"And Lazare?"

Bill was silent.

"Bill, tell me. What is it?"

"They've traced him, and Nadine—all three of them, in fact—"

"Well? Oh, Bill, you're not telling me. What has happened?"

Bill Armitage hesitated.

"Look here, Sally, you've got a right to know in a way, but it's fearfully confidential. I can't tell you the whole thing. They traced them, as I say; and I know now why Lazare said he didn't care a damn what happened if he had twelve hours' start. Half that would have done him. I might have known that they had big backing—"

"What? Oh, Bill—"

Bill paused. "They *did* have big backing," he said briefly. "And that is every word I can tell you, Sally."

Sally pursed up her lips and whistled.

"Well, I'm not surprised," she said at last. "At least, not so dreadfully. I had a feeling all the time."

They were both silent for a moment, Sally leaning against his shoulder. All at once she said:

"What about Etta Shaw—and Sascha?"

"The whole thing will drop. The Ledlington people think they were after a gang of motor thieves. My car comes in uncommon useful. Etta Shaw has pulled herself together. The fight will do her good, I expect. What a woman!"

"And my poor Sascha. I've got a lovely plan for him."

"Your Sascha?"

"He'd love to be," said Sally wickedly. "He adores me. He'll write a Sally Symphony I expect. I think it's frightfully romantic."

"Sally!"

Sally made a face.

"I shall give him a letter to Papa Lemoine. He doesn't take pupils, as a rule, you know, but he'll take Sascha if I write to him. My ambulance happened to pick him up when he was wounded, and he swears I saved his arm. Also he loves me a little, so he'll be nice to Sascha. I think the boy really has genius, and if he is a pupil of Lemoine's it will give him a start, and he won't have time to get messing about with conspiracies and things. Isn't it a lovely plan?"

"Beautiful," said Bill a thought drily.

"Sally, am I going to marry a flirt?"

"I expect so," said Sally, rubbing her head against his arm. "Shall you mind *much*, Bill, *darling*?"

It was a little later on that Bill said, "Sally, you're distracting my mind. I've come here on business, and not to make love to you. Now be good and attend."

He dived into an inner pocket and produced the red lacquer case.

Sally stepped back quickly.

"Put it away," she said, in a funny, choked voice. "Put it away, Bill. I told you I didn't ever want to see it again."

"Well, you needn't after this. Just open it and get out the formula, darling, and I'll smash the beastly thing with Eleanor's poker."

Sally shook her head.

"Sally, you goose, what is it? Come along, it won't take you a minute. You haven't forgotten?" His voice was suddenly anxious.

The anxiety touched Sally and made her feel cold. It would have been quite easy to say that she had forgotten, but she couldn't lie to him. She lifted honest eyes to his, and said:

"I haven't forgotten, but—I can't do it."

"Why on earth not? What's the matter?"

"I can't do it, Bill."

"But why not?"

Sally was growing paler and paler.

"There was such a lot of time to think whilst I was at Charnwood. I didn't make up my mind in a hurry. I thought and thought about it. Bill, it's a horrible devil of a thing. If I just put out my hand and do what Fritzi showed me, I'll be letting it out, and no one, no one in the whole world can chain it up again. No, wait, let me tell you. I meant to let you have it, but in the end I knew that I couldn't. It's a devil, and I can't let it out."

Her voice went away to a whisper. Her eye searched Bill's face, and found no understanding there.

"But Sally," he said, "you can't mean it. It's—it's ridiculous. Lasalle was committed to us—he—"

"He couldn't face it when it came to the point, and I can't either. Bill, don't look like that."

"I'm not," said Bill impatiently. "Look here, Sally, you're overwrought and worked up. I oughtn't to have come today, I suppose, but of course I'm mad keen to know if the formula is intact. After all, the case has had some pretty rough handling. Now look here, darling, you just open it, and I'll take all the responsibility, you needn't worry about it or think of it again."

"I can't," said Sally, and saw his frown deepen, his face flush.

"You mean you *won't.*"

At that she fired up, too.

"I mean what I say. I can't open it, and I won't open it."

"Etta Shaw has converted you, in fact?"

Sally flung her head up.

"Why do you stop there? Why don't you ask me if I sold the paper to Lazare?"

"You've no right to say that to me, Sally. Take it back."

"No, why should I?"

"Sally!"

"Why should I?"

The angry tears were hot in her eyes, but her heart was sick and cold. The anger was her defence against Bill, but her heart felt the shadow of estrangement and separation, and sickened.

If she held out, if she refused to open the case, or opened it only to destroy the paper within, it would be the old story over again. Bill didn't understand. He couldn't understand; perhaps no soldier could. It wasn't to be expected. He would think her a crank and obstinate; and the wall of separation would rise between them again, and this time for ever.

Bill Armitage, frowning angrily, saw that she was whiter than ever she had been at Charnwood, and under his anger something smote in upon his heart and touched the deep wells of tenderness there. Oddly enough, for the moment this made him furious.

"Of all the damned, morbid nonsense," he began, and saw the quick colour flame and die again in Sally's face.

"If you take it like that, you must," she said hopelessly.

"How do you expect me to take it? You say you've thought the whole thing out so carefully, but have you given one moment's consideration to my position—the position you are putting me in? I may say that I've been building a good deal on pulling this thing off. It means a lot to me, personally, and I believe it means a lot to the country. I've reported the recovery of the case. Do you realise that I shall have to go back and say, 'Miss Meredith has changed her mind. It seems to run in the family, and she has destroyed the formula.' A nice, easy job for me, isn't it? My dear girl, do have a little common sense. The thing is War Office property."

"No," said Sally, very short and sharp. "No, it's not. It's mine." She put out her hand. "I think you forget that, Bill. It's mine. Please give it to me."

He reddened to the very roots of his hair. There was an endless pause. Sally's outstretched hand shook more and more. Suddenly Bill thrust the case into it, and turned his back.

"Take your property then," he said, between his teeth, and walked to the window.

Sally took the case.

The afternoon sunshine was all gone. The grey light that goes before the dusk made the room look cold.

She stood with the case in her hand and looked at Bill's back. He didn't move or turn round. He would never forgive her—not a second time. Oh, well, what did it matter? He would marry a woman who would say "Yes," when he said "Yes," and "No," when he said "No." Sally hoped viciously that he would find it deadly dull.

She said "Bill," in a little shaking voice, but he did not move. Only after what seemed like a long time, he said gruffly:

"What are you going to do?"

"Bill, *do* turn round."

He turned then, showing a red face of wrath. "Why don't you get it over? Destroy the damned thing and have done with it. I take it you mean to destroy it?" Sally nodded, biting her lip. "Yes, I must, Bill."

"Well do it. What are you waiting for?"

"I don't know," said Sally very miserably. She walked over to the fire and stood there. "I suppose I'd better open the case first, and then—and then burn the paper."

"I should think that would be the best plan." Bill's voice was polite and stiff. He spoke apparently to some acquaintance whom he disliked a good deal.

"You—you won't—"

"I beg your pardon?"

"No," said Sally, with half a sob, "of course you won't. Well, here goes."

She took the case in both hands, and pressed as Fritzi had showed her how to press. The lacquer cracked, the crack widened, the case divided. A folded paper showed against the steel lining.

Bill came a step nearer. Sally took out the paper, and let the case fall upon the floor at her feet. She stretched out her hand over the flames, stretched it out and drew it back again.

Something in the colour of the paper, in the writing half seen by firelight, something made her draw her hand back. Bill saw her open the paper and look at it. He heard her gasp, and saw the colour rush scarlet to her cheeks. She gave a laugh and a sob, and then she called his name, "Oh, Bill," and, as he came a long step nearer, she began to read aloud in a trembling, laughing voice: "'My honoured grandmother's recipe for making black-currant jelly, *very economical.*'" She turned the paper and waved it at him. "'Take nine pounds of black currants'—Oh, Bill! Bill! Bill!"

Bill Armitage gave a shout of laughter, and caught her in his arms. They rocked together, the tears running fast down Sally's face.

"Fritzi," she sobbed, "he had the recipe—he was fiddling with it—the case was open. He must have put the wrong paper back. Oh, Bill, do you think he meant to?"

Bill hugged her, still laughing unsteadily.

"I shouldn't wonder. I shouldn't wonder a bit. The old fox! I never told you I found him, Sally."

"Fritzi?"

"Yes, Fritzi, the old ruffian. He's inventing a food for infants; swears the gas formula is wiped from his memory. He isn't interested in you, or me, or in the War Office, or anything except his new invention."

"Yes, he's like that, Bill. Oh, Bill, I thought—"

"Sally, *darling*, don't cry."

"I must. I thought you'd never forgive me. I thought you'd go away again for seven years, and—and—"

"Seven years is too long," said Bill gravely. "You'd get into mischief."

Sally began to shake with laughter.

"What is it?"

"Lazare," she said. "Oh, Bill, if I had opened the case at Charnwood! Oh, why didn't I? Think of Lazare's face if I had! 'Take nine pounds of black currants'—Oh, Bill, *darling*, I've changed my mind. I'm converted. The War Office *shall* have the formula. I'll give it to them for nothing. Black-currant jelly is so *much* nicer than plum and apple!"

THE END

Lightning Source UK Ltd.
Milton Keynes UK
UKOW01f1830070817
306865UK00004B/310/P